Warning!
Malfunctions May Occur

B.J Valli

To My wife Christy,
Thank you for all your patience and understanding
for allowing me to write this book,
and to my two boys
Alec and Blake
for all the times you gave me much needed
Daddy hugs at my writing desk.
Never stop reaching for the stars.

Chapter One

The battered little spaceship slipped and spun through the asteroid field. Only narrowly avoiding several devastating collisions with chaotically spinning, blue chunks of jagged rock, its engines whined and strained under the stress of the radical manoeuvres the pilot continued to put it through in his attempt to escape the deadly field. Inside the cockpit of *The White Vulture*, steadfastly ignoring a variety of alarms and warning lights, the pilot slammed the accelerator lever down hard into reverse, then threw the lever forward again.

"You really might have to rethink this 'no questions asked' policy of yours, Johnny," Tyson said, flinching as they passed a particularly large asteroid with only inches to spare.

"Oh, I don't know, Ty. It brings with it...certain benefits," John replied, emphasizing the phrase "certain benefits" with a forced smile.

"What? Like being pursued by bounty hunters?"

"I was more thinking along the lines of the pile of credits we got upfront for taking on such a simple, straightforward job."

"Simple? Straightforward? You know that 'delivery job' we picked up? Well, he just ejected himself out of our airlock."

"He did what?" John swore as he took his eyes briefly off the screens, and a split second later the ship shuddered as one of the asteroids glanced off their faltering shields. He refocused his efforts back on the spinning rocks outside of the cockpit's windows.

"I guess we'll be delivering that package ourselves now," said Tyson, as he pointed at the silver briefcase that had been hastily jammed under John's chair earlier that day.

"Well, you know, that's the thing about no questions asked." John gave his co-pilot an apologetic look. "I didn't ask."

"What? So, where are we supposed to deliver it to then? And to whom? You didn't ask anything?!"

"Of course, I did. I'm not a total idiot, you know."

Tyson fought the urge to correct the captain on his last statement. Instead, he asked slowly, "Okay, fine. So what do you have?"

"I have a name," John said, flashing a grin.

"A name. Great. That is just great, Johnny." The sarcasm in Tyson's voice was unmistakable. "Well done, now all our problems are solved. Please tell me, exactly how are we going to locate this name? They could be in any of the seven systems."

"Six systems," John corrected him. "No one is stupid enough to enter the Zeta system. Besides, I have a plan."

Before Tyson could reply, the captain threw the little ship into a hard spin, expertly threading it between two wildly spinning asteroids, abruptly ending the conversation.

The captain eased up on the throttle, pulled up sharply and banked hard to avoid another incoming rock. Then, still ignoring the multiple, flashing warning lights, John pushed the nimble little ship back up to full power. It shuddered briefly in protest then shot forwards, the engines belching out a thick plume of smoke that swiftly dissipated, swallowed up by the blackness between the stars.

"That should do it," John released the restraints on his chair and leaned forward into a flamboyant bow, the smug grin on his face not missed by his co-pilot.

"I'm curious," his co-pilot asked, not looking the slightest bit impressed by the captain's gesture, "what does 'left' mean to you? Is it still that way?" His aggravation was clear in his voice as he pointed vehemently to his left, knocking an array of dangling cables as he did so.

"I have told you before," John retaliated, gesturing to his left. "This way is port," he paused before pointing to his right, "And that way is starboard."

"Port, starboard, left, right, whatever in the seven moons you want to call it, you almost got us killed!" said Tyson with growing frustration.

"What are you trying to say? It worked, didn't it?"

"But I nearly died, and I can tell you right now, if I *do* die, I will not be happy!" The co-pilot resigned to the captain's unwavering overconfidence in his own abilities, gave his head a shake and got to work checking his instrument panel, currently lit up like the end of year celebrations on Earth Prime.

A voice hailed over the ship's intercom, interrupting them, "This is Captain Breanna Gomez of *The Scarlet Blade*.

Captain John Alexander and Tyson Blake of *The White Vulture,* please bring your ship to a complete stop. My contract authorises the use of deadly force if necessary."

"Lost them, did you?" said Tyson sarcastically as he gave John a withering look. "Good job. Well done."

"Look on the bright side, she said 'please'," John replied as he pressed his ship-to-ship intercom button. "Captain Gomez, how nice it is to hear from you again. How long has it been?"

No one replied.

"Before she starts shooting at us again, can you at least tell me the name you were given?"

"Sure, but first," John paused for a moment before continuing, "Promise me you won't get mad."

Tyson's response was slow and filled with forced restraint. "Whatever you say," he agreed at last, one eye on the ship's still silent intercom button. "So, what's the name?"

"Hector Gibbs."

"What?!"

"Hector Gibbs," said the Captain a second time as he leaned over and lifted a glass panel on the main console between the two men. The console had the words "Let's Go Baby" written on it in the captain's untidy scrawl. Under the lid was a big red button and now his hand hovered above it.

"Oh, no you don't!" Tyson said firmly. "The last time you used that, we ended up in the middle of dead space. We spent two weeks living off Aloe Vera juice before we found a station. I still have nightmares about the smell of the ship!" He had removed his cybernetic eye from its socket and was inspecting it, a habit he had developed whenever he was feeling nervous.

"Don't be so dramatic. You promised not to get mad, remember. Besides, I'm not the one who was found in bed with a senator's daughter on Renus, am I?" John paused, his eyes flicking to the intercom button briefly before he continued, "The same senator, I might add, that broadcasted our names and faces over every channel he could find."

Tyson shrugged as he held his eye up in front of him, feigning indifference.

John creased up his face in frustration as he went on, "This woman is the most tenacious bounty hunter I have ever encountered. Need I remind you she has been chasing us for more than five weeks now?"

"Hey, it was a great party and you know how it goes. Pretty girls, drinks, music, and me being my usual handsome and charming self," Tyson smirked as he finished polishing his eye and popped it back into place. "I was bound to end up naked with someone at some point. How was I supposed to know she was betrothed?"

"If it wasn't for you, we would have been in and out of the planet without anyone knowing any better," countered the captain.

"Who would have thought her father would have the power to lock down the entire starport?" Tyson mumbled.

"Me! I knew who everyone was at that party; that's why I told you to keep a low profile. Now, thanks to you, this Gomez bloodhound has found us again. For a smart guy Ty, you can be seriously thick at times. Just assume she has eyes on every planet in every system."

"Liebecker really isn't screwing around by selling our debt to a bounty hunter like Breanna Gomez," said Tyson, looking every bit as guilty as he felt.

"Well, do you really blame him after we dumped his cargo from the last job he gave us?" John ran a hand through his long brown hair. "One way or another he will want the debt paid, by either credits or our lives. And if he's really pissed off, he'll take both."

The intercom interrupted them, cutting their conversation off.

"Captain Alexander, I strongly advise you to stop your ship. I would prefer to take you alive, as I have no desire to further damage your vessel. But I warn you; do not test me. I will not hesitate to destroy that little ship if you continue to run."

"Well, you heard the woman; stop the ship," said the captain.

"Oh shit, I really hate this part," Tyson screwed his eyes shut and shook his head, easing the ship to a slow stop.

John's hand still hovered above the red button. It was a piece of alien technology they had found on a salvage mission. It had been identified by a contact of Tyson's and had been guaranteed to make their warp jump untraceable. John, a gifted mechanic, had fitted it to the ship himself. Unfortunately, what the contact had failed to mention was that, when fitted to a ship with incompatible navigational systems, the ship would be hurtled randomly through space.

After the first few jumps, the two men had spent a full week parked up in one of John's safe zones. After a complete system-wide diagnostic check, they finally located the flaw. A few modifications were done, including a refit of a new upgraded navigation system. It was yet to be tested.

Using it had saved them on more than one occasion. However, it had two major drawbacks. The first was that the ship had to be fully stopped before it could be activated. The second was that when they arrived at whatever system they jumped to, they often did not have the correct star charts.

Captain Gomez's voice came over the intercom, "Wise choice Captain, we are approaching you now and deploying our immobilizer cables. We will be escorting you to the closest outpost for processing. Thank you for your cooperation."

The two men heard the cables slap against the Vulture's hull, followed by the dull groan of metal as they gripped the ship. There was a brief, jerking twist as the cables tightened their hold.

"Thank you for your cooperation! She's a funny woman!" John said sarcastically as he rolled his eyes and brought his hand down hard on the big red button. He hurried back to his seat and buckled himself in, just as the ship's mechanical countdown began.

5—4—3…

Tyson, who was fumbling to secure his chair's harness, snapped, "You do know I only have one eye, right?" There were many things about his artificial eye that Tyson loved; including enhanced vision, along with his advanced data interpretation and processing speeds. Unfortunately, his depth perception had never recovered. As a result, he had always struggled with his seat buckles. "A little more warning would be nice!"

The cockpit of *The White Vulture* was plunged into darkness. Tyson swore.

The only light in the cramped quarters came from the big red button and he continued to battle with his harness. The button's pulse grew in intensity until it filled the entire room.

2—1.

Tyson heard the satisfying click of his restraints. Then *The Vulture* winked out as it made its warp jump, leaving behind the immobilizer cables floating lazily, holding nothing but empty space.

*****

"Captain Gomez," the youngest of the crew members stammered.

Captain Gomez stood in the centre of the bridge. Her black knee-high boot tapped impatiently as she turned to face the young man. Her long black hair flicked over her shoulder with the sudden movement.

"Yes, yes, what is it?" she replied tetchily.

The young navigator cleared his throat and said, "The ship. It just…vanished."

"How does he keep doing that?" The captain swore under her breath before mumbling to herself, "Next time, I'm going to shoot first."

Chapter Two

Captain Alexander woke to find himself upside down and weightless, still securely strapped into his harness, his arms drifted above his head and various items floated aimlessly around the cockpit. He gave his head a quick shake. Slowly, the realization that the antigravity stabilizers must have shorted out again began to dawn in his foggy brain.

"Tyson," he called to his friend. "Hey, Tyson wake up!"

There was no response from the co-pilot.

John was a strong believer in the philosophy: *if at first you don't succeed, try harder.* He took a deep breath and yelled, "Cyclops. Hey, Cyclops, you useless sack of monkey crap, wake up!"

Tyson slowly regained consciousness and looked around. His good eye blinked with befuddlement as his data pad drifted past his face. "Stabilizers failed again, huh?" he replied.

"No shit, Sherlock. Can you reach the lever from there?"

"Well, you're the genius who hit your precious button before I had time to check that all the systems would reboot properly," Tyson replied. He flicked the antigravity lever up twice and reset it.

As the cockpit returned to normal, John unfastened his harness and stood up and began picking up all the items that had dropped with a clatter onto the cockpit's floor. "So, where are we?"

"This can't be right," Tyson muttered as his fingers frantically attacked the navigation computer's keyboard.

"Don't be so dramatic, it can't be that bad. After all, we got away, didn't we? We have a fully stocked ship. We'll be fine. So, where are we?" John repeated, trying to sound as cheerful as he could.

Tyson frowned, "There is a problem."

John stepped across to the navigation panel to peer over Tyson's shoulder to see what he was looking at. "What problem?"

Tyson unbuckled his harness and leaned closer to the data screen. "We have no star charts for this sector. What I mean to say is, judging from the nearest star constellation, we are..." his voice trailed off.

"Come on! The suspense is killing me!" pressed John, starting to grow uneasy. It was unlike Tyson to ignore his insults.

"Okay, after a careful study of all the systems and sectors, then cross-matching those with our current position..." His cybernetic eye darted over the flashing data too fast for his friend to follow.

"Yes, yes, well?" said John, who had started to pace back and forth in the cramped cockpit..

"It seems we have landed in the Omega System," Tyson finally announced, stunned.

"No, no, that's not possible. Double-check it! We couldn't have been thrown that far. We don't have the power to generate a jump from the Alpha system!" Hoping that Tyson's calculations were wrong, John insisted the co-pilot check his calculations again, "You must have made a mistake."

"It's no mistake. I have quadruple checked it! That's what took me so long, you ass hat." Tyson's face flushed red with anger as he continued, "Look, we're lost, and it's all because of you and your beloved red button!"

John's jaw dropped open in stunned silence and Tyson took full advantage of the moment. "This system hasn't even been fully charted yet!" he shouted. "You do realize every explorer who has ever gone beyond the outer edge planets has vanished without exception?" Spent in defeat, his shoulders slumped as he finished.

John cleared his throat, "Okay, Ty. I get it… now let's see if we can find anything that can help us."

Tyson tapped away on his keyboard. A moment later, he brought up an old report. "Here, read this."

Obediently, John read the screen and then said, "So, years ago, some famous explorers got lost and the military sent a couple of vessels on a search and rescue mission and, from what I'm reading, with some very impressive gear."

"Did you even read all of the reports?" said Tyson shaking his head.

"I skipped a bit until I got to the good parts," John admitted with a grin.

"Okay," said Tyson with growing frustration creeping into his voice. "All that was recovered was a section of its hull. No signs of life."

"What you're saying is, some explorers got lost? That's not so unusual, is it?" John said.

"You know you really are an uneducated dung farmer, don't you? And yes, it is very unusual!" Tyson said, slapping his forehead with the palm of his hand in frustration.

"Hey, there's no need for name-calling. We can figure this out. You need to relax." John walked back over to his own chair and sat down. He rubbed his right hand behind his neck- a mannerism he had developed over the last few weeks of being chased. "So, what do we know about this system?" he asked, dragging his hands down his face as the seriousness of their predicament finally sank in.

"Right, okay. What we know is we have no way of getting back to our system or even close to it. Well, not anytime soon, without the proper ship upgrades and fittings," said Tyson, scratching at the stubble on his chin. "Which, I might add, we don't have."

"If it's really that bad we can always use the button again. How much worse can it get, right?" said his friend, flashing a smile in an attempt to lift Tyson's spirit.

"I don't know, Johnny. Our last modifications didn't work. We could end up worse off than we are now," said Tyson, scanning through more data.

"Okay, I'm open to any suggestions."

Tyson stopped sifting through all of the data relating to the Omega System. He hesitantly glanced at John and said, "There is something we can try, but I can't promise you anything." He paused before adding in a hardened tone, "And if we do try my idea, the next time that button is pressed, I'm going to be the one to press it. Deal?"

"Sure, but if it doesn't work, I get to do it my way," John countered, folding his arms across his chest. The silence in the cockpit stretched out for several long minutes before John spoke again as he looked out the cockpit's window. "So, what have you got?"

Tyson smiled at his victory but said nothing. Instead, he just flicked the accelerator lever, and the little ship shot forward as he entered coordinates into the navigation computer.

Seconds later a dull, blue light lit up on the panel. Their new course had been plotted. John secured himself into his seat before reaching out and pressing the blue light with a tight smile.

The co-pilot fumbled with his own buckle as he cursed the captain, "You really are a bastard, you know that, right?" Swearing loudly, he fought with his harness straps, eventually snapping them closed, but unable to tighten them properly before he was thrust savagely back into his seat as the ship's main drives came online.

John was still laughing at the sight of Tyson struggling against the thrust of the engines when the gravity stabilisers kicked in. "So, where are we going?"

"Before I answer that, you know you're a prick, right?" Tyson retaliated. A small smile played upon his lips as he appreciated the joke of the harness, this time as John barked out a short laugh in reply.

"I found a log entry of a trading ship in this system," he explained. "On a military channel, which is strange, but maybe they had clearance for some reason." He shrugged and waited for John to respond, but his friend remained silent. "Something must have happened to its warp drive, because once the main drive was activated, it just…kept going. But then, something must have caused it to stop here." He paused again, this time just making sure he still had John's attention. "The distress beacon was briefly set off but then it stopped. Anyway, it was activated not far from here and that's where we are headed."

"That sounds all very interesting, but how exactly does that help us?"

Tyson let out a long slow breath and continued, "By tracking the distress signal's path, I can tell that, although it entered the system differently to us, all we have to do is follow the trail and we'll find the ship," he said, looking extremely smug.

It took John a moment to fully comprehend what Tyson was getting at. "Oh, right. I get it! We can access the ship's logs and download all its star charts. That's brilliant!" He unbuckled his harness and started walking off down toward the galley, pausing briefly to deal the co-pilot a slap on his shoulder," Nice work."

"Exactly, my addlepated friend," said Tyson after him.

John had no idea what his friend had just called him, and he didn't care much. If Tyson had really found a way out of the Omega System, he could call him all the names he wanted.

It didn't take him long to reach the galley. He opened the refrigerator and took out two small silver bags with straws taped on the outside of them. He carried them back into the cockpit and tossed one across to Tyson, before lounging back down in his chair.

Tyson removed the straw from the packet and pierced it, reading the label as he did so.

At the same time, John opened his. It was a ritual they always followed after a big win.

"How's the spiced iced coffee?"

"Good, thanks, my friend, and your scotch with dry ginger and lime?" inquired Tyson as they saluted each other with their drinks.

"It's the best drink I've had in this sector," grinned John.

Chapter Three

The trading ship came slowly into view. It was a light freighter and looked enormous compared to the *White Vulture*. There were several large holes torn into its hull, unmistakably made by missiles. Scorch marks were etched liberally over its surface, biting into the ship's outer hull, creating a chaotic pattern. John rubbed his forehead, thinking. To an untrained eye, the marks looked random, but John knew better. They were precise strikes, aimed to knock out every system on the ship. Even from his time in the military, John had never seen a ship with such extensive damage still holding together in one piece.

The Vulture slowed and matched the rotation of the trading ship before approaching it cautiously, coming to a complete stop a few hundred metres away.

Tyson let out a whistle and shook his head, "What in the seven moons is holding it together?"

When he had found the initial distress signal, all that was allocated to the ship was its tracking number and class. Now, in such close proximity, they could clearly read the call sign on the hull —*The Trading Winds.*

While John busied himself by trying to establish a data link between the two ships, Tyson checked the data banks of the spare drives of the Vulture. He had no idea how much room would be required to hold the uploaded information, and there was no way to tell how much data the trading ship had stored.

"Something serious went down here, that's for sure."

John nodded his response, still deep in thought.

"I'm just dumping another set of drives just in case it has close to our capacity. Although, I doubt it," Tyson smirked. "No one has our quality of system. After all, I designed it."

There were times that when the captain could quite happily have smacked the smugness right off of his co-pilot's face, and this was one of them. Unfortunately, Tyson was a gifted hacker; the best John had ever seen during his long, 'illustrious' career. He would be much easier to tolerate, however, if he wasn't so aware of his own skills.

"How long do you think it will take?" John enquired.

"I'll have it done before you can recite Jacques' 'Crossings of the Five Systems'," boasted Tyson.

As if to prove a point, it took him barely twenty minutes to hack the security systems of the trading ship and break the access codes. "Hey, Johnny! We're in! Although," he added, scanning the data as it was transferred to their backup drives, "Something feels weird here. I've seen security systems on banks that were easier to hack."

"Really?" John asked without looking up from his own task.

"There's a lot of stuff in here, Johnny. The Captain's log. Personal mail entries. Crap that we don't need but at least if it's recorded, we won't miss anything. Hang on a minute." Tyson broke off as he swore softly. "There's a hidden file in here and it's locked."

"Locked? As in, you can't open it?" asked John, who was now out of his chair once again and starting to pace.

"Of course, I can open it. It's just that I can only copy it from here. Its code is different, very old. I'll have to be plugged into the terminal on the ship to retrieve it, which means it's likely to be very valuable."

John stopped pacing and looked directly at his friend. "I don't care how valuable it is, we're not going over there to that death trap. I'm astounded it's still holding together. All we need are the star charts," John reminded him. "Just find them so we can leave."

The co- pilot's hands began flying over the keyboard once again, pressing buttons here and moving files there.

"There! Done!" He hit the last sequence of buttons with an exaggerated flourish and sat back to announce, "All of The Trading Winds files are safely stored. Well, except for our mystery one. All that is left for me to do now is sort through them to see what we have."

"Nice work! But before you get lost in the files, find me the charts so we can plot a course out of here to the Delta system. It will be our new home for a while."

It was too late. His friend was already thoroughly absorbed in the data on his screens.

"Tyson? Hello? John to Tyson! Hello!?" he said with rising frustration, tapping the screen in front of the co-pilot's face.

"Oh...yeah. Okay, hang on." After a long minute of silence, Tyson spoke again. "This is fascinating, Johnny," he said excitedly as he drummed out a quick tune on this keyboard with his index fingers. "Every file has been encrypted. If I didn't know any better, I would say it's a military-grade." Tyson threw a look of deep concern at his friend.

"Relax, that ship out there is far from anything the military would use. Look here and here," John said, pointing at the ship that floated in front of them. "Any ship in military service must have a minimum of two forward weapon placements and one aft. That ship only had the one," John gestured at the front of the ship once again. "That gaping hole there is where it was, and my guess would be that it was destroyed first, followed by its main thrusters."

Tyson nodded thoughtfully "Well, in any case, whoever secured these files did a very good job."

"Tyson," John said as slowly and as calmly as he could. "I understand this is all very exciting, but priority one is, we need those star maps so we can plot our way to the Delta system."

Silence followed his order and, frustration getting the better of him, John dealt his friend a hefty slap to his shoulder, "Ty! Can you do that for me?"

The co-pilot snapped out of his daze. "Yeah, sure Johnny, no problem. But I will need some uninterrupted time at some point to check out the rest of these files."

"Sure, you can have all the time you need when we are safely out of this system. Now, bring the maps up, if you please," said John, trying to remain patient as he pointed to the navigation systems console.

Tyson flicked over to the screen onto the navigation systems page and flashes of data filled the screen. He sped through the files and paused, "There's a problem. I found the star charts but they're not for this sector. Either they are hidden somewhere in the other files we took or...they are in that file we couldn't move."

The captain let out an impressive string of swear words. "Scour all the files we took and pray that it's buried in amongst them. Otherwise, we will be going over to retrieve that cursed file from that pile of space scrap," John grimaced, pointing over at *The Trading Winds*.

"I'm on it," Tyson replied, his eyes never leaving the screen. "Like I said, every file is encrypted. This is going to take me awhile."

John sighed, mumbled his acknowledgement, and headed off in the direction of the galley. Still grumbling a little to himself, he selected some food cubes, arranged them onto a plate and then put them into the rehydrator. A few seconds later the machine beeped, and he removed the plate now filled with perfectly cooked bacon - his favourite - over-easy eggs, spicy baked beans, two hash browns, field mushrooms and French toast. Figuring it had to be breakfast time somewhere in the galaxy, John carried his meal to the small table across the room and sat down.

When he had finished eating, he was tempted to leave his dirty dishes, knowing how much it would annoy his co-pilot. John resisted the temptation and carefully placed the plate in the cleaner before he sauntered down to the ship's small recreation room.

'Small' was a generous description of the area, and there wasn't much for John to do there other than pull out his data pad and begin poking through its contents. He had read all the eBooks and watched the entire movie list that he had several times over. His favourite ones were from Earth prime from the 19th to the 21st century – *the classics*.

He found himself hoping that *The Trading Winds* had more of a selection and he tossed the data pad aside, wishing he was better at navigation computer systems so he could have something to do. But John knew his own limitations, and besides, that was Tyson's field of expertise and one of the main reasons he had taken him on board in the first place.

Bored and a little restless now, he wandered down the narrow walkway and opened the cargo bay door. It was empty. John gave a small, wry grin. At least he hadn't lost a ton of credits by taking a fully stocked cargo bay into a system that had no market for it.

He closed the door again and kept walking towards the engine room. When he opened the door, a wave of heat hit him, along with the smell of grease, engine oil, and hydraulic fluids. He breathed it in, a wave of nostalgia washing over him. He had made all of the modifications to the aging spaceship himself and saved a small fortune in doing so.

There was no denying he loved the old ship. There was no part of her that he hadn't either modified or built with his own two hands. It gave him a sense of freedom like he had never known before. After spending so long in the military, it was exciting to be able to choose his own destiny, to take the path of the less travelled, to go anywhere he wanted, and more importantly, to not follow any order he didn't agree with. This ship was the one thing in his life he could truly call his own.

He walked up to the main panel, more through habit than necessity, and inspected it, expecting nothing amiss, as it ran like clockwork in there. A small green light immediately caught his attention. It was flashing frantically. John froze.

It was something he had hurriedly tacked to the side of the secondary panel some time ago, and while he had been in here thousands of times since, he had never seen the light blink like that before. It was normally a solid green light. John moved closer, inspecting the beacon in more detail.

There was silver tape underneath the button. Written on it, in his own handwriting, were the words "RED BUTTON. If flashing, malfunctions may occur. Do not use."

"I knew I had forgotten something," he berated himself softly. "I never did get around to installing a relay light on the navigation console." Reluctantly, he headed back up to the cockpit. "Shit. I guess I had better go tell Tyson."

Chapter Four

Tyson had his earbuds in, and as soon as the cockpit door slid open, John could hear the faint, tinny sound of music coming from them. Tyson didn't acknowledge the captain's arrival and continued tapping away on the console, staring intently at the screen.

John didn't disturb him and sat in his pilot's chair to complete the weekly flight check, which was only a couple of weeks overdue. He completed the task with more attention than the usual tick and flick that he did, knowing it could be a long time before his ship would be docked at a decent port. He was good at resolving most electrical faults, but if anything major happened, they would be stuck in the middle of nowhere.

He glanced across at the navigation light. It was still unlit.

Tyson sat up abruptly, yanked out his earbuds, and startled his friend. His long fingers a flurry of motion over the keyboard as he crowed triumphantly, "It's taken a while, but I've done it."

"You found the star charts?"

"No, I have decrypted all the files so I can search for them!" Tyson started the search program with a flourish and sat back in his chair, the music from his discarded earbuds spilling out into the cockpit. "Shouldn't be too long now."

"That's great, Tyson," John nodded, one eye still on the navigation light. "Let's just hope they're in there. Hey, you know when we had the red button installed and I said I would put a relay light right here next to the navigation one?" he asked, tapping the spot he referred to with a casual air.

"Yeah, sure," said Tyson, who was more interested in the data flickering across his screen.

"Well, anyway, as you know, I never got around to it, right? And there might be a slight malfunction with it that we didn't know about, until now," he finished sheepishly.

Tyson stopped what he was doing, his focus now well and truly on his friend. "What kind of malfunction exactly?" he asked slowly.

"Oh, the light's not red or anything!" John hastily assured him. "But when it was installed, I wrote a short note under it on the panel in the engine room that said if it starts flashing red, don't use it." He kept his tone flippant, determined to play the situation down.

"Right, okay then, how long has it been flashing for?" Sounding a little more concerned than John and, for once, giving his friend his full attention, Tyson finally turned off his music and an eerie silence settled over the cockpit.

In truth, John had had no idea when the light had begun winking out its warning. He hadn't been down to the engine room since he made the latest modifications to the engines, and that was at least a month previously. There was no way, however, he was going to tell Tyson that - *the man's head would most likely explode* - so he took the only avenue open to all good men in charge when breaking news to someone that they didn't want to hear. He lied.

"It just started doing it, and you know, I just thought you should know because you're the one who will be using it next," he said dismissively.

"Maybe it would be best if you disconnected the button. Just in case," Tyson said after a moment's silence.

John got up and walked over to the big red button. He studied it for a while. "Simple enough really," he shrugged. "I just have to remove the housing, separate it at the hub here, and then disconnect and isolate these four groups of wires here," he turned to Tyson, who looked totally confused.

Tyson simply nodded in mute agreement. Mechanics, and to a lesser extent, electronics, were a mystery to him. He watched his friend walk off down to the toolbox. That was what Johnny called his impressive collection of tools. Tyson had to admit that if it wasn't for Johnny and his knowledge of the ship's drives and electronic systems, chances were they would have died long ago floating around in dead space. There was no way he was ever going to admit it to him though.

John returned whistling and with an assortment of tools in an old canvas bag. He chose one, climbed under the main panel, and started working on dismantling the big red button.

Tyson, feeling oddly useless, stood up to watch what his friend was doing. He still had no idea what going on but felt as if he should at least appear as if he did.

"Right, that's done," John said as he was crawling back out from beneath the console.

"That didn't take as long as I thought," Tyson mused as he lifted the lid over the button and slapped his hand down on it.

"What are you doing?" John yelled the nanosecond Tyson's hand made contact.

The White Vulture's engines fired up for a split second, then stopped abruptly, catapulting them both into the cockpit's window. Everything went black. Then, slowly and steadily, the red button's light started to pulse.

They scrambled into their seats and fought with their harnesses to get themselves secured in. John was the first to hear the dull metal click of his harness. A few seconds later, he heard Tyson's click into place.

"Why in the seven moons, did you do that for?" he yelled once he was sure his friend was locked in. "You know it needs time to recharge before using it again! A minimum of six hours, remember? Otherwise, the ship could pull itself apart under the stress! You know this. So, why would you do that?"

"You said it was my turn, and you were done, so I pressed the button. How am I supposed to know that when you say you're done you don't mean completely DONE!" Tyson shot back angrily.

"*Done?* I was done with removing the screws from the housing you idiot!"

All Tyson could think of saying to that was, "By the seven moons, this can't be good."

The light from the big red button grew brighter until it illuminated the whole cockpit. Then, it went out.

The two men sat, harnessed in, both gripping the arms of their chairs tightly for several minutes, in total darkness and silence. Then, when it became apparent nothing further was going to happen, they looked at each other and laughed. It was a nervous laugh, but it was enough to break the tension between them.

"Well, that was anticlimactic," John said. "I guess it needs longer to build up a full charge."

"Yeah, lucky for us! And on the bright side, it's your turn to use it next."

For a moment, as if to make sure nothing was going to happen, the pair stayed strapped into their seats.

"Hey!" Tyson broke the silence with a sudden shout. "Look at the button. It's stuck down," he shot the captain a wry grin. "Can I suggest we try and lift it back up again? Then, maybe we just leave it alone for a while?"

"Yep, sounds like a plan to me," John nodded. "Although maybe you should stay strapped in. You know, just in case..."

"Just in case it starts up?" Tyson sounded almost nervous and John laughed.

"No, just in case you get the urge to press it again!"

"You know, I've thought about it, and you're not funny," said Tyson, shaking his head.

"Sure I am. I'm hilarious." John shucked off his harness and stepped over to the console. He reached down and selected a broad-bladed knife from the old canvas bag. He then carefully slid the blade under the bottom of the button and pried it up gently. It didn't move.

He pushed down harder. Still nothing. He stopped, worried that he would break off the red button and make things worse.

"It's not moving," John returned the knife to the bag then turned to Tyson. "Stay strapped in. I'm going to go down to the engine room and try and take it off-line from there."

Tyson nodded and tightened his harness as John headed towards the rear of the vessel, promising, "I won't be long," as he did so.

Tyson puffed out his cheeks thoughtfully and figured he was probably going to be there a while, despite John's optimism. So, he opened up the newly hacked files and began sifting through the data. As he searched, he noticed there were inconsistencies throughout the stored information. It appeared from the registration of *The Trading Winds*, that the type and class of ship it was listed as had been changed several times. That was odd.

After checking his own files, which were quite extensive, Tyson could find no match whatsoever to the ship that was floating in space just a few hundred metres away from him. He scratched his head, flexed his shoulders, cracked out his knuckles, and then set to work with renewed vigour.

For once, the task was challenging his skills, the process hampered by the fact he kept finding viruses that had to be carefully and thoroughly neutralized before he could proceed. With his cybernetic eye, he scanned the data rapidly; not for the first time, wishing he had cybernetic hands so they could keep up.

Time, as is often the case when drifting in foreign, empty space, passed in a meaningless blur, until John's voice jolted him back sharply to his surroundings.

"You are not going to believe what I found when disabling the red button!"

Tyson looked up. John was brandishing an object roughly the size of a billiard ball, a black frame that had a conglomeration of wires in a myriad of different colours inside of it.

"It's been a while since I last saw this," He tossed the ball-like thing into the air and caught it again. "Say hello to the heart of the red button." Grinning like an idiot, he placed it down on the console in front of Tyson. "I have absolutely no idea how it works. It is alien tech, after all."

Ignoring Tyson's cynical, raised eyebrow, John continued, "You see this?" He pointed at a small, purple broken wire inside the ball. "I'm thinking that's the fault. It was probably on its way out and that's what started the green light flashing. It must have burnt all the way through when you hit the button again because it didn't have time to cool down enough," he concluded, looking rather pleased with himself.

"So, you're saying that it's totally disconnected now; non-functional, right?" asked Tyson, eyeing the device on his console curiously.

"Well, once alien tech is correctly installed, it integrates and adapts to the ship it's installed in." He walked over and, in an exaggerated motion, pressed one finger hard against the button. The button stayed stuck. "And it uses the ship's capabilities to execute said function."

Tyson rolled his eye at his friend, not believing a word he said.

The captain continued his lecture, "Unless the ship has a stored-up charge, it should be rendered non-functional." John grabbed the button and gave it a sharp twist. It then popped up with a click. Determined to prove his point, the captain pressed it again four more times, looking across at

Tyson with a grin. "See? Harmless." On the last press, however, the button stayed half-way up and began emitting a dull, red glow.

Neither John nor Tyson noticed.

"Okay, okay, I believe you, Johnny! You can stop pressing the button now. Hey, listen to what I've found in the files."

Tyson handed him back the caged ball of wires that was the heart of the red button and launched into a description of what he had found on the trading ship's drives, including his theory on why certain files had been deliberately separated for increased security. He explained how, from what he could tell, the ship had been trading in Alien tech. This sort of highly illegal but very lucrative trade would account for the changing of ship's names and profiles he had found in the logs and registry files. However, the star maps they were after were missing.

With a wry grin, Tyson concluded that they must be still on the ship in the file they couldn't move, and the only way to get the charts now was for one of them to go over and manually retrieve it.

Chapter Five

Tyson knew that John wasn't keen on docking the ship on anything other than a space station or outpost, where the docking computers could interface and guide them in. Free docking was very dangerous, and most pilots refused to do it. There were too many variables involved in lining up the other docking port, timing the thrust, and judging distances and rotation. It was only attempted as a last resort as most of the time it destroyed both ships.

"Before I make any decisions, I want a thorough scan of the ship. And I mean, the full workup. Not just the normal crap like life signs and oxygen levels. We did that already. And don't take this as a 'yes' either. I want to know everything – power distribution, fuel cell type, all the way down to the last time someone ejected the waste – before I even consider going over there!" John said, lowering himself slowly into his captain's chair.

"Yeah, I figured you would say that, so I started the scan about 15 minutes ago. It should be ready soon. Level with me, Johnny, what's really the matter? You seem nervous about this ship," asked Tyson looking at the captain.

"Don't you think it's a little weird that the very file we need is the one we can't move? Whoever was after the ship didn't want it destroyed, they blew holes in it so they could board it. They wanted what was on it," John was grim as the data on the ship began to flash up on his screen.

Tyson scratched his head. "I've been wondering about that myself and I think I know why. My guess is whoever attacked the ship boarded it and copied the files they wanted. That's why we could move them over to our ship, the pinning program had already been cracked. The only file they didn't need was the one they already had."

John had to admit, his friend's line of reasoning made sense. He nodded his agreement, then set to work, breaking down the data files on his screen.

Tyson knew John would be looking for any reason not to free dock the ship. He would scrutinize every last bit of the report, twice if necessary.

After what seemed a lifetime the captain stood up, stretched and said, "And you're positive the navigation files are over there?"

Tyson had been anticipating the question, but he still scratched his head and looked into thoughtfully out into space for a few seconds. "Well they are not here and it's the only thing that makes sense. Besides, if we are really lucky, we might find something worth salvaging for a few extra credits. These guys were into smuggling alien artefacts. If we make a find like that, all we have to do is match it up with the right buyer and start planning our joint retirements."

"Is it really that easy to sell?" John asked doubtfully.

"Easy? No. Not for just anyone. Luckily for you I'm not just anyone. So, for me, yes, it will be easy," said Tyson, looking rather superior.

"Alright, let's get this over with. I need your full attention on the rotation and speed of the approach. One mistake and it will be all over," John strapped himself into his harness and fingered the throttle forward, at the same time delicately engaging the secondary reverse thrusters.

He glanced across at the co-pilot who was focused on the screen in front of him.

The atmosphere had changed perceptibly. Gone was the bantering and name-calling. Now, it was all business.

"Okay, Johnny. Quarter thrusters until my mark, then on my mark, rotate one eighteenth to the right and match to 763.6. Confirm?" The co-pilot spoke slowly and purposefully.

"Copy that. Quarter thrusters, then one eighteenth to the right, match at 763.6. Check."

"You're good to go, Johnny," said Tyson.

Beads of sweat breaking out on his forehead, John eased off the reverse thrusters and crept forward to a quarter on the secondary thrusters.

Tyson continued, watching his read-outs like a hawk. "3-2-1. Mark."

The captain rotated the ship one eighteenth to the right and held it steady.

It always fascinated Tyson how John always made it look so effortless. Although John had tried to show Tyson on many occasions the advanced manoeuvres of flying, unlike his friend, he just didn't have the natural talent needed.

"Matching to 763.6," said Johnny, putting a slow clockwise rotation on the ship. They now matched *The Trading*

Winds' perfectly. The only task left was for them to close the gap between the two craft and secure the docking chute.

"Good luck, Johnny," muttered Tyson as he unfastened his harness and headed off down towards the docking hatch.

" Thanks. And remember, if it doesn't seal on the first try, that's it, we will have to try something else."

Tyson turned back to answer but decided against it, as he could see more sweat beading on John's face from the intense concentration.

The captain eased on the secondary reverse thrusters. Smoothly and slowly, the battered hull of *The Trading Winds* filled the cockpit window.

It was a much bigger ship than *The White Vulture* and, with the ships almost touching, John gently eased the reverse thrusters on to a fraction just off the maximum setting. They were now moving so slow it was impossible to measure the speed.

Over the ship's intercom came Tyson's voice, "Johnny, we are nearly there, I'm looking at it through the hatch. On my mark, pull to 0.6222 thrust. Confirm?"

John pressed the button for the intercom, chanting, "Copy that, slow to 0.6222 on your mark," without moving his eyes off the screen.

Tyson could now see where the individual panels on the big ship joined and called, "3 … 2 … 1. Mark!"

Immediately, the ship's reverse thrusters were smoothly eased on fully. John touched the forward thrusters' lever forward slightly. So slightly, he almost did it twice. Fortunately, he stopped himself just in time.

Movement this slow and precise meant the computer couldn't calculate the distance between the ships accurately.

However, Tyson's cybernetic eye could do it within the time needed to avoid a collision. "Excellent," he said. "Hold it there."

Both ships' rotations were now matched perfectly, barely a metre apart. A green light just above the docking hatch flared to life a moment later, confirming that they had alignment.

Tyson operated the panel to extend the docking chute. The hard, flexi-chute crossed the distance between the ships and locked in place. Once Tyson was satisfied with the seal, he used the same process for the second chute that completely enclosed the first one. This second chute was made of a much harder composite and made a loud click that echoed through the tubes.

"How's it looking down there?" asked the captain.

"Excellent, Johnny. It was your best one yet!" praised Tyson.

"Okay, great. I will lock the rotation in. I'll be there in a minute or two. I just want to do a final check before we head on over," replied John.

"Sure, no problem. Oh, and can you grab my yellow drive on the panel and my data pad on your way?" asked Tyson, hardly able to contain his excitement. He loved exploring other ships, although they rarely got to do so.

"Yeah, can do." John did his final checks, pleased with the rotation and speed parameters he had set on the computer. On the slight chance there was any change, both ships would move as one unit.

John cast his eyes around the cockpit one last time; it was then he saw the silver briefcase under his chair. He knelt and tugged at its handle. The case was wedged in tight. The owner of the case, who was now certainly dead and floating off somewhere in the depths of space, had given two strict instructions before handing it over into the care of John and his crew. The first was for it to be kept in a secure location; the second was for it not to be open under any circumstances. In John's mind, there was nowhere more secure than under his seat, so he had mentally ticked off that box. As far as opening it up, that was something he just wouldn't do. What sort of no-questions-asked courier would he be if he peeked inside every delivery he had ever been in possession of? The word would spread throughout the systems like wild fire. He would be labelled untrustworthy and his business would be ruined.

He pulled again at the handle, harder this time. The case groaned at first, then released its hold on the underside of John's chair, smashing into the space between his nose and mouth with a dull thud. He instantly recognised the tangy taste of blood inside his mouth. He blinked several times trying to chase the tears out of his watering eyes. Swearing, he threw the case aside and buried his face in the sleeve of his shirt.

When his eyes cleared, he looked over at the now dislodged briefcase. The silver cased lid now sat at an odd angle. John swore again, reached out and dragged it over to where he sat. Gently he removed the broken lid and placed it on the floor to his left.

Inside, surrounded by a thick red layer of protective foam, nestled a small vial. Luckily it was intact, however, the thick rubber stopper at the top had become dislodged and at least at third of the thick dark grey contents had seeped out. John felt a pang of guilt. Never before had he delivered an item not fully intact.

Instinctively, he reached out to wipe up the spilt grey liquid but stopped himself just in time, realising that he had no idea what the substance was or what it might do to him. Gripping the broken briefcase with both hands, he stood up carefully and walked purposefully to the medical bay. He carefully placed the case on top of one of the workstations, before searching every storage locker. He quickly located the hazardous materials gloves, along with silver, long-handled oval-shaped ladle.

He fitted the gloves on and picked up the spoon. Carefully, he scraped up as much of the spilt dark grey liquid as he could and deposited it back into the vial. He then replaced the stopper in the vial, and he dropped the ladle down into the waste disposal unit.

For a second time, John searched the room, this time looking for a new suitable container to hold the little bottle more securely. Finally, he located the perfect thing - a small, silver box that was lined with foam. After fitting the vial snugly inside the box, he removed one of the gloves and, with his un-gloved hand, fastened it closed before pushing it deep inside one of his pockets. He then removed the other glove with practiced care and dropped them both into the waste chute.

With a sigh of relief, John collected the broken briefcase and carried it over to the disposal unit and tossed it in after the gloves. Unfortunately, he misjudged the throw and one of the corners of the case hit the edge of the chute, flipping loose the thick foam insert. John watched helplessly as it bounced up off the wall and slapped down on the back of his left hand, slowly sliding over his hand and his fingers before dropping into the bin below.

He felt burning instantly. John looked on in horror as, within seconds, his flesh began to turn white and blister. His mind raced, then he remembered the neutralising agent that was standard on every ship. He had been the one who had insisted several bottles of them be kept in the medical bay's cool room.

John exploded into action as his eyes filled with tears and his ruined skin began to swell with large grey blisters. He threw open the doors of the cold storage area and, with one hand, savagely ripped the top off the nearest bottle of neutraliser, plunging his hand deep inside its gooey, white contents.

Gradually the burning slowed to a dull throbbing pain. With gritted teeth, John carried the bottle, his hand still firmly inside it, out to the main medical bay and located the medical packs. Gingerly, he removed his blistered hand from the cylinder of now pink-coloured liquid and wrapped it carefully with the packs. Tears of pain were still streaming down his face as he collapsed to the floor.

John fought to blink away his tears as he stood, peering around the room once more. He strode across the room with purpose and pulled open a drawer, popped several pain suppressant pills out of a blister pack, and swallowed them in one fluid motion. It didn't take long for the medication to take effect. His whole body felt light, but now his injured hand had gone partially numb. Hoping he had been quick enough to avoid any permanent damage, he slowly made his way back to the cockpit.

Tyson's voice chimed in over the ship's internal com system. "Hey, Johnny, what is taking you so long?"

John keyed the intercom from his screen and replied, "Sorry, was just taking care of a few last-minute things. I'll be there soon."

He turned, knocking the red buttons' "brain" off the panel as he did so.

Luckily his lightening quick reflexes kicked in just before it hit the floor. "Gotcha!" he smiled, praising himself on his catch before putting it in the opposite pocket to the vial.

Reaching over to the console, he picked up the two data pads along with the yellow drive Tyson had requested and walked out towards the docking chute's hatch.

Chapter Six

The two men fitted their bio-suits while they waited for the chute to pressurize. They both carried fully stocked backpacks, John having also stashed the box containing the vial and the heart ball of the red button into his without Tyson noticing. He even managed to carefully conceal his injured hand inside the glove of his bio-suit without his co-pilot seeing the bandaging he had applied.

Tyson checked the status on the wall panel light was still green. "We are good to go. You ready?" he asked.

John would never have admitted it to his friend, but on rare occasions, he suffered from claustrophobia. He hated walking the docking chute. It was one of the times he felt it clawing at him most. Unfortunately, for reasons of safety, it was necessary to make the long walk as slowly and as evenly as was possible. This only made things worse for John, as it only lengthened the time spent inside the confines of the chute. He took a slow breath and tried to think of something else.

Once the correct code was put in, the hatch slid open with a soft whoosh. Tyson entered the chute first and flicked on the small light that was clipped to the side of his helmet. A narrow beam of light pierced the darkness. Cautiously, he placed one outstretched hand on the wall and started walking at a slow, measured pace along the dimly lit corridor.

It was only a few minutes later when he reached the other end of the chute where he then touched his data pad to the trader ship's hatch and pressed in the override code. A loud click echoed down the chute as the hatch opened.

"Come on, hurry up!" he called back over his shoulder as he entered the ship.

John turned on his torch and stepped into the chute. After his first few nervous steps, he soon gained a rhythm, and before he knew it, he was half-way in. Breathing heavily, he became aware that his bio-suit was now stuck to him, through all of his sweating, like a second skin. "Focus, Johnny. Not far now," he reassured himself.

He could feel his blood pounding in his ears as his face grew hot, small balls of light formed in front of his eyes. John swore. He knew what was coming next. As he closed his eyes a memory sliced through his brain – *He was back on the "Red Jackal" with his old team. Holes were being punched into the cockpit and his team leader Mystic Fox was screaming at him to get them out of firing range; then, a blinding flash.*

John reopened his eyes; his head was pounding as he struggled to focus. A few moments passed before he continued pushing forward. He could see Tyson's silhouette inside the doorway waiting for him and he kept moving with slow, deliberate steps.

Somewhere in his mind, John registered that a red glow was coming from behind him. At first, he ignored it. He forced down the rising panic he was feeling and focused on his destination.

He was only a few metres shy of the door when he heard the ship's mechanical countdown start. That was when he realized what was happening. He abandoned all caution and started to run the rest of the way down the chute.

He knew what the countdown signalled. *The Vulture* was about to wink out.

5...4...

Tyson realized immediately what was happening, and he gripped at the doorway with one hand, the other reaching out towards his friend. John leapt towards Tyson's outstretched hand just as the red light went out. In his panic, he completely miscalculated the jump, however, and he flew in over Tyson's head, slamming into the wall and knocking himself unconscious.

Ignoring his friend's slumped body, Tyson tapped his data pad to the open hatch. The door struggled to move at first, but then slowly slid shut.

3...2...1...

John was soon awake and struggling to his feet. He was, however, still a little unsteady as he joined Tyson at the door. Both men watched, in stunned silence, through the hatch window as their ship winked out.

The disconnected docking chute drifted off into empty space.

"My ship!" John leaned against the wall; his voice heavy with defeat. "Everything I own is on that ship. It was nothing but a shell when my uncle bought it for me. We spent years building it together. It's the first thing I have truly ever owned. The one true thing in the galaxy I could call mine."

"Well, look on the bright side," Tyson quipped, in an attempt to try and cheer his still-lamenting friend up.

"Really? There's a bright side? And what exactly would that be?" John asked bitterly.

"Actually, you will find it's a bit better than a bright side," Tyson said, looking at his friend and grinning.

John stared blankly back at Tyson, "Okay sure, I know we are still alive. But tell me, what in all of this could possibly be good news?"

"You still have me!" Tyson's grin stretched even wider as slapped his friend heartedly on the back.

"Oh yeah, you're right. I feel so much better," John said, his voice thick with sarcasm as he wondered, and not for the first time either, why he hadn't yet killed his co-pilot.

Tyson shrugged, "It's true what they say, you know, there really is no cheering some people up." He set to work on his data pad, trying to plot their way forward, although he was not entirely sure what they were going to do next.

John said nothing. He just shook his head and sighed.

In a heavy silence, they both accessed their data pads. Fortunately, Tyson had thought to download the ship's schematic onto his data pad, complete with all the security codes for each of the rooms.

As they had suspected from the start, the ship was a wreck. Not only did it have multiple hull breaches, but there was also minimal power throughout, and all systems were offline, including life support, which meant there was no breathable air. Their bio-suits held a maximum of two hours supply; less if the user's needs were higher than normal. They had already been in them for over half an hour.

The plan was simple. First, they had to seal the holes and get the essential life support back online. For maximum efficiency, the two men agreed to split up. Tyson elected to head to the bridge to see if he could get the computer systems to boot up, leaving John to seal the hull breaches on his own.

It was a sensible division of labour, but John still sighed as he headed for the engine room. At least there was always the manual override, should any emergencies arise.

Tyson veered off down a second corridor, his helmet light illuminating the darkness barely more than a metre or so in front of him. "Good luck," he called over the intercom. John didn't bother with a reply.

It took much more time than Tyson would have liked to reboot the systems. He found he had to reroute what little power they had to be able to run a diagnostic check from the main computer hub. Glancing down to confirm his bio-suit's status, it dawned on him that John had maintained his intercom silence for over half an hour.

Normally it was near on impossible to shut the cocky captain up.

"Johnny!" he hailed him over the intercom. "The power readings are at twelve percent. I have them holding steady. The life support system is ready to come online."

John sealed the last of the holes in the hull, amazed that there was no major damage to the engine. Sure, a few parts would need replacing, but with work, he was certain it would run. "Okay. It's all good down here. Breaches are sealed. Bring life support online," he verified with a sigh of relief. He was looking forward to getting out of his clingy bio-suit and into some fresher air.

Fingers-crossed, Tyson activated the life support systems. The ship was big, and Tyson knew it would be awhile before they could tell if his friend's leak-fixes had been successful. Or if any new holes had happened to spring up in the meantime. It wasn't long, however, before the panel in front of him blinked to life and indicated the colour he had hoped for.

Tyson smiled and removed his helmet, a hiss of air blasting out as he did so. "02 is all green up here!" he called as he tapped the panel on the suit that turned off the oxygen supply.

Over in his sector of the ship, John removed his helmet gratefully and turned off the oxygen supply from his suit. He breathed deeply.

His friend's voice crackled to him over the suit's still-activated intercom. "Okay Johnny, what's our next move?"

"Check out the status of all the escape pods. We may still need them in case this crate doesn't hold together."

"Roger that. Anything else?"

"Yeah, see if there are any recordings of the attack. It might give us an idea of what happened to this ship and why," replied John.

"Okay, all the escape pods have been jettisoned and I managed to retrieve part of one of the recordings. It's bad, Johnny. Real bad."

"Tell me," John set his jaw, expecting the worst. They had encountered no bodies on the ship, so that meant one of two things. The first being they all fled in escape pods. Although, he thought that it was highly unlikely that, in the middle of an attack, everyone would get away safely. The second option was unthinkable.

"By the seven moons, Johnny, they killed them all. The whole crew. They dumped as many as they could into the evacuation pods and the rest they jettisoned out into space," Tyson's voice was strained with emotion. "Who does that, Johnny? Who does that?"

John didn't answer him. He had heard of similar things being done during his time in the Elite Special Forces, but he couldn't see any point in telling his friend. He would only worry more. "Whoever it was is long gone now, Ty. Sit tight, I'm on my way."

As soon as John stepped inside the cockpit, Tyson began talking. "I got busy while I was waiting for you. All the system screens are up and running," he said, obviously pleased with himself. "Oh wow! Man, you don't mess around when you sweat," he laughed suddenly at John's appearance.

John wiped his long, damp hair out of his face and gave a weak grin. "I will visit a personal grooming stylist just as soon as we find a system that has one," he vowed as he yanked off his bio-suit's gloves and stashed them in his helmet.

"I'll make the appointment for you myself. You look a mess without your designer clothes," laughed Tyson.

John was too tired to respond with anything other than an obscene hand gesture. He was well aware he had watched his favourite clothes wink out of his life along with *The Vulture*. His trademark was well-worn blue jeans with the back pocket that had been ripped off, any T-shirt from his collection that looked clean and, of course, his faithful grey bomber jacket.

"I know one thing," John fell into the vacant captain's seat with a sudden grin. "My style will always better than yours, mister 'look-at-me-I'm-wearing-the-same-black-t-shirt-and-green-jeans-for-the- last-three-years'," he teased, feeling a surge of finally returning to his normal self.

"I'm just ahead of my time, but you're right. We better find ourselves some other clothes. And soon. These bio suits are not meant to be lived in." Tyson looked down at the suit he was wearing with a grimace.

"Yes, very true. After that, one of us had better look into how much food and water is on this wreck." John sat up straighter and looked pointedly across at Tyson, who simply sighed and nodded. "And you know what else?" John slapped his hands against the arms of the chair as if staking his claim on it. "I want to have a really good go over the engine room as well." He got back to his feet and referenced his data pad for a moment before striding off. "My intercom is on. Keep in touch, okay?"

Tyson's thoughts had turned to food and, by the time he nodded, "Sure," John was already out of earshot.

***

It didn't take John long to find the engine room. He opened the door and stepped inside. A wave of nostalgia washed over him. It smelt just like his uncle's workshop back home; all grease and worn metal.

He wandered around the room, checking the equipment with a practiced eye. Two of the three main panels were definitely showing signs of damage. Closer inspection showed there had been a major power surge at some point, probably during the attack. John surmised that several critical components were beyond repair and would have to be replaced.

"Nothing too hard to fix ... providing we can find the parts," he mused to himself. He tapped the intercom. "Tyson, do you copy?"

"Copy, Johnny. What's up?" replied Tyson without missing a beat.

"What power percentage are we at now? And how long is it likely going to support us? Best guess."

"Sorry, Johnny, the engine's producing less than thirteen percent of power. At the rate we're going at, you're looking at around thirty-two hours and that is the best-case scenario. There is a power drain showing somewhere down in the cargo hold. If you could find a way to stop it, life support should stabilise, and we'll be okay."

"Right," John rubbed his hand behind his neck. "Can you see if there is a storeroom somewhere, where they might keep spare parts and tools?"

It took Tyson a moment or two to reply, "Sorry, Johnny, the layout is very different from *The Vulture's*. But there should be an unlocked door at the far end of your room. Can you see it?"

"On my way there now," John confirmed.

"Okay, well it looks like it leads out into an area that could hold what you're after."

John walked towards the only door he could see that looked promising, then stopped, catching sight of another leading off to his left. Instinct was telling him it was the better option. So, with a shrug, he turned and tried to open that one instead.

It swung inwards with a dull groan. John took a few steps inside and stopped. The holes in the hull made perfect sense to him now. Although he had never seen this particular type before, he knew in an instant what it was he was looking at. He stood and just stared at it with a dazed expression on his face.

There, right in front of him, was one of the biggest shield generators he had ever seen. It was so huge that the machine and its control console filled the entire room.

John could see immediately that it had been disconnected, rendering the whole thing non-functional. But if it had been operational during the attack, the firepower required to wear down the shields it generated, let alone tear massive holes in the ship's hull, must have been phenomenal.

John didn't know if he felt lucky or unlucky right at that moment. He settled on unlucky, because if they hadn't found this ship, he would still have *The White Vulture*. However, it still was an impressive find.

An idea suddenly formed in his mind; one he was sure would be worth a shot. With a grin, he contacted Tyson. "Copy, bridge."

"Go for Tyson. Hey, I'm heading down to the cargo bay to see what's causing the power drain," the co-pilot replied from the bridge in a burst of static.

"Good job. Quick question, are we using much power for heating? And would a big shield generator help?" John enquired mildly, already knowing and not waiting for Tyson to respond. "Well, hypothetically," he answered himself, "if we had a big ass shield generator, not just the standard sized one, I estimate we would save between fifteen and twenty percent power usage, depending on the output yield of the generator."

Still grinning, he walked over to the shield generator. After a few minutes, he had it all connected up. After doing a quick visual check and, being happy with what he saw, he pressed in the reset button.

Every single light on the generator's display panel turned green. He waited a full minute before he pressed in the start button, immediately the vast machinery roared to life, the deafening sound lasting somewhere around thirty seconds before it wound itself out and settled down into producing little more than a gentle hum.

A voice erupted over the intercom, "Johnny! The readings just went nuts! The power dropped down to eight percent and then rebounded to thirty-seven and it's still climbing! Are you telling me we have a shield generator? That's fantastic news!" Tyson said excitedly. "We just might live through this after all!"

'Hey, I heard that. Your intercom is still on," John shot back.

His friend didn't reply. He knew what he had said. It was what they both had been thinking ever since the disappearance of *The White Vulture*.

John closed the door behind him and headed up to the storeroom, unsurprisingly where Tyson had said it would be. He pushed the door open and went inside.

It was a mess. Supplies were scattered everywhere. Obviously whoever had left the ship had done so not expecting to return. He rummaged through all the parts, finally finding what he needed to finish patching the ship, and headed back to the engine room.

It was hard work and he had to make several trips back and forth for more parts, but already bonding with the busted-up beast, John did the best repair job he could do on the two damaged panels. It took every part he could find and some impressive ingenuity and creativity, but in the end he had just enough spare parts to patch them both. Even one-eyed Tyson wouldn't have called it pretty, but John was convinced it would hold for a while.

"You there, Johnny?" Tyson asked after neither of them had spoken for some time.

"Yeah mate, I have just finished up repairing the damaged panels," he replied, wiping the sweat off his face and smearing it with grease as he did so.

"Good stuff but do me a favour and don't try turning anything on just yet."

John frowned. Was that Tyson sounding nervous? Or was he hearing things now? "Too late," he said slowly. "I turned them on before I put the tools away."

"You did? And you're okay?" asked Tyson.

This time John was certain it was rising concern he was hearing in his friend's words. "Sure, why wouldn't I be?"

"Well, I'm in the cargo bay," Tyson replied cryptically. "And I think you better get your ass over here and take a look at what I have found."

Chapter Seven

The captain made his way to the cargo hold, a mixture of intrigue and trepidation turning his stomach into a tight ball. The sight of Tyson, standing in the doorway of another room, leaning off to the side looking very nervous, did little to calm his growing concern.

"Take a look in there. I think we might just have found out what caused the power surge," Tyson said, hooking a thumb back over his shoulder into the room.

"What is it, drama queen?" Forcing a flippancy into his voice he didn't quite feel, John shoved past his co-pilot and entered the room.

He froze. In the centre was a large steel cage, the bars were over two inches thick and wired to a separate backup generator that was powering a containment field. On the floor of the cage, curled into a ball and unmoving, was a man. While tall and lean himself, John could see that, if he had been standing alongside him, his new shipmate would have been much thinner and a lot taller than he was.

It was an unsettling thought, and John flicked his gaze over to the generator once more. It appeared to be working, although currently, it was drawing its power from the ship's main engines.

That wasn't a good sign.

Tyson was more interested in the man than the cage. "He must be at least ten feet tall, Johnny," he hissed, scanning the inert body with his cybernetic eye. "I'm not picking up any life signs though. He's got to be dead, right?"

"There's only one way to find out," John countered, maintaining his air of nonchalance.

"Careful, Johnny. Someone went to an awful lot of trouble to make sure that guy stayed put!"

John entered the room with a disdainful, "Pffft," and walked around the large cage, considering it from all angles. It had been battered with incredible force. The bars were bent and misshapen, stretched to their very limit. Little wonder then; whoever had imprisoned the man had erected the force field!

John looked but couldn't see a weapon anywhere in the cell that would explain any of the damage. Tyson stayed in the doorway, watching the man closely for any signs of life. "Johnny, I really think he's dead."

John reached the same conclusion, and with a nod, he walked across to the generator to turn it off. Slowly and noisily, the machinery wound down and John paused, waiting with his hand hovering above the buttons, ready to restart it all at a moment's notice should the need have arisen. The figure inside the cage, however, remained motionless.

John stepped away from the now-silent generator. "Tyson, stop being such a chicken shit and get over here and help me!"

Tyson shot the captain a sheepish look and finally inched his way into the cargo hold.

"And find me something to break this," John gestured towards the huge metal lock that was hanging from the cage's door.

With hesitation Tyson inched closer, examining first the door, then the lock. "Wow! How old school can you get? Sorry Johnny, nothing I have will open that. Brute force is all that's going to crack that thing." He swept his cybernetic eye around the room. "Maybe we can find the key."

"I'm going to go out on a limb here and say, whoever locked this man up wasn't that kind to just leave a key just hanging out in the open," John returned sarcastically.

"Yeah, right...I'll go find something heavy so you can smash it off. At least that's something even you can do without screwing it up," Tyson said with a grin as he headed off into a small room just off to the side of the main cargo area. "Don't go anywhere."

John rolled his eyes. "Move your ass, Ty. I have a really bad feeling about this."

***

Tyson entered the little room, looked around, and immediately began swearing quietly under his breath. Almost every available surface was covered with dozens upon dozens of varying pieces of counterfeit Alien Tech. High quality but still fakes. Even without his enhanced vision, Tyson could tell none of it was authentic.

Highly prized, much sought after and extremely rare, what gave genuine Alien Tech its uniqueness was that, no matter what the object was, from a simple part to detailed electronics, it always exhibited the same rough, pitted texture that made it stand out from anything else. People had tried over and over to successfully recreate this unusual desirable appearance, but none could match the craftsmanship of an original piece. Unfortunately, while some of the forgeries came close, most of the time it didn't take a genius to spot the imitators. Real Alien Tech was made of a vastly superior, and still mostly unknown, alloy that could not be cut or scratched or modified with any kind of tool or weaponry.

There were a handful of interesting looking pieces on one of the long benches, and Tyson wandered over to examine them in greater detail. He dismissed them quickly as the usual poor imitations and, with a disappointed groan, set about searching for something to break the lock with.

It didn't take him long to uncover a large ball hammer amongst the rest of the junk. He shrugged, picking it up. He would really prefer something a bit more heavy-duty, but he was pretty sure it would do the job.

***

John was studying the force field generator when his co-pilot returned with the hammer. "This thing is quite clever," he began before Tyson had even reached his side. "It's designed to run on the ship's power supply. However, if the ship can no longer supply a full charge, it switches over to its own power and look, see here," John gestured to a section of the console that Tyson dutifully looked at, even though he had no idea what he was supposed to be understanding, "It then recharges itself automatically as the ship's power becomes available again." Admiration for the designer of the system was obvious in his voice. "Someone went to a lot of trouble to make sure this guy was secure at all times, Ty."

Tyson scratched his chin as he handed John the hammer. "Maybe it wasn't such a good idea turning it off, then?"

John's expression darkened. "Look at him, Ty. I don't care what he's done. No one deserves to be treated like this. You don't need cybernetic sight to see his body is covered in bruises and he has clearly been beaten, starved, not to mention, he's naked and probably dead." John took a deep breath and hung his head. "Ty, I've seen the worst of slave traders treat their merchandise better. If you don't want to help, fine. Leave! LEAVE!"

"I'm not saying don't help," Tyson hastily assured his friend, a little taken aback by the outburst. He didn't know a lot of John's history, but he did know from past conversations, that it was best to tread carefully whenever slavers were mentioned. "I'm just saying be careful, that's all."

John moved around to the front of the cage and began wielding the hammer like a man possessed.

The lock was very strong and, even after five solid minutes of pounding at it with the heavy tool, it was completely mangled and misshapen, but still held firm. John roared in frustration then, red-faced and dripping with sweat, he renewed his assault. Tyson stood by in silence as his friend unleashed his full fury upon the sturdy restraint. Never before had he seen him look so determined.

Finally, after what seemed like a lifetime, the lock gave a long, metallic groan and dropped to the floor, the loud 'clang' echoing throughout the whole ship.

Dropping the hammer, John swung the cage door open and cautiously approached the now-slowly moving form. "Hello," he said softly, leaning in closer. "Can you hear me?"

The man tenderly eased himself over onto his back, gulped in a few deep breaths and opened his eyes, looking up directly into John's. "How could I not?" he queried in a hoarse whisper. "You were making sufficient noise to wake me from the dead."

"Sorry." John took a hurried step backward at the intense stare from the stranger.

The man nodded and rolled his head to the side to look at Tyson through the caged bars. "Your friend over there, he is not as brave as you, it would seem." He returned his gaze to John. "Are you not afraid of me?"

John wavered. He didn't recognize the man's accent and there was something quite disturbing about his unblinking, black-rimmed eyes.

"Look what I have done to this cage," he went on, his voice cracked and heavy. "Imagine what I could do to your fragile body."

Beginning to rethink his rash behaviour, John examined the cage again. The man was right. All of the damage had definitely been inflicted from the inside. "All I was concerned about was you; not what danger I might be in," he answered truthfully.

The man moved with unnatural grace; uncoiling his long limbs from the floor, moving fluidly up onto his knees, and then stretching himself upright, the top of his head mere inches from the roof of the cage.

Tyson finally found his voice, "Who put you in there? And who attacked this ship?"

The man's next move was like liquid lightning. He was upon John in an instant, pinning him against the side of the cage with incredible strength. Tyson swore.

The man spoke fast and loud, his yellow eyes frantic and pleading, "Human, I do not have much time. I believe my life force is about to extinguish."

"Okay," John gave a small nod. "I'm listening."

"I am Esheel. Remember my name, for it will be important for you to do so. I am one of those you call the Ancients. I was taken from a planet. A planet that was home to me and my family for many years. The ones who captured me discovered what I was. For a while, they treated me kindly to gain information, until they realized I would not tell them the birthplace of my race. After that, they began torturing me for my secrets." He took a deep shuddering breath. "They were not successful."

John had a thousand questions buzzing through his head, but there was that look in the man's eyes that rendered him speechless.

"I require you to take my body back to the planet I call my home, Caxton. Will you honour this request for me?"

While the man had been speaking, Tyson had been moving towards the cage door, and now he reached down, picked up the ball hammer, and brandished it at him. "Let him go," he hissed. "Or I'll cave your skull in."

"It's okay, Ty." John found his voice again. "He's not hurting me." He directed his next words at the man, still gripping the front of his bio-suit. "Yes. Okay. We will take you back to your home. That is," he added with a wry grin, "if we can keep this pile of space junk together long enough to fly there."

The man calmed visibly, letting go of John and taking a step back. "Your scent is unusual for a human, however my other senses tell me your word is your bond. Thank you."

"Sure, no problem," John finally allowed himself to relax a little. "Now, let's get you out of this cage."

He peeled himself off the bars and turned his back on the man, intending to lead the way out. He didn't get very far before he felt a piercing pain in the right side of his neck. He opened his mouth to scream, but nothing came out. He felt his blood begin to flow out of his body, as his attacker dug deep with three fingers. John could feel the man's fingers moving beneath his skin with purpose.

The man was right behind him now, whispering into his ear, "I do not know how this will affect you, but I give you my gift. It will help you in your task. To my knowledge, it has never been given to a human before. I have great strength. Others of my kind possess different types of abilities; on rare occasions, some are blessed with more than one. Its manifestation is random, and it may only be temporary. I give you this to aid you only in returning me to my home. On completion of your task, a further reward will be bestowed on you, if you survive the bonding trial."

As his last words ebbed away from his lips, the tall naked man slumped to the floor. His body paled in colour to an ash white. His cheeks hollowed as his whole body contracted tightly into a foetal position, his skin shrinking back to the bones. Blue blood bubbled out of his mouth and stained his chest. His body had mummified itself within seconds.

Chapter Eight

John was woken up by several violent jolts. For some reason, he couldn't immediately fathom why he was harnessed into the co-pilot's chair and the whole ship was shaking violently. He looked around, totally disoriented at first, and slowly the memory of all that had happened returned to his fuzzy brain.

His ship, *The Vulture*, was gone. He and Tyson had boarded the floating death trap of a ship, *The Trading Winds*, to find some star charts. There he had made a deal with a tall, clearly insane, skinny naked man who had been held prisoner on the ship who claimed to be an Ancient.

John moved to raise a hand to rub the back of his neck and winced. Shortly after he had agreed to take the crazy bastard home, he'd attacked him viciously from behind and then died…? A nanosecond before, he himself had blacked out.

What the …? Tyson was flying?

Tyson was, in fact, not so much flying the ship as fighting the controls of the severely damaged craft. He glanced across at his wounded friend, relieved to see he was finally conscious. "I've found a port we can dock at. All we have to do is get there in one piece."

John wasn't sure if it was his eyes not focusing properly or if it was the shuddering of the ship, but it looked like Tyson had three faces. It took him several moments to decide it was the latter. He rubbed at his neck again. At the spot where the crazy guy had cut him with his razor-sharp nails, his fingers brushed a med-pack bandage and he realised Tyson had patched him up.

"Good thing you always put those in your pack," Tyson nodded. "It probably saved your life."

"Thanks, and you were right," John sighed, lowering his hand. "I should never have gone into that cage."

Tyson grinned. "Look on the bright side ..."

John rolled his eyes. "You and your bright sides!"

"Hey! This is a good one!" The ship gave another violent lurch and Tyson strained and wrestled it back under control before continuing, "You're always saying I need more practice flying and here I am – flying!"

"You call this shuddering through space 'flying'?" John raised an eyebrow, amused.

"You would think a guy would be grateful after his best friend saves his life. But OH NO. All I get is criticism!" Tyson laughed as he added, "Some people are never happy."

John tried to sit up but found that he couldn't. His whole body felt like it was on fire and he was tired; very tired. He reached out and pressed a finger against the panel's display in front of him. Slowly, he found the correct menu, selected the stabiliser settings and increased them as best he could without overcompensating and causing more damage.

He managed to apply the new settings and both men immediately noticed the difference: the ship was still running very rough, but now it wasn't trying to throw them out of the chairs anymore. John had overexerted himself by making the adjustments to the ship and passed out once again.

Tyson was doing his best to pilot the wrecked vessel. Whatever John had done before going back to sleep had worked. It still wasn't what anyone would call a smooth ride, but at least the ship didn't feel like it was trying to shake itself apart anymore.

He headed for the port, praying he managed to get them there in one piece. For the following three days, John slept fitfully, alternating between raging sweats and shivering with extreme cold. Sometimes he yelled things out in a strange language.

Tyson did what he could do to help. Once he had successfully plotted their course into the navigation system and figured out how to engage the autopilot, he spent his days alone making himself familiar with all the ship's systems and complicated layout.

He then went out on 'salvage missions', scrounging up a few thin blankets and other meagre supplies; even managing to find some fresh clothes for him and John to change into from one of the crew's quarters that he could still get access to.

The galley, he had discovered, had been badly damaged in the attack, but he did find a food hydrator that was still functional. Unfortunately, after a few days, the only food cubes he could find amongst the rubble were sweet saffron porridge with lemon syrup.

Once he was satisfied with all the settings and had checked that John had food and water within easy reach, Tyson slept.

***

The sound of chaotic alarms going off woke him sometime later. He sat up straight, blinking, taking a moment to comprehend what was taking up the whole cockpit window in front of him. It was a space station and it was getting closer by the second!

Suddenly very alert and awake, Tyson threw on the reverse thrusters and killed the main engine as he threw the ship into a violent left banking manoeuvre, barely missing the station.

The ship shuddered and lurched to a stop.

The motion was enough to wake John, who lifted his head groggily to ask, "Where are we?"

"The seven moons if I know," answered Tyson. "I just woke up myself. If it wasn't for the alarm," he reached across to switch the ear-piercing wailing off, "we would've crashed right into it." Frowning, he set the ship into an orbiting pattern and then accessed the system's star maps. "We are in the outer sector of the Omega System, and that is Harmon Station, the third biggest in this system," he informed his puzzled-looking friend.

"How long were we asleep?" asked John as he reached for the drink on the console in front of him.

"You, about four days, on and off. Me, for about eleven hours. Not a bad nap," said Tyson, who was now standing up and stretching out his aching muscles.

"Okay, let's take a look at this station," said John, scanning the station's stats on his display. "This is good. This is *very* good. This place has all the gear we need: refuelling station, repair dock and spray booth. Now, all we need are the credits to pay for it." He waved the back of his left hand over a scanner next to the screen.

At John's insistence, both he and Tyson had credit circuits fitted just under their skin. When scanned, they displayed the balance of their credit accounts. The rest of their readily negotiable, portable credit sticks had been stashed onboard *The Vulture* and were all probably off drifting in some unknown quadrant right at that moment.

After a quick calculation he figured they were short, very short, of the required credits for everything they needed to repair.

"So…any chance you've found something on this wreck we can sell?" he asked with a hopeful look across at Tyson. "Well, I was considering selling off your internal organs if you croaked it, but unfortunately, it looks like you're going to pull through."

John started laughing, but it quickly turned into a coughing fit. It took him a moment or two to get it under control, but once he had stopped coughing, he unbuckled himself out of the chair's harness for the first time in almost four days.

The movement puffed the stale, sweaty air out of the bunched-up bio suit right into his face. "What in the seven moons of Cryos is that smell?" he grimaced, turning his head to try and escape the foul odour.

"That would be you, my smelly friend," replied Tyson, a wide grin plastered across his face and knowing very well what a hygiene conscious person John was normally.

Disgusted with his own odour and barely able to breathe through it, John pleaded with his friend. "Tell me we have a working shower on this wreck of a ship."

"As it so happens, we have many," Tyson's smile was almost serene. "Complete with hot water and full massage functions. And because I can't stand that stink either, I'll just get you the directions to the nearest one."

***

Following his hot shower, after which he felt much better, John replaced the med-pack on his neck with a fresh one. He was pleased to see the wound was healing nicely, although it would probably leave another scar, he could add to his already impressive collection.

Tyson had thoughtfully laid out some fresh clothes for him on the bunk he had allocated him. Grateful to be out of the bio-suit at least, John still cringed as he changed into the black and silver jumpsuit his friend had chosen.

John shuddered. What he objected to more were the vibrant purple and white sneakers that accompanied it. Now he understood why his co-pilot had pointed the phrase "beggars can't be choosers" out to him before he left.

His stench under control, , John turned his attention to their other pressing predicament and he poked around the broken ship, assessing every room he was able to, looking for something to sell in order to scrape up some much needed credits. He had little success, however, as Tyson had already found and bagged everything of any value.

John made his way slowly down to the cargo hold. There, in the centre of the steel cage, was the lifeless body of the strange man, wrapped tightly in some bedsheets Tyson had found. As John moved closer, he noticed Tyson had taken the added precaution of chaining the door to the cage shut.

Turning away from the corpse, John looked at the force field generator. He was sure it would fetch them a good price - enough for some of the more urgent repairs, anyway.

A voice crackled over the ship's intercom: "This is Pilot Tyson Blake. Would all breathing passengers report to the cockpit immediately? Thank you for your compliance."

Heading back to the bridge, John shook his head, wondering if there was anything worse than his friend being in charge. There probably was, but nothing immediately came into his mind.

***

Tyson had been busy while John had been away.

He had hacked the station's files and added a few new ones; including travel documents, ownership of the vessel, insurances, trading licences and up to date quarantine medical reports on he and John.

He had also learnt more about the type of ship that they were on. It was a class titled *Pioneer,* not one he was familiar with, and it was reportedly the smallest of that class. When John entered the cockpit, he found his friend sitting in the co-pilot's chair, looking rather pleased with himself. He took the pilot's seat with a relieved sigh and asked, amusement in his voice, "What have you done? And should I be worried?"

"Johnny, I found him."

"Found who exactly?"

"Hector Gibbs. I found him."

It was the name that had haunted John, ever since he had learnt it. It was the contact of Wayde Dempsey, the man that had thrown himself out of their airlock while being pursued by Captain Gomez of the Scarlet Blade. All John knew was that the package he had been given was to be delivered to Hector Gibbs.

"Where is he? Let's get this thing delivered and off my ship as soon as possible."

"He isn't here but I know where he is headed. I found his flight log registration."

John smiled. "Excellent work, Ty. Now, let's get this heap patched up, deliver the package, get paid and get Breanna Gomez off our tail once and for all."

"It's always nice to be appreciated, and there is more," grinned Tyson.

"Two great deeds in one day? Hmm. Now I am worried," teased the captain.

Tyson feigned astonishment, "I have no idea what you mean. I'll have you know I may have just solved all of our problems. Okay, maybe not all of them, but it will certainly help us a great deal."

"I repeat," John gave a small groan. "What have you done? And should I be worried?" It made him nervous when his friend 'fixed' problems. He almost always made things worse. A lot worse.

"I've just been in contact with a small and exclusive firm that trades in exotic goods. They're very interested in obtaining new up to date star maps from the Alpha and Beta systems," Tyson explained with a grin. "Lucky for us, I back up all our star map files on this," he waved his data pad in his friend's direction.

"I don't know," John sighed, a familiar feeling of impending doom washing over him. "It's highly illegal to sell anyone maps of another system without going through the proper channels."

"I know that, but it's highly profitable. The number of credits we could get from this *one* sale would be enough to repair most of the ship." Tyson leaned back in his chair as he continued, "It's not like we have a lot of options here, Johnny."

"Yeah. Okay. You're right. How do they want the exchange to be done?" asked John.

Tyson went back to the keyboard, a moment later, announcing, "In person. A place called *The Nobles Bar*. Twenty-seventh floor. Observation deck."

"Good. And instead of throwing figures at them, ask if they have a dress code," John said with a nod.

"You seriously want me to ask them that?" Tyson looked at John as if he were nuts. "If there's a dress code?"

"Mention dress code only. I have done this sort of thing before. Just do it. You'll see."

Shaking his head in disbelief, Tyson sent the message. The rapid reply was not what he expected, and he read it aloud, unable to hide the surprise in his voice:

"Thank you for not being so common as to ask what we would offer for such an item. Smart formal attire is required as usual; High-line neckties are not necessary for the establishment we have chosen. We would appreciate you bringing the map data on small L2 drive…"

"…Your contact is Mr. Rodney," Tyson finished reading, continuing to scan the display for any further information. "Hey, they've sent us a picture!" he said suddenly. "I gather it's of our esteemed Mr. Rodney."

John got up from his chair and walked over to Tyson's screen to look at the image shown there. "Good," he nodded. "Set up the meeting for 2330 hours."

Concealing his curiosity at his normally verbose friend's briefly worded orders, Tyson relayed the message and promptly received confirmation.

The meeting set, Tyson copied the required system's star maps onto a small portable drive that was no bigger than his thumbnail and handed it mutely across to John.

John contacted the station and received docking authorization. Still refusing to share even small talk with his co-pilot, he edged the busted-up ship into the docking port with the help of the station's guidance system. After successfully docking, a confirmation notice flashed up on his screen.

"Welcome crew of *The Broken Eye* to Harmon station. We hope you have a pleasant stay."

The welcome message was repeated in at least three different languages and John reached over and shut it off. "The Broken Eye?" he finally spoke, punctuating his query with a single, raised eyebrow.

Tyson put on his most innocent face and said, "We did vote on it and when it was suggested, you didn't answer. So…I took that as a yes."

"I see," replied John. "And exactly when was it suggested and decided upon?"

The co-pilot looked up at the ceiling of the cockpit, apparently deep in thought for a moment before he replied, "Come to think of it, you may have been unconscious for that conversation. Oh well, never mind that now. Great name though, huh?!"

John couldn't help himself. He fought the urge for as long as he could, but a smile betrayed him and split his face. He tried to count to ten is his head trying to control himself, but he only reached an eight-count before he exploded into laughter at his friend's explanation.

"I guess I had better go find myself more appropriate clothing for this meeting." He shook his head with a resigned sigh and checked his watch. He still had plenty of time.

"Have fun!" Tyson called at his departing back. "And don't sweat it! I'll organize everything else from here as soon as you have secured the payment."

Chapter Nine

John had been to many space stations before but none quite like Harmon. He had never been to the Omega system before and he took his time following the directions Tyson had uploaded to his data pad, checking out as much of the scenery as he could.

It certainly had its own flavour. Part social hub, part retail and part watering hole, it was huge and there were people everywhere. The station's primary function was to supply travellers and local traffic with anything their heart may have desired and John peeked into shops that were not in Tyson's directions but that were selling a wide variety of interesting items – from system upgrade programs to exotic foods to imitation Alien jewellery.

Eventually, John found the store Tyson had selected for him that sold a range of clothing from overalls to chameleon suits. The staff ignored him for the first few minutes until finally a reluctant young woman approached him and said, "Good morning, Sir. My name is Shayla. May I help you choose something for today?"

John couldn't blame her for her hesitation in approaching him. What he was wearing didn't mark him as someone with either taste or credits, and he shot her a charming grin by way of apology, quickly appraising her.

She was certainly very attractive; a human with long, blonde silky hair and wearing a black suit with a tight, bright pink shirt underneath that emphasized her ample bust.

"You certainly can," John said finally with a wolfish grin. "As you can see, I am in dire need for some help with my fashion sense."

"Well, let's see if you can be saved or not," she said, smiling sweetly back.

"Nice to meet you Shayla. My name is John," he reached out his hand, ditching his usual casual air for a more business-like persona. Shayla offered hers in return.

John took it and gently brushed his lips across the back of her hand. "I have a business meeting tonight," he explained, looking around at the racks of clothing. "And I require some more suitable clothing."

Shayla smiled at him, running a critical eye over his 'borrowed' outfit, then she winked.

If John hadn't known better, he would have sworn she meant something by it, but he knew that salespeople were chosen for their looks and were trained to extract the maximum amount of credits from their customers. He was sure, however, that the mention of the Nobles Bar had got her attention.

"Certainly, John. Please follow me," Shayla replied with an efficient flick of her hair, leading him straight in the direction of the higher end of the store.

John frowned to himself, annoyed that he wasn't able to get his usual style of clothing. He had to remind himself several times that credits were short and they needed the transaction to go smoothly. Like it or not, he had to dress as a successful businessman.

Shayla had bombarded him with a mountain of choices. He had never seen so many colours and styles of suits in his life and hoped never to again. She had tried her best to influence him towards the higher end of suits and seemed a little disappointed with what he finally chose: dark grey pants, white shirt with a black, silver-buttoned vest, and a long, dark maroon jacket.

"Traders," she gave her head a shake, totalling up the bill.

John wasn't sure if she was annoyed by the minimal commission she'd earn or because what he settled on wasn't technically a complete suit but a cross match of three.

He left his old clothes behind and paid, cringing as it very nearly wiped out all the credits he had. He had taken barely a dozen or so steps back into the mall area before he realized he hadn't bought new shoes. He was still wearing the purple and white joggers! He shrugged and headed off for his meeting.

***

John reached the Nobles Bar early and bought himself a drink. It wasn't long before he was approached by the Maître d' and quietly informed that his contact had yet to arrive. He had expected to wait and had to mask his surprise at being led, only moments later, by an impeccably dressed but expressionless waiter into the private booth section. It was a large, spotlessly clean but also noticeably empty area with its own separate, gleaming bar.

John was shown to a table, the still silent waiter bringing him another Daylarian scotch with dry ginger without bothering to ask if he wished to change his order. He then returned to his position behind the bar.

It was a short time later that a stocky man with a wide barrel chest, closely cropped white hair and neatly trimmed black beard entered the room. Everything from his intricately woven black-rimmed glasses to his perfectly tailored three-piece suit oozed wealth and power, and John guessed immediately that it had to be Oberon Rodney.

The man walked over to the table and wordlessly extended his hand. John stood and accepted the firm shake. "Mr. Rodney, I presume. How very nice to meet you. I'm Captain Alexander. I believe my associate has contacted your office about some items you may have some interest in."

"Captain Alexander. Please, call me Oberon," Mr. Rodney said, sitting down.

Within seconds, the waiter had placed a drink in front of him and Oberon smiled, thanking the man before he once again returned silently to the bar in the corner.

John's smile was equally charming, and he replied without dropping his business-like facade for a second. "My friends call me John."

"Very well, John, how long have you been on Harmon? Do you like our little station?"

John took a purposeful sip of his drink and waited until he had placed his glass back on the table before answering, "To be honest, we haven't been here very long. We only stopped fora few minor repairs and to restock our supplies. But I must say, so far, I've been quite impressed by it."

"Good. Good," Mr. Rodney nodded, pride resonating in his voice. "We do our best to keep this station up to the highest standards. It is our wish for it to be among the greatest of attractions this system has to offer. That brings us to our meeting today," he paused. "Have you brought the item to be reviewed?" he enquired politely.

John inclined his head, keeping his expression neutral. He knew Tyson had put two files on the drive. One, an open sample drive, the other, a complete file that had been locked and encrypted. The only way to get the information out of the secure file was with the correct cipher key. Otherwise, it could take years to crack his friend's locking program.

Mr. Rodney put a credit stick on the table and said, "We believe in paying well for information, but of course, we need to check the quality."

John nodded again in agreement and passed the little drive across the table.

Mr. Rodney produced a data pad and inserted the drive. His eyes widened as he scanned the information the sample file flashed up on the data pad. "My word, I must say these appear very thorough. May I ask where you acquired them from?" A look of surprise crossed his face, which he quickly smothered and abruptly changed his tone. "Captain Alexander, excuse my manners. I do not need to know how you obtained these maps. I would pay you a handsome bonus if you would keep the sale of the maps exclusive to us."

He didn't need it, but John still took a moment to consider the offer. "I would like to think we are going to be good friends and can come to a mutual agreement, Mr. Rodney," he finally nodded. "And please, call me John. I will warn you though, it may take some persuading to convince my associate not to set up other business meetings with other interested buyers."

Far from appearing concerned, Oberon brightened at the news and took two more credit sticks from his breast pocket and placed them on the table. "John, please, I insist you check the balance and hope you find the amount satisfactory."

John took out his data pad, slowly reached across the table and swiped it over all three. The data pad beeped and, fighting to control his expression, he looked down at the amount. A lump caught in his throat and he swallowed hard.

"I believe we have reached an understanding, Oberon," John said with a warm smile.

Oberon gestured above his head with his hand and the waiter immediately came over with two fresh drinks. "Let us celebrate a satisfactory transaction," he announced loudly, raising his glass to shoulder height.

John lifted his drink off the table, his grin not wavering for an instant as he transferred the unlocking code across to his new 'friend's' data pad. "I hope we have an opportunity to do business again together."

Oberon smiled, "Speaking of new business, I have a contract you may be interested in."

John took a long, slow sip from his glass and nodded thoughtfully for Oberon to continue.

"It's a simple enough task, a drop off assignment. I would use my normal couriers, but discretion is of the utmost importance," he emphasized with a brief adjustment of his glasses.

"I see. Is the delivery time-sensitive?" enquired John.

"No," Oberon replied with a quick shake of his head. "Secrecy, however, is paramount. The item is quite small but contains, shall we say, delicate contents. It also requires a DNA signature on acceptance of the item."

"Nothing that will land me in trouble with the local authorities, I hope," half-joked John.

"I assure you it is all perfectly legal," Oberon insisted. "It is simply the fewer people that know about it, the better. You will be well compensated for your time."

John smiled. Extra credits were always attractive. "I think we can help each other out," he replied with a smile.

"Excellent. I shall have the item and all pertinent details delivered to your ship within the hour."

"My ship is undergoing repairs at the moment. I can depart as soon as they are completed."

Oberon nodded and slid two more credit sticks across the table. John scanned them over his pad. Another generous amount appeared but he managed to keep his expression neutral as he slid the sticks into his jacket pocket.

"It goes without saying, you will get the balance of the amount on confirmation of delivery," said Oberon.

"Of course,"

"Please, take this," John stood up and, as he reached out to shake Oberon's hand, he felt the other man press something into his palm. He looked down and saw he had been given an old-fashioned holographic business card.

"Thank you," he nodded and pocketed it along with the credit sticks. "I look forward to seeing you again on my return."

Then, without looking back, he strode out of the booth, nodded at the waiter and made a beeline straight for *The Broken Eye*.

***

Gesturing for another drink, Oberon watched John leave. He liked the man, even if he was not the business type he tried to portray. *"Nice try Captain Alexander,"* Oberon smirked. Even without prior research, he knew ex-military when he saw it. John Alexander, specialising in acquisitions and delivery of rare items. Word from his underground contacts assured him he was reliable and dependable.

The waiter swapped Oberon's empty glass for a full one, enquiring mildly, "Is there anything else I can get you, Mr. Rodney?"

Oberon lifted the whiskey tumbler to his lips and smiled, "No thank you. I believe I have everything I need."

The waiter backed away and Oberon reached inside his jacket pocket, taking out a small data pad and typing a brief message into it. Almost immediately a response came back on the pad. The result was positive. Captain Alexander showed recent traces of the Penchell serum in his blood. A very good sign, Oberon thought to himself. John may have lost the ship he left the Beta system with, but he had retained the vial. It mattered not that he had somehow come into contact with the contents, Oberon had been promised it was harmless until it was combined with its sister vial. Even then, one had to know what it was capable of, which the Captain most certainly wasn't.

Smiling broadly to himself, Oberon drained his glass and considered the situation more fully. He had always believed in luck, but how glorious fate was that they now had Captain Alexander couriering *both* vials for them.

***

While making his way back to the ship, John kept getting the feeling he was being followed. He quickened his pace for a good hundred metres, then suddenly stopped and turned around. He saw no one out of place, however, and put it down to his imagination. Trying to dismiss the thought, he continued down to *The Broken Eye*.

On his approach to the docking port, he stopped and again and he looked around. Still, there was no one there. Frowning slightly, he checked for any sign of surveillance cameras.

He soon spotted two sets on the wall and, putting his back to them, he pretended to have a coughing fit. While in the throes of apparent discomfort, he was able to discreetly transfer the value of all the credit sticks to his hand chip. It beeped softly three times to acknowledge the transactions, each one covered up with more coughing.

Finally, seeming to get himself back under control, John pushed off the wall with his foot and continued toward his ship. As he rounded the last corner, he was greeted by several soldiers who were standing in formation, blocking his path to the docking port.

The highest-ranking officer stepped forward and said, "Captain Alexander, I am Sergeant Wheeler and I would very much like a word with you."

John had spent many years attached to the military as a pilot and knew exactly the type of man standing in front of him – a career man. One who did everything by the book, his book, and one who had probably written a few extra pages into it regarding the appropriation of funds, or rather redirection of funds into filling his own pockets.

"Sorry, Sergeant," he said without the slightest hint of respect. "I'm retired. If you want to talk, you'll have to make an appointment with my secretary."

He made as if to shove his way past the soldiers, but the Sergeant grabbed his arm. "I'm afraid I must insist, *Captain*."

John knew he was outnumbered, and he stopped, turning to face the soldiers with a small, frustrated sigh, "What can I do for you, Sergeant Wheeler?"

Wheeler released his arm and said, "Captain Alexander. It has come to my attention that you have recently come into the possession of some credit sticks. Allow me to relieve you of them. Let's call it a visitor's tax."

John knew enough to recognize a shakedown when he saw one and he hesitated.

"Sergeant, why are you really here?" He handed over one of the empty credit sticks with a raised eyebrow.

The Sergeant looked down at the chip and said smoothly, "I'm glad you are being so cooperative. Where are the others? I believe there were several."

John cursed loudly, remembering the security camera nodes that he had spotted on the walls of the bar, making a show of anger as he handed them over.

"We have checked you out, Captain. You and your co-pilot, Tyson Blake. Aside from a few minor warrants in the Alpha and Beta systems you are, for the most part, clean."

"If that's all, Sergeant, I have to see about some repairs to my ship," John said bitterly as he started walking away.

Wheeler waved his hand and the soldiers stepped back to clear him a path. "One more thing, Captain," he added with a tight smile. "I'm the senior officer on this station. I want you and your crew off my station within four hours or there will be consequences."

"Any particular reason why?" enquired John with a brief look back over his shoulder.

"Let's just say … I don't like your purple shoes!"

John could tell this man was as particular to detail as he was corrupt, and he quipped, "Yes Sergeant, message understood," without breaking his stride towards the station's main hanger.

***

When John arrived at *The Broken Eye*, a man in a crisp black suit with swept-back dark hair was waiting for him. "Can I help you?" he enquired pleasantly.

"Captain Alexander?"

John nodded.

"Mr. Rodney asked me to deliver this to you and you alone."

The man reached out and handed John a small envelope along with a thin, bronze briefcase. He then produced a data pad with a DNA scanner and motioned for John to place his hand on it.

The scanner beeped, a series of lights flashed in confirmation and the case unlocked, revealing another smaller, bronze rectangular box inside.

John removed his hand from the scanner and put the smaller of the boxes in his pocket.

"Thank you. I will inform Mr. Rodney that the package was delivered into your care." Abruptly, the young man turned and departed the hanger bay.

Once he was safe aboard his ship, John relayed to Tyson the details of his meeting with Mr. Rodney and the subsequent encounter between him and Sergeant Wheeler.

Tyson looked puzzled by the news. "We haven't been flagged for anything. We have had several scans and checks run over us in the last few minutes, but if there was a problem, we would know about it by now. Relax," he assured his friend, checking the station's data flow. "Our cover is solid."

"Good. Let's just get out of here as soon as possible after the repairs are done," John said with an uneasy grin. "When Sergeant Wheeler realizes that he has empty credit sticks in his possession, he won't be happy."

"I hate to admit it but that was a smooth move transferring those credits like you did," Tyson said, nodding his approval.

John smiled smugly.

Tyson rolled his eyes. "I did say I hated to admit it."

***

Unbeknownst to John, Tyson had been busy while his friend had been away. Guessing their time at Harmon was limited, he had called on structural engineers from several different companies to scan the ship and submit their repair proposals, complete with refitting.

He quickly filled John in on what he had done, and they were in the middle of considering which tender offered the best value for credits when a third engineering submission flashed up on their screens.

It was a radical proposal. Instead of removing and replacing all the damaged panels, it advised cutting and reshaping the hull using the existing panels and the application of a newly formulated, heavy-duty Tycolp patch sealer over the scorch marks.

Tycolp patches, the submission insisted, were very effective in repairing blemishes on a ship's surface. There was a slight downside in that it took three hours to harden. However, once it did, it was as strong as the original hull.

John stared at the three-dimensional model that accompanied the third proposal. The overall shape of the vessel would be very different, much smoother and sleeker. Sure, they would lose about a quarter of their current cargo space, but it would still leave them with over double what *The White Vulture* had held.

The cost of the first two tenders was roughly the same, while the third tender's price was almost a third cheaper, a discount with the complements of Mr. Oberon Rodney.

It didn't take John and Tyson long to agree the third proposal was their best choice. Not only because it included a full trim, but its estimated completion time fell neatly within the four-hour deadline they had been presented with to vacate the space station. Within minutes Tyson had forwarded payment to their chosen company. He also arranged a small army of specialized contractors to carry out a refurbish, repair and restock of the ship.

It cost them a substantial amount of the credits they had just acquired, and before they could let anyone on board, they realised they had the little matter of the body in the cargo hold to address.

After a brief discussion, Tyson suggested they store the body in the ship's crew shower room. It was lockable, he pointed out, and it was out of the way. It was one of the few areas that hadn't been damaged so, theoretically, no one should have the need to access it. John, mostly because he couldn't be bothered coming up with a better plan, agreed.

It hadn't taken them long to relocate their 'guest'. Although John had to send Tyson off to try and find something to mask the smell, for even in its mummified condition, the body had begun to stink quite a bit. Tyson soon returned with a box of hang able air fresheners and the two men set to work decorating the room.

Once they were happy he was safely secured in his new, scented accommodation, John left the shower block, leaving Tyson to lock the doors with one of his elaborate alphanumeric codes, just in case someone on the outside should go wandering. After all, a naked dead man wrapped in a bedsheet would be a little hard to explain.

***

A sophisticated symphony of professional efficiency buzzed to life both inside and outside the ship. There were several different groups of engineering and repair droids assigned to the work, and all were extremely well-organized. A group of twelve began the re-design and rebuild of the exterior of the ship, while a smaller group of nine set to work on the inside.

The outer droids worked quickly and methodically, lifting and cutting away the damaged parts of the hull and replacing them perfectly in line with the newly modified shape of the hull that the team on the inside had created.

The secondary team replaced all the damaged interior wiring and components before joining their mechanical teammates outside to work on the multiple scorch marks. This was a much slower process as each section had to be thoroughly carbon scrubbed and undercoated with a bonding agent before the final layer of Tycolp could be applied.

John oversaw the work with a practised eye, the bond with his new ship deepening with each modification. Tyson took a nap.

Once the remodel was complete, four brightly coloured bots escorted the ship to the station's custom spray booth and went to work on the final trim. Tyson had already selected the new colour scheme from the colour pallet on offer – a grey camouflage design. He had chosen it more for John than anything else; knowing that, even though he complained about it frequently, he had enjoyed at least some of his time in the military.

The ship's new external paint job was completed in fifteen minutes and included a scrolled *The Broken Eye* in vibrant red on the hull.

John was more than happy with the final result. He had been watching the clock and was relieved when he calculated the entire process had taken only a little over three and a half hours. Once the coloured bots had escorted the ship safely back to its docking port, Tyson, fresh from his nap, requested a station exit permit.

The completed exit permit flashed up on John's screen a moment before an alert, complete with arrest warrants for Tyson and himself, lit up his screen.

Courtesy of one Sergeant Wheeler.

It seemed the four-hour warning he had given John was up. Tyson scowled as he read through the fabricated charges about not paying a service registration docking fee to the station. "It'll be dismissed," he insisted after a string of swear words.

John, having already made up his mind about the Sergeant, shook his head and took control of his ship. "Not before Wheeler gets his hands on our credits! Buckle up, Ty. This could get ugly." Tyson reached for his harness as John disengaged the docking clamps and headed towards the station's exit port.

Seconds later, the ship had edged its way past the other docked ships. John issued a sigh of relief as the sound of Tyson securing himself into the newly fitted and far less complicated harness on his co-pilot's chair coincided with *The Broken Eye* reaching open space. "Plot a course out of here. I think we've worn out our welcome already."

"Do you have someplace in mind?"

"Surprise me…Crap!" John glanced down at his screen. Four military police ships had left the space station and were heading straight for them. "Just set a course to the nearest quadrant. We have company." He pressed the engage button on his chair and activated his own harness.

Tyson was already scanning the screens in front of him, entering coordinates swiftly into the navigation computer. The captain slammed the main thrusters on full and both men were flung powerfully back in their seats.

Even with the burst of power, one of the four ships had managed to keep pace with them, and a voice came over their ship-to-ship intercom: "Captain John Alexander and Tyson Blake. This is Sergeant Wheeler. I have a warrant for your arrest. Slow your engines and prepare to be escorted back to Harmon Station for questioning."

"It's for you," said Tyson chuckling.

"It's nice to have a fan," said John.

The Broken Eye shot forward again as he engaged the afterburners to add even more speed to their attempted getaway. The ship responded instantly and seamlessly, and John looked at Tyson with a raised eyebrow.

"Oh yeah," said Tyson, looking rather pleased with himself. "I had a little extra work done to the ship's thrusters."

"*You* had some work done?"

"Okay. Okay. The work was recommended," Tyson confessed with a grin. "But I approved it. That has to count for something, right?"

The captain chuckled softly to himself, shaking his head as he checked the scanners. "I've got some good news and some bad news," he said. "The good news is only two of them were quick enough to follow us. The bad news," John looked across at Tyson with a forced smile, "The bad news is that they are charging their weapons."

"You sure do know how to make friends," sighed Tyson, reaching across to press the shield activator, only to mutter, "Oh no. We might have a little problem," a moment later.

"Problem? What problem?" asked John, trying to ignore the incoming threat still flashing resolutely on his screen.

"The adjustment I made to the thrusters," Tyson said, searching his own screens frantically for a solution, "They may have affected our shields."

"How?"

"They may not be working right about now."

"*Little* problem?" John echoed his friend's earlier statement. "That's a bit more than a little problem, Cyclops! We have two military-grade fighters behind us with their weapons powered up," he snarled. "We have to get the shields up or get out of here – *fast!*"

The Broken Eye was a fast ship but not as quick or responsive as a military fighter. John could see both pursuit crafts were gaining rapidly on them and would be in weapons range in under a minute.

Sergeant Wheeler's voice hailed them over the com once again, "Captain Alexander, your actions have allowed us to use any force necessary to bring you in for questioning. We will disable your engines and tow you back to the port if you do not acquiesce. As you know, targeting an engine at this speed can be hazardous and ships have been known to be accidentally destroyed as a result."

John scoffed at Wheeler's comment but didn't slow his ship.

"On a personal note, I would hate for that to happen to either of you," Sergeant Wheeler added, not sounding the least bit concerned.

Tyson looked at John in a combination of surprise and awe, "Wow, you really pissed this guy off."

"Yeah, yeah. You know how I feel about assholes with a power complex," John shrugged. "How long until we have shields?"

"I think I've found the problem."

"*Think?*"

"No, I know," Tyson corrected himself quickly. "It was just a small programming conflict. All we need to do is reset the shield generator."

"You do know it's about a three-minute walk down to the engine bay to do that, right?" John pointed out.

Sergeant Wheeler's voice filled the cockpit for the third time, "Captain Alexander of *The Broken Eye*, we will be firing on you in eight seconds if you do not slow your vessel to a stop immediately. This is your last warning."

"Shit, Johnny. We're done for. This is it."

John could tell from his tone that Tyson was starting to freak out. He threw the ship into a roll as two beams flashed past, missing them by inches. "I've had enough of this shit. Tyson, we need weapons. *Now!*"

As John continued to pilot the ship through an impressive array of evasive manoeuvres, Tyson's fingers flew over the keyboard. "Our weapons are online, and auto-targeting is engaged," he announced.

"Good." John banked left and then right in quick succession to avoid more deadly blasts, ordering, "Target the lead ship's engines. Maximum burst!" as he did so.

Tyson fed the information into the targeting system and hit engage. He pulled up the aft camera on his screen so he could see the action, right at the exact moment, the beam weapon was discharged.

The result was spectacular as the beam nailed the fighter head-on. The craft's engine exploded, sending it spinning sideways. The fighter behind was unable to avoid a collision, slammed into it and somersaulted, sending out a wide arc of sparks and debris.

The navigation light started flashing and, without a second thought, John brought his hand down hard onto it, while, Tyson who was still watching the destruction left in their wake, unleashed a loud, victorious roar of joy.

Chapter Ten

John regained consciousness slowly. Tyson was still asleep, his head lolling forward onto his chest, which was rising and falling methodically. Satisfied they had both survived the trip, John accessed his screen and put up the sector's star maps, studying them closely. According to the charts, they were orbiting Trevell, the innermost planet of the quadrant.

A thought hit him, and he went searching through the computer system. Normally Tyson's field of expertise, it took John a minute or two to find what he was looking for. But when he did, he smiled. The newly repaired ship could achieve planet landings.

Tyson woke up abruptly and stared around the cockpit blankly for a couple of seconds, before checking his screens and pressing the button on his chair to release his harness.

His captain followed suit, shaking himself free of his restraints and bringing upon his screens the planet specs on Trevell. "Tyson, welcome back buddy! Can you check if our little encounter with our favourite sergeant has been reported yet? Oh, and while you're at it, transfer these credits into our accounts." He waved the back of his hand at his co-pilot, "I'm not happy walking around with it all on me."

With some reluctance, Tyson went to work, soon discovering that not only had the incident been reported, but they were now also wanted for the wilful destruction of military property. He swallowed hard. It was a capital offense.

He read further into the report, relieved to see no officers had been killed. One fighter craft had been destroyed and a second, reduced to scrap, but both pilots had ejected from the ships in time and had been rescued. They were listed as being in serious but stable conditions, recovering in the Harmon medical bay.

A warrant for their detainment was in effect, pending a full investigation. Tyson knew that meant all dealings of the incident would be scrutinized; in detail and at length. It was a serious crime against the military, and it covered all systems.

Tyson had been in trouble before but not on this scale. He rechecked the files on the ship that he had changed earlier. They were air-tight, he noted with a relieved sigh.

Then, as an afterthought and while he was in the ship's systems, he added their video mail addresses, so they could send and receive messages.

"Johnny, you need to see this," Tyson threw the warrant information over to the captain's screen.

John read it and swore, "Shit. We are in it deep, Ty." He rubbed at the scar above his eye with his finger as was his habit when under pressure. "Tell me we have a recording of the whole thing."

Tyson checked the ship's cameras and skimmed through the footage. In under a minute, he had found the section he was after. It was crisp and clear; showing the pursuing ships opening fire on *The Broken Eye*. "This is good, Johnny. It might be our get out of jail free card. You can tell that these are not warning blasts. They shot at us at least a dozen times before we returned fire." He sat back in his chair, feeling slightly better about the situation. Sure, they still faced imminent arrest and lengthy detention until the footage could be properly investigated; which could take weeks or months.

John's screen beeped at him. He looked down at it and then did a double-take. It was telling him he had seven, unopened video mails. "*Seven?* I see you got the video mail to work," he said to his co-pilot who was still looking despondent.

"I thought it was a good idea. This being our new home and all," Tyson was checking his own mail in a bid to lift his spirits. "Now we have a ship it will work on."

The only message that caught John's attention was from Lyle Gregson, his ex-army instructor who was now a Lieutenant Colonel.

The message was brief. It had the standard greeting at the top, with the usual 'next time you're in the sector we should catch up', but after that, it was all business. Lyle wasted no time stating that he had already heard about the outstanding warrants and went on to point out that Sergeant Derrick Wheeler was under internal investigation, suspected of "larceny and theft." He was also considered a person of interest in many missing person reports, with allegations being thrown around that people who did not give up their credits as he demanded tended to go 'missing'. Permanently.

The video mail continued, "My office is responsible for his prosecution and would be very interested if you have a recording of your meeting in the hallway outside your ship, and one of your alleged attack on the two fighters. The one recording we have is of low-quality audio and will not hold up in a court-martial. The report I received about you damaging two fighters without reason and leaving the crew for dead just doesn't sound like the man I trained in the corps. I know there is more to the story John, so please forward me all the recordings you may have so I can clear your name. Send it through to my personal mail. I have made sure your clearance is still valid. Even though you have left the corps, it's the least I can do after what you did for my boy and his team. If it is as I suspect - that Sergeant Wheeler acted beyond the scope of his duties - I will take great pleasure in dishonourably discharging him from the service."

John relayed the information to Tyson, then set to work gathering and viewing the highlights of data streams from the past few months of news feeds on the Omega System, hoping to get a feel for what type of system they had landed in. From what he could tell, the trouble in the system had started many years previously, after a spike in illegal activity had resulted in an increase in the Military presence in the area. It seemed pretty obvious that the Military wasn't much better, widely accused of being rotten to the core with corruption. This left the inhabitants caught choosing between whatever they viewed as the lesser of the two evils.

For a while, the Military had turned a blind eye to the practice, but eventually, the pirates had become so bold that some of them had overthrown a number of the Military's own ships. In retaliation, they threatened war. After many months of negotiations with the group known as the *Kings*, they sent an envoy and a treaty had been agreed upon.

The *Kings* released all captured military vessels intact and a strict mandate was put in place. They agreed they would no longer target military ships, and if at any time any captured ships were used in acts of aggression against the military, the treaty would be broken and there would be a war until all pirate activity and presence were crushed and the military-controlled the system once again.

Both sides had honoured the agreement. Nothing had changed. From what John could see, it had held strong and had continued to do so for over fifteen years.

"Ty, I think we should go into hiding for a while until this all blows over. Somewhere the Military won't think to look for us. What do you think?"

Tyson nodded, "Yeah, that might be a good idea. Any suggestions where?"

"Well, we do have this package to deliver," said John glancing over at where he had put the bronze briefcase. He opened up the envelope the man had given him with it. Inside was a card with brief instruction scrawled onto it.

A lump formed in John's throat and rose. He coughed several times to clear the obstruction. After gaining his composure once again, he swore and said, "Hey, Ty, you are not going to believe this."

Once he was satisfied, he had his co-pilot's attention, John read: *"Deliver the package to Hector Gibbs, located on Caxton, in the Omega system. Package has a removable DNA scanner for proof of delivery."*

Tyson said nothing.

"You know me, Ty," John said after a brief pause. "I don't believe in coincidences, and our luck lately hasn't been good. It could be a setup."

This time Tyson swore, agreeing with John's assessment. He closed his mail and began pulling up all data he could find relating to the history of Caxton. It was not good news.

Originally colonized as a mining outpost, within three years of it opening, the mining company had made a killing in credits, and by the end of the following two years, had doubled the size of the mine. Soon they were sending out numerous, specifically programmed probes to scan further areas of the planet. Due to an unknown technical issue, however, they lost contact with the probes.

The most recent information Tyson could find was that the planet had been placed under quarantine and had apparently remained so ever since. A poisonous gas of unknown origin was blamed for the death of every human on the planet. Curiously though, all indigenous fauna and flora were unaffected by what had to have been a massive atmospheric change.

A vein in Tyson's forehead stuck out and throbbed bright red. It was something that only happened in moments when he was under extreme stress. "You have got to be shitting me?" He cursed and flicked the data across to John.

The captain read the screen with interest but remained silent. Nothing was going to stop him from completing the delivery and he still had a promise to fulfil to the Ancient man's corpse. Besides, they had their bio suits. Finally, he stood up and declared, "I'm going to reset the shield generator and bring us a couple of drinks on the way back up. What's your poison?"

Tyson winced at the poor choice of words, still trying to get over the fact that John was obviously determined that they attempt a landing on Caxton's toxic surface. He took out his cybernetic eye and began polishing it on his shirt, shaking his head in thorough disbelief.

John left the cockpit and headed down to the shield generator. The light on the side was orange – a good sign. He pressed the reset button. The orange light went off and the generator restarted, soon settling down into a reassuring hum. After a few seconds, the panel lit up green.

John touched the intercom unit on the wall and said, "How is it looking up there, mate? Do we have shields again?"

"We're good to go again, Johnny," Tyson replied, his voice still thick with worry. "Oh, and that drink? Make it a double blended Lishten ice coffee. Actually no, make it a triple."

John stopped off at the freshly repaired crew's quarters. He found the captain's room and took off his coat and laid it across the bed. He thought about taking off his vest also, but beginning to like his new style, decided to keep it on.

It was all very clinical in the cabin: stark, white walls stared back at him everywhere he looked. Even the freshly painted room smell lingered in the air.

He crumpled up his nose in distaste and made a mental note to pick up a few things to give his quarters a more personal touch. He always liked keeping a few select souvenirs and mementoes in his room.

A wave of nostalgia washed over him. The first time he had his own room that wasn't part of a barracks was after he had left the military, when he had returned home to help his uncle save his failing business.

His uncle's space dock repair-shop had fallen into disrepair. His uncle's declining health had resulted in the failure to complete jobs on time, and as a result he has lost all but his most loyal customers. It had taken John two full years to rebuild the business, while his uncle recovered. Over time, the word had spread all over the system about the quality of work being produced out of the little starport. They even expanded the floor space and added a design and modifications workshop, to help keep up with the now flourishing business. In his spare time, he and his uncle had worked on their own special project, modifying and customising an Orion class ship.

John smiled, recalling how his uncle had presented him the papers of ownership once it was registered, with one small stipulation. A promise to explore the systems and see all the wonders that they each had to offer. John knew that due to his uncle's health in the last few years, any chance of space travel was now lost to him.

Altren had been like a father to John from the moment he had found him in the burnt-out wreckage of the crash site; the only survivor. For five years, John had been kept as a slave. As a boy, John had told him stories of wearing only filthy rags for clothes, being starved for insubordination and savagely beaten every time he attempted to escape. He had lost count of how many times he had been sold and resold over the years. His collection of scars grew thicker and uglier with each attempt for freedom and so did his resolve to escape.

It was by pure luck that John had managed to escape. The slavers ship had been in a battle and was badly damaged. Forced to make an emergency landing, the craft was ripped apart on impact. Altren had been on his way home from work and had seen the ship hurtling through the night sky, shortly followed by a flash of light and flames. The shockwave and the sound of a heavy, wet impact that came next, was unmistakable. Altren had once told John that he had heard the sounds before, many times during the time he had spent in the military, for there to be any mistake.

John had spent the first two years of his freedom either in hospital, being 'upgraded and repaired', as Altren called it, or being tutored in all core subjects. John struggled with language and calculus the most. When he did well, he was rewarded by being allowed to do his favourite thing: helping out in the old man's workshop. John had little in the way of formal education, but even at that young age he displayed an uncanny ability to understand machinery.

The trouble began with the change of local government. They ordered a census to correctly gauge the needs of the people. Altren did not include John in the census report as he was neither a blood relative or a visitor on the night of the lodging, and DNA samples had to be provided for each person on the form. Two days later, officers of the court appeared at Altren's door, reporting that they had been notified that he was harbouring an illegal resident of the state.

Altren had objected and drove the officers off of his property with his service pulse rifle and blaster. A week later, a team of armed officers surrounded the old man's home and threatened to take the child, explaining that they would do so by force if necessary, and that if they were made to do so, the state would seize his home.

But they were too late.

Altren had already made an arrangement with an old military friend, a Major from his own time in the military, and had cashed in a favour that was owed to him. As a result, John was entered in as a "special entry" military cadet. However, because John could no longer remember his family name, Altren offered to rename the boy after his own. From that day onwards, John began calling him Uncle. Even though he insisted it wasn't necessary, John knew it meant the world to the old man.

***

John returned to the cockpit and handed Tyson his drink. The two men opened them thirstily and sat in silence. Tyson took a sip of his beverage and coughed suddenly as it burned its way down his throat. He waited for the drink to work magic and spread its warmth through his body. A realisation suddenly occurred to Tyson; he knew very little about John, but he wasn't the sort to ask. He liked the fact that John never pried into his past either and that he respected his privacy. He repaid that by not asking any questions of his own.

John offered to drop his co-pilot off on a planet with a pocketful of credits until he had delivered the package.

Tyson's response was immediate, "I'm not letting you go in there by yourself! Besides, how hard can it be to deliver one small briefcase?"

John was glad that his friend was joining him. He wasn't entirely comfortable about going by himself, but he did understand Tyson's reasons for maybe wanting to take a pass on this one.

Although not willing to let John go it alone, Tyson was not happy at all about heading to Caxton. It was deep inside the system, in the third sector – a long, *long* way to travel. It was unrealistic to believe that they wouldn't run into pirates.

The two men checked over the ship's operating systems thoroughly, making a few minor adjustments as they did so.

By the time they were finished, they had reset just about everything at least twice.

John was waiting for the computer to complete the calculations for the jump when he had an idea. He checked his screen. There were several leftover redundant data cables after the repairs had been made. He looked around and spotted his backpack on the bench seat along the wall behind their two chairs. He stood up and walked the several paces over to it, rummaging through it until he found what he was looking for.

"I'm just going down to the engine room to do a final check," he announced as he stuffed the item into his pants' pocket. "I won't be long."

He hadn't made it out of the cockpit before Tyson asked, "Johnny, what are you up too?"

"Nothing. Nothing at all," a look of guilt flashed across John's face as he answered, "I just want to give it one last check over. That's all."

"Yeah right. Okay. So, what have you got there?" queried Tyson, pointing at his friend's bulging pocket.

John reached into his pocket and took out the heart of the locator.

"I thought as much," Tyson rolled his eye. "Do you even know how to fit that thing to this ship?"

"Of course I do," said the captain, examining the heart's purple, broken wire as he turned it over in his hand. "I just thought it might be good to have it installed in case of an emergency."

Both men let the last statement hang in the air for several moments.

"Fine, go ahead and plug it in!" Tyson said, clearly not impressed at all with the plan. "But if we die because of it, I'm blaming you!"

It took John a little over three hours to successfully fit the heart of the relocator under the watchful eye of his frowning co-pilot. Many of the computer systems had to be reset and diagnostics run and re-run to make sure there would be no conflicts or unexpected surprises with the new alien tech. He also fitted a new big red button, complete with a cover that he claimed to have salvaged from some unused equipment on one of the ship's lower levels. When Tyson pressed him for more precise details on where he had found it, John was annoyingly vague in his reply, pointing out instead the newly installed warning light that Tyson had insisted on.

John, satisfied with the relocator's refit, wandered off to the galley for sustenance and returned, still chewing a mouthful of rehydrated food, as Tyson was entering their target planet into the navigational system. He sat in his captain's chair and looked over at his co-pilot.

Tyson's face was uncharacteristically flushed. As each attempt he made at entering the planet's coordinates, resulted in the same error – "Destination: *unavailable*."

Bringing his hand down hard on one of his armrests, Tyson finally broke into a round of frustrated swearing. "I don't believe it! This cannot be happening!"

"Problem?" John asked through a half-mouthful of chilli mushrooms.

"I thought it was all just, you know, rumours. Hang on, let me try something different," Tyson entered another planet location from the Omega System into the navigational computer. The result was the same.

Slowly and methodically, his frown darkened with each subsequent error reading. He worked his way outwards, planet by planet, inputting new co-ordinates until the navigation computer finally accepted a destination.

"YES!" Tyson exclaimed, sounding cheerful at last. "We have a winner!"

The planet Haskain. It was the closest he could get them to Caxton.

Tyson had heard stories of how pirates had developed a new type of tech – disruptor beacons that sent out silent energy waves that distorted map data. It was rumoured to have been developed to stop the military gaining unwanted access to the Omega System, just in case they got any ideas about trying to retake it.

"Well?" John enquired, now swigging down a drink. "You want to tell me about it yet? Or do you want to keep playing with your keyboard a little more?"

"I have good news and bad news."

"You know me, always lead with the bad and finish on a high note," John quipped.

"Well, in that case," Tyson paused for effect. "It appears that the closest we can get to Caxton in a single jump is to a planet on the outer edge of the third sector."

John let out an impressive string of swear words before finally asking, "Why?"

"It looks like the *Kings* have managed to place disruptor beacons in key locations around the Omega System to prevent unwanted visitors."

"That's just frigging great! How long under normal flight will it take us to reach Caxton from there then?"

Tyson paused again, only this time because he didn't want to have to relay the news, which wasn't exactly ending on a high note, to John. "Eight days, give or take a few hours."

With an impatient grumble, John brought up the ship's shields and weapons screens. There was some good news. At least with the size of their shield generator, they were unlikely to sustain much damage, even if they came under heavy fire. Unfortunately, there was more bad news in that they only had two forward-facing D class beam lasers and one rear E class pulse laser. Both were more deterrents rather than actual combat weapons.

He flicked his screens to the generators and power consumption data. The ship was running on less than forty percent usage. It wasn't enough. John knew they were going to have to either land on a planet or dock at a station before they reached their final destination

They needed weapons. There was no way of telling what they might find when they landed on Caxton. John knew from experience that a simple package drop-off was rarely that. A full upgrade of the ship's offensive systems would be their best option. There was a very real possibility that they would run into pirates at some stage.

Space stations were run by common laws, almost identical across all systems. Planets, however, had their own rules and these varied from planet to planet. Moreover, some had laws that were strictly administered and adhered to while others had barely any laws at all. John, naturally enough, was looking for one of the latter. A planet where credits talked and no questions were asked. Now, all he had to do was hope Tyson had found them one.

Chapter Eleven

After a successful planet landing on Haskain, John was happy to discover not only did it have a fully equipped space port, it also had a thriving business hub that traded absolutely everything a pirate's heart might desire – ranging from powerful hand-held data pads to the massive Merloc missile systems. He and Tyson took their time browsing through an area of ship components, meticulously comparing systems and prices.

John's weapon of choice was the Merloc. It was an impressive piece of engineering. Any size, range and type of missile could be fired from it without compromising its performance. Unfortunately, the system cost the price of an average cruiser-classed vessel, and every single time John mentioned it, Tyson would point out with increasing frustration that they didn't have the money for one.

***

After they had carefully selected the appropriate, affordable weapon upgrades for *The Broken Eye*, John left it to Tyson to oversee the fitting of the equipment and reprogramming of the ship's computers, reminding his co-pilot not to touch any of the new parts himself, before heading off alone to scout for smaller firearms.

After an hour or so of browsing the other stores and making some discreet, and some not so discreet enquiries, John was finally directed to a large, Rillion class freighter. The ship was huge, dwarfing the pair of Archer class fighters that sat either side of it. The big freighters landing ramp was down and two men stood guard at the bottom of it; one on either side, both holding modified pulse rifles. As John approached, he took the time to nod to each of the security guards but walked up the ramp and into the cargo bay without breaking his stride.

John made his way through the rows of tables that had been set out. From handguns to turret mounted Ion cannons, it was an impressive display of equipment. He remembered once, seeing a demonstration of an ion cannon as it decimated a twelve-story office block. It was a very impressive weapon indeed.

Taking his time, John inspected each of the various weapons on offer. They were of the highest quality. Some were clearly modified, but most were left in stock condition. He felt, stripped, and reassembled the ones he had selected to buy with practiced efficiency, much to the surprise of several onlookers.

It wasn't long before a woman approached him. She had dark skin with black close-cropped hair and a petite frame. Her high cheekbones framed her light hazel eyes, and she had a warm and welcoming smile on her face as she spoke.

"Greetings. My name is Lyella Birch. Welcome to my marketplace. May I ask if you are buying or selling today?"

John put down the weapon he was holding, "Hello, Lyella. I'm John. It's quite a collection you have here. I'm looking to make a few small purchases today."

Her eyes gave him a once over, "Please let me know if I can be of any assistance."

He was about to answer when a young woman called out for Lyella's help.

"Excuse me," she adjusted the black tinted welding goggles on her forehead. "It seems I'm needed elsewhere." She paused for a moment, handing him one of her hologram cards, before spinning on her heel and walking away.

He watched her leave, weaving her way between the various tables; her red and black jumpsuit standing out in contrast to the bulky, dark brown welding jacket she wore over the top. He examined the card she had given him with interest. It was similar to Oberon's, but not as finely made. There was a small hologram of the ship he was standing in on the top right hand corner of the card. The rest was a simple message: *Best mods in the system. We buy, sell and trade. Owner Lyella Birch.*

With a nod, John slipped the card into one of his pockets then calmly picked up a black duffle bag and began loading it up. He had chosen a tactical pulse rifle, a disrupter rifle and one eighteen shot blaster with three backup cartridges complete with a hip holster. The blaster was one of his favourites, having been the same type of sidearm that the military had assigned him while he was serving. Next, he added a stun pistol with a matching shoulder holster. The stunner held fifteen charges and was not a bad little weapon. John shrugged and swiftly located four more clips for it, tossing them into the bag as well.

He then selected several small throwing knives and two fold-away knives, each with a four-inch blade. He paused for a split second before putting them into his duffle bag too. John knew Tyson didn't like the idea of killing people, even if they were trying to kill him. He didn't understand it at all. His firm belief was that if someone was trying to take him out, he sure as hell was going to return the sentiment!

John had tried to convince Tyson many times that death was always a possibility in their business and would be preferable if it were someone else that died instead of them. Tyson had tried to defend his stance, but had stopped arguing in the end. As for John, he'd been forced to put Tyson's reluctance to kill down to nothing less than him being a weak-assed, spoiled, rich kid.

Still, thinking about his friend now, John looked around one last time. He knew Tyson was not a fighter. He could handle a gun okay but was next to useless in a fistfight. That was when John spotted the perfect, close quarter's weapon for his friend and tossed it into the bag as well, before making his way to the transaction clerk.

Once more Lyella came over to him, "I hope you found all that you needed."

"Yes, thank you," John nodded, watching her gaze sweep across his purchases. "But if I have a need for anything else, I will definitely return."

"Perhaps you may have something to sell us next time?" she smiled. "You know, John, I don't believe I've seen you before, though I have the feeling I'll be seeing you again."

John chuckled softly at her careful use of his name, "I guess we'll have to wait and see, won't we?"

She patted him lightly on the arm, "Take care. See you again, sometime." Then she winked before walking off again, this time disappearing into the back of the ship.

***

Work on *The Broken Eye* had been completed by the time John made his way back to the ship and Tyson was just doing the final diagnostic checks when he reached the cockpit. He dropped the bag between the chairs, sat in his captain's chair, and brought up their joint credit account balance. There were only a few thousand credits remaining. Frowning heavily, he shut it down and opened up the ship's weapon screen instead. His frown slowly disappeared as he read their new offensive load off the screen.

They now had two forward-facing B class pulse lasers, accompanied by two rear mounted C class beam lasers; complete, charged, and ready to go. John nodded to himself happily, feeling finally prepared for their travel to Caxton.

Tyson's screen flashed up the ship's diagnostic result. It was all green. He too smiled triumphantly then looked over at the black duffle bag that the captain had dropped on the floor. "It's a bit early for Christmas, isn't it, Johnny?"

John peered down at the bag and then gave his friend a confused look, "I have no idea what you're talking about."

"Christmas. You know, the jolly fat man that has a long white beard? Wears a red suit with fluffy white collar and cuffs. He hands out presents to children to mark the end of the year? *Really*?"

John continued to look confused and remained silent.

"Sometimes I think you grew up under a rock!" said Tyson. It wasn't the first time he had tried to explain old Earth

108

traditions to his friend. This one though, he thought, was surely the most basic of all of them.

"You do realize that those traditions you grew up with on your home planet are all really bizarre, right?" retorted John, who, based on all that Tyson had told him of his early years, had concluded that Earth 2 must have been a very odd place to live. Wealthy and luxurious but definitely odd.

Tyson laughed, "I suppose having running water and electricity was a real treat on your planet."

John countered with a rude, one finger gesture that was universally accepted throughout all known systems, before asking, "What's electricity?"

Tyson laughed again. This time, even louder.

The captain slipped out of his seat and gathered up the black bag in one swift movement. He strode across the cockpit and carefully laid out the contents on the bench behind their chairs. When he had finished arranging the weapons, it made quite an impressive display.

"Since we will be landing on Caxton very soon, and we don't know what we will find there, I thought we might need these." John picked up the disrupter rifle, stun gun, holster, and clips. Finally, he picked up one of the small fold away knives and handed them all across to Tyson.

"Johnny, I appreciate the thought, but you know how I feel about guns," said Tyson as he pushed them back towards his friend.

"Relax, Ty, they are only stun weapons. *Non*-lethal. They just put the target to sleep for a while," John explained with a wink. "They will wake up with a nasty headache, but that's about it."

"Oh, right. Well, I can live with that," Tyson smiled and accepted the armament.

Not wishing to have his co-pilot accidentally injure himself with any of them, John ran through the basics with him, carefully showing him how to release the safety on each firearm and how to recharge, load, and prime each one. He even offered to teach him how to field strip and clean them all, but every time he started to disassemble one of the guns, Tyson just looked confused. Eventually, John gave up, happy in the knowledge that his friend at least would be competent at reloading and firing them and was unlikely to kill himself in the process.

John collected his own weapons and fitted his holster to his right thigh. After a few minor adjustments, he soon also had three throwing knives secured into his gun belt. It fit snugly against his body; the weight of his new sidearm feeling very comforting and familiar. It was like being reunited with a long-lost friend.

Tyson pointed at the item that was left on the bench, "And what is that?"

John picked it up and grinned. It was a sleek black glove. A very thin wire had been wound in an apparent chaotic pattern all over its entire surface. Set into the back of the glove was a red disk.

"It's a shock glove," John enlightened his puzzled looking counterpart. "It will deliver a charge to stun your target." He put the glove on and powered it up. A meter appeared in a display panel on the red disk.

"This," he said. "Displays the battery's charge and the power level setting."

Tyson nodded his understanding for two reasons. The first was acknowledging that he understood the operations of the glove, the second was that he appreciated the fact that John knew him so well.

"It also scans the user's DNA profile when it's fitted and powered up, to ensure that you can't shock yourself by mistake."

"I can see how that would be an advantage," said Tyson. He smiled, wondering how many times people had shocked themselves before the safety feature had been fitted.

"And again, it's non-lethal," John reiterated, powering off the unit. He removed the glove and he handed it over to his friend.

Tyson took the glove and powered it up. Immediately, it began to inflate, resizing to remould itself to the exact contours of his larger, meatier hand. He smiled and flexed his fingers.

The weapon had been cleverly designed so the wearer could still throw a punch while it was recharged, and Tyson took a few practice swings while the glove pulsed yellow, then orange, then red. It then went back to its original shiny black, innocuous appearance.

"Whatever colour the glove's meter shows is the intensity of the power setting," John explained. "Yellow is mild. Orange is medium. Red is full power, and that one could knock someone out for a day or so. It delivers the best charge with an open hand," he went on while Tyson continued to admire his new acquisition, "The more surface area that touches your target, the stronger the shock."

"This is because I can't fight like a common thug, isn't it?" Tyson raised an eyebrow even though he was quite impressed with the device and was already beginning to grin over his latest toy.

John flashed a smile and said, "It's not that at all. It's more because you hit like a ten-year-old girl with a sprained wrist."

Mutely, Tyson dialled the power to yellow, the lowest setting, and reached out and touched John's arm. John, who hadn't anticipated the move, was thrown backward across the room, sliding on his backside across the floor. He stopped with a dull thud against the bottom of the cockpit's window.

"Hey, what do you know? It works!" Tyson said, unable to hide his joy at, what was now, his favourite toy.

Thoroughly dazed, it took John a few moments to stand up, and even when he could, his legs still felt rubbery and he brushed himself off with extra care. "And you call me an asshole! If you keep this shit up, I won't bring you any more fun things to play with," he berated the still grinning Tyson.

As he walked out of the cockpit on his wobbly legs, John bumped into the wall several times and Tyson started laughing so hard tears ran down his face. He only stopped when he found it hard to breathe.

John bounced his way from wall to wall, all the way down to his room. His whole body felt like it was on fire. He stripped off his clothes, dumped them on his bed and staggered into his bathroom. He threw the showers setting to cold then turned it on full. The icy water helped a little, but his muscles were still tense. He felt a bit like he had just finished an intense workout in the gym.

A few minutes later, his head had stopped buzzing, so he increased the water temperature up to a warmer setting. His neck throbbed in pain as he removed the medical pack.

John ran his hand over the tiles on the shower wall, activating them.

They changed from standard white to a shiny mirrored surface and he was able to better inspect the wound on his shoulder in them. It looked almost fully healed. John sighed and the rest of his muscles slowly loosened up under the hot water. He cupped some of the soapy water in his hands and began massaging out what was left of the tension in his shoulders, his arms, and then his legs.

He washed his long brown hair and brushed his teeth. Then he turned off the water and selected the Air jet on the shower's console. After only a few seconds, he was completely dry. The shower had certainly helped a little to ease his discomfort, but he still felt like he had stuck his tongue on a live power Hub.

Re-dressing took John a lot longer than it usually did, and he had to sit on the bed in the end to accomplish it. Even just pulling on his pants was proving difficult as the muscles in his arms and legs that had cooled down from the hot shower would periodically spasm, throwing him sideways.

Waiting until the worst of the spasms had stopped, John sat dressed in his room for over an hour. Finally deciding his muscles were able to carry him safely, he walked slowly up to the galley and hydrated up a plate of roast beef and gravy with crisply roasted pumpkin and potato. To complement his meal, he selected a dry ginger ale with lime and carried it into the dining room.

Tyson was already sitting at the table, enjoying his own meal. John sat across from him with a gruff expression, "Great minds think alike."

The co-pilot merely nodded his agreement. Not much got in the way of Tyson and his food. John had always thought that out of all the things anyone could possibly want to do to Tyson, starvation would be the worst. The man had an unnatural love of food. John had once seen him travel half a planet to dine at its best authentic Chinese cuisine restaurant.

John smiled at the unexpected memory but continued to eat his roast beef in silence. Much to his annoyance, his face kept making involuntary twitches every few seconds or so and his grin soon faded.

Seeing this, Tyson smiled smugly to himself, *'Revenge is a dish best served cold'*. John had been giving him a hard time for a while now and they both knew how the game worked.

The captain did so many little things to piss Tyson off that, after a while, it became necessary for Tyson to even the score. It was a task he took seriously. So seriously, it usually ended up with John needing medical treatment of some type. His most recent exacted revenge had resulted in John's pilot's chair becoming 'mysteriously' partially un-bolted from the cockpit's floor while the captain had been doing his routine inspections of the ship. John had returned to his seat without noticing the problem. Until that is, the main engines had engaged, and he had been thrown side-ways, out of the chair and into the rear of the cockpit. It had left him with a badly bruised shoulder and a broken rib.

It had been one of Tyson's finer moments.

They both sat quietly for a while, enjoying their meals in companionable silence. It was a rare moment indeed, and it was Tyson who broke the peace first.

"Let me see if I've got this right," he began thoughtfully. "First, we make our way to the quarantined planet, cleverly evading any confrontations with pirates as we do so. Take the dead guy's body to its final resting place. Then, we find Hector Gibbs somewhere on the poisoned surface of an inhospitable planet."

John quietly drained the last of his drink.

"After that," Tyson removed his cybernetic eye and inspected it, "We go back and get our names completely cleared of the incident at Harmon station, avoiding destroying any more military fighters as we do so." He gave his eye one last polish on his shirt and popped it back into place. "Then lastly, but by no means least, we find our way back to the Beta system, pay Liebecker the credits we owe him, and *finally* get that bounty hunter Breanna Gomez off our asses."

Wordlessly, the captain finished his meal and stacked his plate on top of the other empty one in the middle of the table. He then ran his hand through his hair and said with a dismissive shrug, "Well, when you put it that way, it sounds so simple."

Tyson stood up and collected the plates, depositing them less than gently into the cleaner. "I'm off to have a shower."

"Make sure you're back in the cockpit in twenty minutes for lift off."

At the order, Tyson stopped in his tracks halfway across the floor. Abruptly, he clicked his heels together and spun around to face John. Next, he executed a sloppy salute and replied, "Sir, yes Sir!"

John chuckled, "That's the sort of respect I have been missing all these years," as he returned a perfect salute in reply.

"Don't get used to it," Tyson laughed as he turned and exited the room.

John was in his captain's chair, harnessed in and ready to go when Tyson joined him. He could see that the blue navigation light was flashing, signalling that the computer had already calculated the shortest flight path to Caxton.

Pushing aside any last-minute nerves, he sat down in his co-pilot's chair and pressed the button to lock him into his own harness. "Any new video mail at all?" he managed to quip, looking across at John who was staring out the cockpit window.

John glanced over at Tyson with a wry grin, "Our luck isn't that good my friend."

"You know lately," Tyson said, as he shook his head, "If it wasn't for having bad luck, we wouldn't have any luck at all."

John reached for the navigation light and pressed it down, engaging the drive.

Chapter Twelve

As always, John's take-off was flawless, and they achieved escape velocity without incident. Even though he made it look easy, successful lift offs from planets were always tricky. Every ship behaved differently, and John paid very close attention to every readout the screens in front of him displayed. All in all, it was a great ship to fly.

Tyson let out a whistle of appreciation. He had never enjoyed planet landings – or take-offs for that matter. They were always bumpy and uncomfortable compared to space stations. Station dockings were always as smooth as Charnard silk. Tyson scratched at his freshly shaved face as he looked out through the cockpit's window. He could see Haskain gradually growing smaller as they pulled away further and further away from the planet.

John wanted to get to Caxton as soon as possible but knew that it was already going to be an eight-day journey and didn't want to risk any further delays by pushing his new ship any harder than was necessary.

After half an hour of watching the stars stream past, Tyson announced he was going for a walk around the ship to inspect all the recent modifications. He collected up his data pad and exited the cockpit, humming to himself as he went.

John gave him a thumbs-up gesture in acknowledgement, then reached down into the side pocket of his chair and fished out his own data pad. With a sly smile, he selected the random setting on his music file and pressed play.

The cockpit erupted in sound. The song was an Earth classic – *'Shout'* by *Johnny O'Keefe*. John could just imagine Tyson cringing at his taste in music, and he chuckled to himself as he piped it through the ship's entire intercom system.

The final bars of the third, equally loud 'classic' were echoing through the corridors when a video mail notification popped up on his screen, pausing the playlist on his data pad. With a softly uttered curse, John opened up the mail. It was from Lyle Gregson and was a thank you for sending the recordings of the incident at Harmon station. In a surprisingly pleasant voice, he went on to inform John that Sergeant Wheeler had been stood down pending further investigations into his conduct.

Closing down the mail and pressing resume on his playlist, John hoped that it would be the last he heard of the matter. He also seriously doubted it.

Tyson, enjoying the sudden quiet, had barely made it past the galley when again the sound of a man screaming erupted through the intercom's speakers. He shook his head, knowing his friend did it more to piss him off than anything else. "Next time I shock glove that guy, it's going up to the orange setting," he promised himself.

He wandered around the ship, admiring the refit and congratulating himself on his decorating choices, eventually ending in the medical bay. The droids at Harmon station had done an excellent job of repairing and restocking it and, as Tyson stood and looked around at all the equipment, a flood of memories washed over him.

When Tyson had been young, his mother had often taken him with her to her workplace. As one of Earth 2's leading experts in genetic erosion, her lab had been one of the finest and best equipped in the sector. If he promised to be quiet while she worked, he would be allowed to sit on her big, brown overstuffed chair and watch her while she busied herself in her many tests and experiments.

He had always known that his mother was important and very well-respected and, even from a very early age, had been able to figure out that all the attention he received from her many students and co-workers wasn't genuine. He had seen through their facades enough to know that they did it only to gain favour with his mother.

A tear slipped down from his eye at the memory. It had been years since he had thought of his parents. Many more since he had seen them. Although his mother had always been warm and comforting, his relationship with his father had been very different and Tyson felt his heart harden at the memory of the man who had always treated him with an aloof indifference. Tyson removed his cybernetic eye, gave it a quick polish on his shirt, and left the room quietly. He didn't look back once.

***

Two days of travel passed without *The Broken Eye* so much as registering the presence of another vessel in their sector. Not willing to take any chances, and given the sector's reputation and the erratic nature of the disruptor beams, Tyson and John took turns sitting in the cockpit, monitoring the ship and its flight path for up to six hours at a time.

As the hours stretched on, they ended up sitting together, their allotted shifts overlapping as they kept each other company. Tyson, quite enjoying the uneventful trip, used the time to share his knowledge of Earth music, art, and culture. John grew increasingly confused on every topic.

Tyson did his best to try and educate his friend on all subjects, but eventually, after a lengthy argument over whether or not Elvis Presley had faked his own death in 1977, he gave up and headed for his quarters for some much needed sleep.

It was some time later when John, snoozing in his captain's chair, awoke gradually.

"What the …?"

It took him a moment to realize his screen was beeping a warning at him. Not a screeching alarm warning, more of a gentle blip that was gradually increasing in pitch and volume.

John looked down at his screen. Sure enough, there was a ship on the outer limit range of their scanners. He glanced across to Tyson's chair. It was still empty.

Shaking himself awake fully, John killed the music on his data pad, which was now only playing through the cockpit's speakers, and hailed Tyson on the ship's intercom.

"Hey Ty, report to the bridge. We have company."

There was no response, but assuming that his co-pilot was still resting in his quarters, he didn't call a second time. It took him another long moment to realise exactly why his screen was continuing to beep at him – *The Broken Eye* was being scanned by the ship behind them.

John examined the data on his screen. The vessel was a Moxal class, which told him very little as every system classified ships differently. What he could tell was that judging by the size and shape, it was a medium-sized freighter. Unfortunately, this still meant essentially nothing as it could well have been upgraded to be anything, from a long-distance hauler to a formidable fighter.

Tyson entered the cockpit and sat in his chair. "What's up Captain?" he asked, looking at the scanner's data.

"We have company."

"So, I heard. It's only a freighter, Johnny. It has more than likely just jumped to its maximum distance before it could re-calculate its navigational computer. Just watch, it'll continue on its trading run."

John nodded and silenced the beeping on his screen. "It scanned us, too."

"You're being paranoid. This system is full of pirates and every pilot will be on edge. It's probably common practice to scan every ship that goes past."

"For a medium freighter, it is moving fast and it's gaining on us."

Tyson was able to initiate a more thorough scan now that the vessel was closer. After a few seconds, he read out the new scan's report. "Ship's name, *Barters Pride*. Moxal class. Medium freighter. Standard shields with two C class Beam forward lasers, one D class at the rear. Not bad for a standard freighter," he mused, as he continued reading. "Fifty-five-ton cargo capacity. Belchar 4 engine. Maximum crew capacity– eleven."

"Our ship has a Belchar 4. How is it gaining on us then? We're a smaller and lighter ship," pointed out the captain.

"Maybe it had some mods done to it. Who knows? You worry too much."

John was still suspicious and kept the scanners read out up on his screen. Finally, though, he had to conclude that Tyson was probably right. It was only the one ship and *The Broken Eye* had far superior shields and weapons.

Still, the two men kept an eye on the ship as it got closer and closer.

The Barters Pride scanned them again as soon as they were within weapons range.

Tyson hastily rechecked all their shields were up and running, while John verified their weapons were online. Together they watched as the ship completed its scan, slowed, then abruptly dropped out of range and made a jump. They both let out a joint sigh of relief.

"I told you so!" Tyson was the first to break the tense silence.

John just rolled his eyes.

The next few days passed slowly and without incident. In response to the monotony, Tyson developed himself a ritual. After eating a meal, he would go on leisurely strolls around the ship. On one such walk, he discovered where John had 'found' the new cover for their big bed Button. He had taken it off of the secondary override for the emergency docking hatch. On seeing his friend's handiwork, Tyson gave his head a quick shake of despair. John had replaced the button with a smaller yellow one and had hastily drawn a large smiley face on it.

"Typical Johnny," Tyson could only groan at the sight as he kept on walking.

Becoming increasingly bored with the trip himself, and tiring of Tyson's criticism at his apparent lack of culture,

John left his friend to do his shift alone in the cockpit for a change and headed down to his quarters. He knew Tyson had taken to walking the ship, and he was beginning to think that it would be a good idea for him to get some much-needed exercise, too.

He had installed a small gymnasium in a corner of the cargo bay onboard *The Vulture*, but *The Broken Eye* had missed out on the addition during its recent upgrade. John missed his daily work out and promised himself that when time and money permitted, he would put a small gym in one of the unused crews' quarters.

Tyson had his head back, eyes closed, earbuds in, and was listening to a lecture about the new, ground-breaking White Lace security system. It was being heralded as such a superior program to its predecessors that it was claimed to be impossible to hack and had recently been installed to all financial and military data and records throughout the Systems for ultimate security and protection.

He was so engrossed in the recording that he didn't see the three ships approach on his scanners. It wasn't until the alarm on his screen got so loud that he could hear it over the sound of the lecture, that he opened his eyes and leaned forward to read his screens.

"You have got to be kidding me?" Tyson swore and went into panic mode instantly. He slapped off the lecture and tapped the ship's intercom in one sharp movement. "Johnny! Three ships are closing on us. Get your ass up here fast!"

John was in the medical bay and had just removed the medical pack from his neck. He was busy convincing himself that his injury wasn't going to heal any better than what it already was when Tyson's voice erupted over the ship's com. Tugging his shirt back into place, he turned and broke into a run, heading as fast as he could towards the bridge.

When John burst through the door, Tyson was already secured in his chair and reading through the scan data he had received on the approaching ships. "Looks like you were right about that ship earlier," he said without looking up. "He's back and he's brought some friends."

John engaged his harness as he brought up the scanner's data on his screen. There were three ships, just out of weapons range, all of them with their weapons charged and all of them heading directly towards them.

The Barters Pride on its own wasn't much of a threat. The two ships that accompanied it, however, were a very different story. The first was a scout class fighter named *The Blue Cobra* and came equipped with a forward-facing A class beam laser, one rear B class, and last, but definitely not least, a Belchar 6 engine. John knew there was no way they could possibly hope to outrun it.

The third ship in pursuit of them was a privateer class, named *The Black Star*. It posed an even bigger danger as it was fully armed with two forward pulse cannons alongside a B class Burst laser. Rear-mounted were two B class pulse lasers, while the whole formidable beast was powered by a Novac 2 engine.

John had never seen a Novac engine used on a non-military vessel before. Not only was it a heavily armed ship, but it was also very, very fast. He could only hope that what it had in speed and weapons, it lacked in manoeuvrability.

"Ty, find me a planet," he ordered, wasting no time taking evasive action as all three ships started firing on them. "Terrestrial, preferably, and the closer the better. Maybe I can lose them on a surface. Because, by the seven moons, I can't outrun them in open space!"

Tyson scanned through the sector on his screens. "There are no habitable planets nearby, Johnny."

"Shit, Tyson, did I say I wanted habitable? I'm not planning on retiring there! I just need one with forests, oceans and if we're lucky a canyon or two!" The captain swore at length, only narrowly avoiding incoming laser fire.

Still working quickly, John activated their ship's lasers. Unfortunately, all three crafts were out of range of the *Eye's* weapons, so he set the rear laser to fire cycling random patterns in an attempt to distract the pilots.

On the very first volley of shots fired from the *Broken Eye*, the pilot of *Barters Pride* panicked and banked sharply. He attempted to right himself, but either through recklessness or sheer stupidity, overcorrected his steering so that his ship clipped the wing of *The Blue Cobra*, sending both vessels spinning off uncontrollably in different directions.

"Nice move," Tyson whistled, admiring the result. "How did you know that would work?"

"I didn't," John shrugged. "Most pilots who haven't seen combat panic when fired upon. I took a gamble that at least one of them would." He turned his attention to *The Black Star*, now within its effective firing range. "Somehow, I don't think this one will fall for the same trick."

"I found something," Tyson announced abruptly. "Planet Wenwik. Plotting a course now."

John flicked his gaze over the new route displayed on his screen. With a quick nod of approval, he turned off the rear lasers and banked sharply, pushing the throttle controls up to one hundred percent power.

The manoeuvre seemed to catch the pilot of *The Black Star* off-guard and the chase ship remained on its original course for several seconds before it slowed and finally altered its course to follow them again. John allowed himself a brief smile. He now knew for sure that the pursuing craft didn't have the manoeuvrability of his Eye.

It wasn't long before he was smiling again as he watched Wenwik come into view; the cloud-covered planet soon filling the entire cockpit window. It wasn't a big planet, but John had been on much smaller ones. Besides, the atmosphere was perfect for what he wanted. It was dense. Far too dense for anyone to attempt a planet fall with their weapons out, as they would most likely be torn clean off the ship's hull during entry. Any ship's hull... including that of *The Black Star*, which was still behind them and rapidly gaining ground.

John knew it was only a matter of minutes before it would be in firing range. *Five, ten maybe, tops.*

Without waiting for the order, Tyson snapped on his harness and retracted *The Broken Eye's* weapons. There was no way he was willing to risk losing any of their brand new – expensive - modifications.

Losing his grin, John selected the fastest and steepest trajectory possible to breach the planet's atmosphere, fitting his own harness in the same fluid motion. He hoped that *The Black Star* would follow his path down, but unfortunately, its pilot wasn't quite as inexperienced as John would have liked and he swore loudly as the pilot corrected his flight path to a safer and more sensible trajectory.

Moments later, *The Broken Eye* burst through Wenwik's upper cloud formations, leaving behind a tell-tale vapour trail as they descended. Tyson was scanning the topography report he had initiated as soon as they had breached the planet's atmosphere.

"Well?" John enquired impatiently, one eye on the screen showing him *The Black Star's* altered path as he unleashed another round of swearing. The pursuing ship was fast. *Too fast.*

Suddenly, all *The Broken Eye's* scanners winked out.

John swore even more, guessing some sort of interference from the planet's surface was to blame. "Ty? Did you get anything?"

"No luck on the canyons or forest, I'm afraid, but I did manage to confirm the location of a desert and maybe a large body of water," Tyson replied looking rather sheepish.

"Let me get this right. The one planet you do find, has no good hiding spots?

"Hey, I only found the place. I didn't make it!"

"Yeah, okay, sorry," John sighed. "Stay buckled in. I have an idea."

"I'm not going like this, am I?"

John threw Tyson a maniacal grin in reply.

"OH SHIT!" Tyson howled as he hurriedly tugged on his harness straps ensuring they were tight. "You are so NOT FUNNY!"

There was no sign of *The Black Star* as John piloted his ship across the planet towards a vast desert wasteland. He checked the outside temperature, pleased to see at least some of the sensors were operational. It was near perfect.

The wide grin still plastered across his face, he positioned the ship, on full throttle, shields off and holding a stationary position, right on the edge of the desert, mere metres from the enormous sandy plain.

The hovering freighter was generating heat quickly. Even without the scanners, both men could clearly see the sand beneath the ship began to liquefy and bubble, rapidly turning into molten glass. Satisfied with the effect, John released the ship inhibitors and *The Broken Eye* shot forward over the surface of the dunes leaving a chaotic landscape of towering glass waves in its wake.

"I don't even want to know what it is you're doing," Tyson said as he screwed his eyes shut.

After several hundred, erratic kilometres, John engaged the shields and slowed the ship to twenty percent speed, before finally turning around in a wide arc to survey his handiwork.

Tyson felt the ship slow and opened up his eyes. The look of wonder and amazement on his face made John laugh.

All the fear and anger drained from Tyson's features as he struggled to find the words befitting the spectacle in front of him. "It's … it's beautiful," was all he could stammer, even after several silent minutes had ticked by.

The massive glass waves stood proud, in a myriad of dazzling colours, enormous and towering over them as far as the eye could see. John nodded, not bothering to suppress his proud smirk. He had to agree with his co-pilot, the view was indeed spectacular.

The bases of the waves started out in deep blues and emerald greens that slowly blended upwards, higher and higher, into burnt reds, sharply giving way to vivid orange crests that were topped off with bright yellow and white caps, that looked almost like clouds in the distance. Each formation shimmered in the light and each was quite unique as here and there, the blues and greens of the base streaked all the way up into the white and yellow peaks.

On the slowest speed *The Broken Eye* was capable of, John picked his way through the chaotic landscape of waves. It was so slow that it barely even registered on the operations screen.

Little by little the ship crept forward, both men watching in silent awe as they progressed into the hazardous glass landscape. Every wave formation was different in colour, shape, and size. Many of them had sharp spikes jutting out of them at odd angles making the navigation challenging, even for the most accomplished pilot. John guessed that they were as sharp and as deadly as they were spectacular and beautiful.

It took Tyson, trying to fully absorb the breathtaking spectacle that his friend had created, several minutes before he was able to speak. "Johnny, how did you know it would do this?"

"One time, back when I was in the military, there was a combat situation on a desert planet," John explained with a shrug, not taking his eyes off the waves. "I was given a report that a squad of ours was pinned down and taking heavy fire. My orders were to do a reconnaissance fly over and report back if a rescue was possible."

Never having heard John talk about this time in the military, Tyson sat in respectful silence as his friend blew out a long breath and then continued, "I will never forget what I saw that day. The intelligence we had been given was wrong. It was a bloodbath. As the light from the planet's twin suns hit the dunes, all I could see was more than a hundred corpses of our men littered across the sand. The white desert sands were crimson. Pools of blood had formed in the natural hollows of the dunes. It was hell, Ty. The most macabre thing I've ever seen."

Tyson sat unmoving, hypnotised in horror as John recounted his memory. He dared almost not breathe as he didn't want to break his friend's concentration; not only in the retelling of his story but also from his piloting the *Eye* through the huge and deadly waves.

"The enemy forces were regrouping before overrunning the dunes in a final push to secure victory. I could see a handful of our soldiers that had survived the initial attack," John went on, his gaze still fixed firmly on the dazzling landscape outside the ship. "From my vantage point, their position was hopeless. I reported back that a full rescue attempt would be futile. Even if the Commander sent in air support, by the time it got there, they would have been dead. So," he gave another shrug. "It was me or nothing."

Tyson could contain himself no longer. "What happened?" he asked.

Almost as if he only just realized his friend was still there, John glanced across at Tyson for a brief moment before turning his attention back to weaving the ship neatly through the towering peaks. "I was in a modified crew transport ship. It was fast but had no weapons. I didn't know what to do until suddenly I remembered that with enough heat you can turn sand to glass. So, I flew in fast and low with my shields on the minimum setting to create as much heat as I could. The ship whipped up the sand as I skimmed the planet's surface and the heat from the rear burners transformed it into glass waves as I raced between our boys and the approaching enemy force."

"So, you planned to do this," Tyson said, nodding his understanding.

"Yes and no," John conceded with a small smile. "I just hoped it would work again. Luckily it did. Although this time it's a little different. Last time, the glass waves were perfectly clear, almost completely colourless and not nearly as big as these. Fortunately, the creation of those waves surprised and shocked the enemy enough to give me time to land and recover the troopers before another shot was fired."

"Are you saying this all was just dumb luck?" Tyson asked, shaking his head with a laugh.

"Hey, we needed a place to hide, so I made one. Most people would consider themselves extremely fortunate to have a pilot so amazing he is able to create such a magnificent hiding place for them," the captain said with a tight smirk. "And you never even said thank you."

"Gee thanks," Tyson rolled his eye and set about getting the scanners back online.

John was busy surveying the biggest of the waves with a critical eye, his face breaking into a wide grin when eventually he found what he was looking for. One of the glass waves directly in front of them had formed a sort of half-bubble in its base.

He brought the ship to a complete stop alongside the cavity, then slowly and gently, manoeuvred *The Broken Eye* inside. Ignoring Tyson's insistence, they look for a bigger opening, the captain guided the ship through the narrow gap with expert precision. The sound of the engines echoed faintly off the thick, glass walls as the big ship landed softly, John powering down the engines to their standby settings.

Immediately, *The Broken Eye* was bathed in a deep green hue, the light from the twin suns amplified through the waves of glass. Tyson rummaged around in the side pocket of his seat and let out a cry of triumph. "I knew I had some of these in here somewhere!" he exclaimed, holding up two thin rolls of plastic.

"I'm so happy for you, I could almost burst," replied John sarcastically, glancing at the objects his friend was holding up.

"And for that remark, I'm having the red pair," Tyson tossed one of the rolls to John, "You get the black ones."

John studied the roll. He had no idea what he was looking at, but he wasn't going to admit that to his friend. "It's just so hard to express how thrilled I am."

He watched Tyson find an edge to the curious roll and hold it up to his ear, the rest of it resting against his cheekbone. He then tapped the roll three times. To John's amazement, it snapped out across his face, neatly unravelling until it stretched from ear to ear, covering his eyes and the bridge of his nose.

"They're sunglasses," John blurted out before realising what he had said.

"Of course, they are. What did you think they were?" said Tyson now admiring his reflection in his screen that he had turned into a mirror so that he could assess his new look.

The captain didn't reply as he activated his own. "Ahh, much better. That green light was beginning to give me a headache."

They heard the incoming ship before they saw its shadow flew over them, the sound of its engines booming off the waves as it passed.

Tyson brought up the scanner screens. Still nothing. The planet's interference was too strong. *The Black Star* could have been in spitting distance and they would never have known it. "Scanners are still non-functional, Johnny."

"With any luck, he doesn't know we're here, and we can slip away when he leaves," replied John.

He had barely finished speaking when a voice crackled over their ship to ship intercom system. "To the occupants of *The Broken Eye*, I am Captain Daylen Rockford of *The Black Star*. I require you to surrender your vessel to the service of the *Kings*. If you comply promptly, I will give you safe passage to the nearest habitable planet."

"He's bluffing. Unless he knows this planet back to front, he can only be guessing we're in here," John reassured his concerned looking friend.

Several long minutes stretched on and the intercom stayed silent. The two men could still hear the dull roar of the ship's engines as it hovered nearby.

"I don't know about that, Johnny. Why hasn't he moved on then?"

"Like I said, he's just…"

Captain Rockford's voice interrupted him. "Do not be fooled into thinking I am merely bluffing. I charted this planet only two days ago and know it inside out."

"He's only guessing, huh?" sneered Tyson.

John ignored the tone and brought the ship's engines back online. "Okay, so we can't outrun him, he has superior firepower, and we can't hide from him. Any ideas?" he asked as he buckled himself into his chair.

Tyson shrugged and hastily fitted his own harness. "Maybe if we can get him to search each of the waves individually, we can buy ourselves some time and trap him in here somehow?"

A moment later two more shadows appeared over the waves where John and Tyson were hiding.

"This is your final chance to surrender your vessel. My fellow captains will not be as lenient as I will upon your impending capture. I am sure you must be aware that you embarrassed them both greatly when you fired on them."

"Oh shit," Tyson tried the scanners once more, this time cycling through the frequencies slowly. "I bet those guys are pissed."

A brief, blurred image popped up on his screen showing three ships mere metres from their location. It was quickly followed by a dull groaning sound that grew louder and louder.

It was John who spoke first, "Tyson, shut down the scanners. I have an idea."

Something in his tone told Tyson it would be unwise to answer with one of his usual remarks, and he complied instantly. Still, by the time the scanners were shut down, the groaning sound had turned into a howl and it now echoed all around them in the cave.

As the sound in the cavern subsided, both men could hear the three ships searching for them. Two of the craft were zig-zagging above the waves and occasionally they would catch a glimpse of one of them as they flew overhead. The third was slowly trawling the waves far below at ground level.

John knew it was only a matter of time before they were found. "Is there any way we can amplify the scanners output?" he asked his co-pilot.

Tyson looked thoughtful for a moment then went to work on his screen. "I get it. You want to try and boost the signal to see who the other two ships are, right?"

"Something like that," answered John, powering up the ship's weapons. He flicked his screen over to the scanners page and locked in the last setting they had used.

"Okay, Johnny. I can boost the scanners all the way up to a thousand percent but I'm sure you didn't mean that much of an increase, right?"

"On my mark, push it all the way up."

"What? Why?"

"If it works, you'll see."

"Oh good! Another one of your PLANS. I can hardly wait," Tyson replied with acid in his voice.

John threw Tyson a rude hand gesture and slid *The Broken Eye* out of its hiding spot out into the open air.

The response from the three ships hunting them was swift and precise. The two that had been patrolling above quickly swooped down, and the third, doing ground control, turned abruptly and accelerated directly toward them.

"They must have boosted their own scanners an incredible amount to synchronise like that," commented Tyson, not bothering to disguise the awe in his voice.

"I know," replied John, with a wry grin. "Hopefully, they sacrificed some of their shielding in order to do so."

"Right, I get it now. You're going to shoot them down while they have no shields."

"Not quite."

The three ships opened fire simultaneously on *The Broken Eye*. *The Barters Pride* raining down on them from above, *The Blue Cobra* blasting away from behind, and *The Black Star* shooting straight at them.

Without showing even a trace of concern John ordered, "Ty, on the count of three. Hit the scanners at full boost."

"Wait. What? Why?"

"One…"

"Johnny, shouldn't we be moving out of the way?"

"Two…"

The Eye was now being peppered with multiple laser shots, but even under the barrage of fire, the shields held firm and the captain didn't move the ship an inch.

"By the seven moons of Cryos!" Tyson cried out. "It's finally happened. You've finally cracked!"

"Three…"

Sending up a silent prayer to whatever gods happened to be in the vicinity, Tyson engaged the scanners at full boost.

Then the sound came. At first, it was nothing more than a gentle *tink, tink, tink*. Soon it grew, louder and louder until it was a roar. A moment later, subtle cracks started to appear in the waves. Then, right before Tyson's eyes, every one of the yellow and white capped waves sheared off and shattered, raining down thousands of deadly razor-sharp shards. Some of the enormous glass structures collapsed on themselves or onto their neighbours. Others exploded and sent huge, jagged chunks spinning out into the air.

One of the airborne missiles slammed into *The Barters Pride*. Black smoke plumed from its fuselage as the ship was flung sideways, its erratic journey coming to a grinding halt as it was speared by a blue and yellow streaked spire.

Watching it hang in the air, more smoke billowing from its whining engines, John winced. "Waste of a good ship," he muttered and turned his attention to the rear screen just in time to witness *The Blue Cobra* being cut in two by a massive hailstorm of beautifully hued shards of red and green.

Tyson had his eye on Captain Daylen Rockford. Clearly, he was a far better pilot than those of the two other ships put together. He had slowed his speed and banked sharply, managing to avoid being crushed instantly by the devastating, avalanching landscape.

Unfortunately for him, it still wasn't enough. The whole wall on his port side was collapsing and the cavern wasn't going to be long enough or straight enough for him to outrun it.

John turned off the scanners and throttled the ship forward, dodging and weaving his way through the chaos of glass at a speed much faster than his co-pilot would have liked.

When they were high enough and out of any immediate danger from the waves that were continuing to shatter and burst, John banked the ship and surveyed the carnage, searching for any sign of *The Black Star*. After several minutes, he spotted it, picking its way under a massive pile of multi-coloured glass.

"And just where do you think you're going?" he muttered and fired the forward laser into a sheet of glass only metres in front of the escaping ship.

The sheet of blood-red glass exploded, caving in right on top of *The Black Star* and pinning it down.

Calmly John opened up an intercom channel, "To the crews of *The Blue Cobra* and *The Barters Pride*. If you require assistance, surrender yourselves without aggression and we will give you safe passage to the nearest habitable planet."

Tyson smothered a laugh.

A moment later the reply came crackling over *The Broken Eye's* intercom. "This is Captain Dauwn Starling of *The Blue Cobra*. Our life support is failing, we require assistance."

Almost immediately, another panicked, faint voice followed. "This is Pilot Lector Craybon of *The Barters Pride*. My ship has critical damage. I accept your offer also."

Smiling smugly John opened up a channel to *The Black Star*. "Captain Rockford, do you require assistance? Will you abandon your ship and accept safe passage also?"

He did not have to wait long for Daylen Rockford's answer, the static-filled connection unable to hide the rage in the other captain's voice, "Thank you for your kind offer. However, believe me, I will find my own way out and when I do, I will track you down and there will be a reckoning."

Tyson chuckled, "You know, Johnny, one of the things I admire most about you is the way that, no matter where you go, you always take the time to make new friends."

John gave his friend a grin, "It's a talent. You either have it or you don't," he said with fake sincerity.

Deciding to give the crew of *The Barters Pride* priority, John relayed instructions for them to kit up in their bio suits so that, once his ship was in position, they would be able to board *The Broken Eye* safely via the cargo bay doors.

Getting the okay from the captain, he expertly manoeuvred the *Eye* closer until they were hovering slightly below the badly damaged ship, several feet from the cockpit's emergency exit plate.

From their vantage point aboard *The Eye*, John and Tyson could see the extensive damage to the other craft. It had multiple lacerations in its hull and a large part of the fuselage had been crushed. The majority of the damage, however, had clearly been caused by it being impaled on the huge bright blue and white, razor-sharp spire.

"I'm amazed that anyone is alive in there at all," commented Tyson as he lowered the docking bay ramp doors.

John hailed *The Barter's Pride*, "We are in position. How many passengers are we to receive?"

Lector Craybon's voice was very faint now and his breathing was shallow, "Just one occupant per vessel, Captain. Our lord, the King, insists on a single pilot per ship for recovery crews such as ours."

"Very well, Captain. Permission to come aboard is granted."

The *Pride's* captain blew open the emergency door. It landed perfectly creating a bridge between the ships.

Tyson whistled, "I'm going to assume that you have done this type of thing before."

"I wasn't always a babysitter for a cyborg," John retaliated.

Far from being insulted, Tyson simply laughed, "I'm not a cyborg. I'm mechanically enhanced."

John smiled and returned his attention to Craybon, creeping out of his battered ship into *The Eye*. Once he was satisfied the captain had crawled safely onto the cargo doors, he set them to close and ensured the double interior cargo doors were securely locked and pressurised. "Ty," he turned back to his co-pilot. "Would you mind relieving our guest of any weapons, concealed or otherwise, before securing him in the cage in the cargo bay?"

"I didn't think you liked locking people up, Johnny?"

John's expression turned serious. "Taking prisoners is not the same as slavery. These people should count themselves lucky that I don't just kill them."

Tyson mutely nodded his understanding and headed out of the cockpit. Before he reached the door, however, John's voice stopped him.

"Take a gun with you. You don't have to use it. It will just show them that you mean business."

"Okay, Johnny," Tyson said, reluctantly picking up his stunner rifle before he left. "And, for the record, I think you're doing the right thing by not killing them."

"I hope you're right, my friend, "John muttered at his departing back. "I really do."

When Tyson reached the cargo bay, he opened the first of two doors by keying a code into his data pad. He stepped through into the little room between the doors, then closed and locked the first one behind him. He made no attempt to open the second door, however, instead he leaned over to peer through the glass panel in the centre of it. Expecting their new guest to be, at the very least, annoyed at having to come aboard, Tyson wasn't taking any chances. He was, therefore, surprised when what he saw was the figure of Lector Craybon lying on the floor, unmoving.

Again, he reached for his data pad and this time opened up a channel to the cockpit. "Johnny, are you seeing what I'm seeing?"

"Yeah, he collapsed a moment ago. Be careful."

"What should I do?"

"You'll be fine, Ty. Start by giving him short, simple, precise instructions to follow."

"And what if he isn't interested in following my simple, precise instructions?"

"Then you shoot him."

"Seriously? That's your answer? *Shoot* him? Listen, Johnny, not everyone is ex-military. This may come as a surprise to you, but normal people don't go around killing people just because they can't follow simple instructions!"

John's exasperated, "Tyson!" and brought the tirade to an abrupt end. "You're holding a STUN rifle."

"Oh…yeah…right. Forget about what I said then."

Tyson felt his cheeks flush in embarrassment as he checked the room was safe to enter. The illuminated display on the side of the door was green, signalling that it was. He opened the second door and stepped through. He heard the snap of the locks engaging as the door immediately slid closed behind him. Acutely aware of the added seconds it would take to get past security should he need to unlock the doors in order to make his escape, Tyson approached the lifeless form.

Nothing happened.

"Captain Craybon," Tyson cleared his throat loudly. "Please stand with your arms above your head."

Still, the man did not move. It was then that Tyson noticed there was a hole in the captain's bio-suit. It looked as if his hand might have slipped away from where he had been trying to maintain a seal as he crossed onto *The Broken Eye*. Tyson promptly lay down his rifle and data pad and removed the man's helmet. His face had turned blue and was barely breathing.

"Johnny!" Tyson shouted, knowing his captain would be listening through the still-open channel. "What should I do?"

"Drag him into the cage and lock it."

"*What?* He needs help. Look at your screen! Can't you see he's dying?"

"TY, drag him into the cage and lock it."

Cursing under his breath, Tyson grabbed the man by his ankles and did as he was instructed.

"Hey, check him for weapons before you lock him in."

Still muttering every swear word he could think of, Tyson obediently patted the man down. He found a small sidearm and a knife tucked in the outer layers of the bio suit's boots which he duly confiscated. It wasn't until he was chaining up the cage, however, that Lector finally started to move.

Tyson faltered, watching as the man's body began convulsing and spluttering. "Johnny…"

There was no reply from the cockpit, but Tyson soon let out a relieved sigh as Lector gave a huge gasp and slumped back into unconsciousness, some of the colour returning to his face, his chest rising and falling again in a rhythmic fashion.

"Okay, Ty," John's voice hailed him. "Good job. Grab your rifle and head back up here. We have another guest to collect."

Tyson entered the cockpit just as the front half of the shattered *Blue Cobra* came into view. "Johnny, how in the seven moons did you know that guy was going to be okay?"

"I've seen it before," John shrugged, more interested in manoeuvring *The Broken Eye* into position alongside the busted-up ship than in discussing Lector Craybon. "It's toxic shock from the planet's air. He's lucky. Exposure to it any longer would have killed him."

Sensing that was all the information he was going to get on that matter, Tyson turned his attention to *The Blue Cobra*. "Looks like the emergency bulkheads sealed before the ship lost all of its breathable atmosphere," he observed.

The two men could see hurried movements going on through the front window of the badly damaged ship.

"So much for Craybon's claims about single occupancy," John noted with a frown. "There's definitely more than one person aboard that ship. Let's see if they feel like being honest with us."

"Why wouldn't they be? Surely they've got to know that without our help, they'll eventually run out of air and suffocate."

"Ty," John said patiently. "To them, we are the bad guys, and they want our ship."

Tyson scratched his head, looking thoughtful for a moment before drawling sarcastically, "You know, Johnny, sometimes you're a real optimist."

"I prefer to think of myself as more of a realist," replied the captain with a grin.

"This is Captain Dauwn Starling of the *Blue Cobra*," a woman's voice crackled over the ship's com. "Captain of *The Broken Eye*, our emergency exit panel had been damaged and is non- functional."

John ran a hand through his long brown hair. "One hundred credits say's they want to exit the ship via the main airlock," he indicated to Tyson where the airlock was positioned on the top of the battered ship. "They'll be hoping that, once we're above them we won't be able to see what's going on down below and we might just miss an extra passenger or two." He activated the intercom to query mildly, "Message received *Blue Cobra*. What systems do you have still functioning?"

There was a long pause. Then a muffled voice responded, "Captain, I have suited up and am ready for extraction from my main airlock. I'm standing by for further instructions."

John held out his hand, palm up, in front of Tyson. "That will be one hundred credits, thank you, sir."

His friend swatted it away with a grunt. "Just because her ship is a wreck, doesn't mean there is a conspiracy going on."

"Sure," John kept his ship port side of The Blue Cobra, checking for any more signs of movement onboard the damaged vessel. "I can't possibly see how she would be upset about having her ship destroyed and being taken captive."

"Not everyone thinks like you, you do know that, right?"

John chuckled and shook his head in disbelief at Tyson's words. *How could his friend be so naïve?* "Okay, fine," he conceded. "We'll do it your way. This time."

"Finally! The voice of reason prevails," Tyson rolled his eye.

"But I'm not locking our airlock onto theirs," the captain clarified, smiling at his own plan. "She can jump onto the cargo doors like her friend Lector did."

"I wouldn't expect you to make things easier for her," Tyson drawled. "That would be far too civilised."

As before, John aligned the two ships then activated one of the bulkheads in the cargo bay, taking care to seal off the cage safely within the ship's breathable air first. He didn't want to kill Craybon; not accidently anyway.

Once everything was in place for the transfer, John hooked a thumb over his shoulder. "It's time for you to make your way down and escort our new guest to her deluxe accommodations."

"What?" Tyson looked incredulous at the instruction. "You want me to give her one of the empty crews' quarters?"

"Yeah, for sure. And put a mint on her pillow while you're at it."

Tyson stared at him for a long moment before groaning, "I'm going to assume you're joking."

"Really? What gave me away? Put her in the cage with the other guy, Ty, and don't forget to check her for weapons."

"And there was I thinking you were going to be a gentleman about this," Tyson said snidely as he collected his stun rifle and exited the cockpit.

Once more John lowered the cargo bay doors and activated the cameras, swearing softly as he realized all they showed him was the view inside the closed bulkhead. He opened a channel to hail Tyson. "This is your captain speaking."

"You do know you're not funny, right?"

John laughed at his friend's almost automatic response. "Just letting you know you're on your own down there. I don't have any cameras working beyond the bulkhead, so I'm not going to be able to see how many people board the ship."

"I understand, Johnny. I'll be careful."

"Any sign of trouble, and I do mean ANY, stun them. I still think it's suspicious."

"Is there anyone you trust? In *any* of the systems?"

John ignored his comment and continued, "Until I close the door and vent the toxic air, do not open the bulky."

"Okay, okay. I get it."

"Ty. I need you to be at the ready."

"I got this, Johnny. Don't worry."

With a short, exasperated sigh, John opened up the ship to ship intercom. "Captain Starling, we are experiencing some electrical difficulties. We are unable to extend the docking chute," he said, the lie slipping off his tongue with the smoothness of a well-oiled crankshaft. "Please access our ship via our cargo bay. We are in position and are ready to receive your crew."

A breathless female voice replied, "Thank you, captain. However, I am the only crew member aboard the ship."

"My associate will meet you once you are safely aboard. Good luck," John cut the communications between the two ships and turned his attention back to the cargo bay cameras.

Tyson had just reached the outer door when he heard pounding coming from inside. He opened up the link to the captain. "Johnny, I believe our guest is safely aboard."

"Copy that. The cargo ramp is closing now."

There was a loud hiss as the ramp sealed shut. "Okay," Tyson relayed back to John. "It's all green down here."

"Copy that. Venting air and pressurising the cargo bay."

Moments later, the third light on the cargo door panel flashed green and stayed solid. Remembering his friend's warning, Tyson checked his weapon. Smiling to himself, he flicked off the safety. He knew John would never let him live it down if something was to happen and he had the safety left on.

With a shudder at the thought, Tyson entered the cargo bay and locked the double doors behind him. He threw a cautious glance at Lector Craybon, who was now sitting up in the cage. His breathing had returned to normal and he was, Tyson noted, watching his every move through narrowed eyes.

Figuring the prisoner was secure and no immediate threat to him, Tyson thought to himself, *let him watch.* He made his way over to the control panel and typed in a code. The bulkhead sprung up suddenly catching him by surprise. Suddenly, two figures in bio suits rushed him as soon as the door lifted. The first tackled him by the legs while the second hit him in the shoulder with such force that he spun around wildly as he fell.

From the safety of his pilot's chair, John saw it all on the cameras and swiftly opened up a channel to his friend. "Ty!" he ordered, "kick down hard with your left foot, then roll to your right and fire at your nine o'clock!"

Tyson obeyed without hesitation. He kicked down savagely with his thick, powerful leg twice, the crunching of the boot against bone muffled only slightly by his attacker's bio suit's helmet. Then, without missing a beat, he spun to his right and fired.

Through sheer luck, more than anything else, the shot hit his approaching target in the legs, the figure giving off a distinctly female cry as she collapsed heavily in a heap on the cargo bay floor.

Watching the action unfold on his screens, John exploded out of his seat, grabbed up his rifle and ran towards the bay. By the time he reached the doors, however, Tyson had stunned all three prisoners and removed their weapons.

Cursing himself for being right – *again* - John punched in the access codes and entered the room. Tyson was already dragging the unconscious Captain Starling into the safety of the cage, so John made his way over to their unexpected third guest and squatted down to gently remove his helmet.

Blood was smeared across his face and it was clear his nose had been badly broken in the scuffle. Although it was difficult to ascertain through all the blood, John guessed he also had at least a fractured cheekbone and was missing more than a couple of front teeth.

He gave a low whistle. "Sheesh, Ty. You might punch like a girl, but you certainly kicked the shit out of this guy."

"I wasn't thinking. I just reacted."

"I wouldn't feel too bad about it," John pointed to the collection of weapons Tyson had confiscated from the pair. "Those are definitely not stun guns."

"I know, but I still feel bad."

"Any particular reason, you felt the need to stun the guy already in the cage?"

Tyson blushed at the question and couldn't quite look John in the eye as he mumbled, "I panicked and shot everyone that wasn't me."

The captain pushed down the urge to laugh and simply nodded his understanding. "Tell you what, I'll finish up while you go rustle up a couple of medical packs for our mangled friend here."

Tyson winced at the word 'mangled' but headed off toward the medical bay without further comment.

John secured the two new prisoners in the cage and was about to walk off when he heard a groan from the man with the crushed face. He turned back with a slow smile. The effects of the stun gun would surely be wearing off him first, due to the pain of his injuries. The man coughed up a wad of blood and spat it through the bars of the cage at John in a show of defiance.

"Name, Soldier!" John barked at him.

Reflexively, the man returned, "Wane Ash."

John smirked, knowing the man must have done some time in the military at some stage due to his swift and very automatic response to the order.

Realisation dawned in the man's eyes that he had just given himself away. He glanced at his fellow captives. They were still out cold.

"How did you know?" he whispered hoarsely. "If they find out, I'm dead."

"Let's just say I've been around enough military personnel to know one when I smell one," John shrugged, taking a step closer to the cage.

"I'm deep undercover. Off the books."

John nodded, apparently unconcerned by the confession. "Is that so? What colour code?"

The man faltered. Uncertain of whom he was speaking to. "How-How could you know about that?" he stammered. "Only people at the highest level know about the codes. Unless …" his voice trailed off into thought.

"Yes," John finished for him. "I'm exactly what you think it means."

Wane let out an impressive flurry of swear words. "My designated code is grey," he finally admitted.

John chuckled at the less than subtle joke. "Ahh, I see. Ash is grey. They haven't lost their sense of humour then. So, they allocate you new names now?"

"Yeah," Wane attempted a sort of a laugh, but his face immediately contorted in pain from the action and he soon stopped. "Someone high up thought it would be clever."

"I'm sure they did. My co-pilot is bringing back some medical packs for your face," John gestured at the man's injuries. "You'll be as good as new in a few days."

"Does he know about you?"

"Let's just say he knows very little, and I intend to keep it that way."

Not missing the intonation in his captor's voice, Wane glanced over his shoulder, checking his associates were still asleep. "Perhaps we can make a deal?"

"Sure, we can. Keep your mouth shut about ever seeing me, and maybe I'll let you live," said John in a whisper as he snapped off the safety on his rifle.

Wane could see the cold look in the captain's eyes. He knew the man had seen death up close, and men like that didn't make idle threats, they stated facts. "Yes, Captain," he nodded. "Understood."

Tyson returned with two fresh medical packs and, once John had introduced them to each other formally, he apologised sincerely for breaking the man's face.

"I would have done the same if given the chance," Wane nodded, gingerly applying the healing packs to his wound. "May I request something, Captain?"

John nodded.

"Can you shoot me again with the stunner? I would rather sleep through the next few hours while these packs do their work."

John grinned. "You heard the man, Ty. Shoot him."

"What?" Tyson could not have looked more appalled by the idea. "Seriously?"

"You heard him. He wants you to do it."

"Am I the only sane person on this ship?"

"Fine," John said, relieving Tyson of his weapon. "I'll do it then."

Before Tyson could blink his one, good eye, John had sighted the man in the cage and blasted him in the face. "Anyone ever tell you, that you're a brutal bastard?" he asked, shaking his head in disbelief.

John chuckled as he said, "No one still alive."

"Why does that answer not surprise me?" Tyson snatched back his stun rifle and marched out of the cargo bay alone.

John calmly stashed the confiscated weapons in the tool room, then ensured everything was locked and secure, before leaving the cargo bay and their three unconscious "guests."

Tyson was staring out the front window when his friend finally joined him in the cockpit. "Johnny," he said, pointing down at *The Black Star*, still largely obscured from view by a mound of the shattered, coloured waves. "What in the seven moons do you think he is up to?"

Following Tyson's finger, John too peered out the window.

Captain Rockford had managed to position his ship horizontally and was hovering above the shattered waves at full thrust. Even from where they were, John could see the glass landscape starting to bubble with the heat the massive engine was generating. "You clever bastard," he swore and sprang into action. "Ty, buckle yourself in! We're getting out of here now!"

"What? Why?" Tyson asked as he ran to his seat.

John was already fitting his harness, one eye still on *The Black Star*. "He's heating up the glass, and with the power of the Novac engine he has, he's likely to create a whole hell of a mess and trap us in there right along with it."

Tyson snapped his chair restraints into place and gave his friend a quick thumbs-up, while simultaneously activating the ship's internal intercoms. "To all of our conscious guests travelling with us today, I hope you are enjoying your stay in our deluxe cage accommodations. Please fasten your seatbelts, place your seats in an upright position, and secure your table trays. If you do not have a seatbelt, chair or table tray, hold on to anything you can. Thank you."

John shot his friend a quizzical look.

"What?" Tyson shrugged. "I just thought I should warn them."

The captain shook his head, too concerned with the ship below them to comment on his co-pilot's sense of humour. A moment later *The Black Star* burst through the molten glass and disappeared from sight. Not to be outdone, John immediately jammed his own thrusters on full and followed him.

Still, by the time *The Broken Eye* reached open space, the other ship was nowhere to be seen. A quick scan of the area showed nothing.

"That is one fast ship," commented Tyson, running a second, futile check and sighing when the screens came up empty.

"Yeah," John sat back in his seat. "And I don't think that's the last we've heard from him. Ty, can you replot a course for the nearest habitable planet?"

Tyson busied himself consulting the local star charts. It wasn't long before he had narrowed it down to several possibilities. "Okay," he began, his cybernetic eye scrolling through all the available information on each. "First up, we have Hepto, a swamp planet, slightly above average population. Or maybe you'd prefer Tarke, a water planet, thirty percent landmass, low population. Then, of course, there's always Mettile, a smaller planet, mostly unexplored jungle terrain, population…looks like only minimal settlers."

John groaned, "Just tell me which is the closest to Caxton."

"Do this, do that, that's all I ever hear. No, 'Thanks Ty', 'Great job, Ty'," Tyson muttered, mostly to himself as he rotated the 3D images on his screen. "Well, none of them really," he finally shrugged. "All are approximately three days travel from here. All in different directions, I guess. Mettile is a little closer in terms of flight time, but not by much."

John shook his head in frustration. "Fine, let's lock in that one"

Silently, Tyson entered the co-ordinates into the computer and a moment later, the navigation light began to blink.

With one last check on the screen, showing him a view of the cargo bay, John pressed the blue flashing button. The lone ship executed a wide, sweeping arc away from the planet and then jumped.

Chapter Thirteen

The Broken Eye slowly approached Mettile, its pilot and co-pilot both relieved that they had not spotted another vessel the whole trip, pirate or otherwise. Mutely, and thoroughly, Tyson scanned the area before they settled into a safe orbit around the green-hued planet. Once the ship's flight path was established, he ran a second scan, just be sure, then, with a weary sigh, took out his cybernetic eye, examining it briefly before giving it a good polish on his sleeve.

John had been quieter than usual during the journey and it was making Tyson feel a little uncomfortable. He knew he was at least partly to blame for the captain's sullenness. But by their standards, there had only been one minor incident and it wasn't like John to hold a grudge against him. John's mood was not entirely the result of the 'minor incident' but he was not about to tell Tyson what was really going on in his head.

The short trip to Mettile had started out quietly enough. Out of a sense of civic duty, the two men had been taking turns to escort the three prisoners to the showers, toilets and kitchen area. John had wanted to take them one at a time, "for security reasons," but Tyson had argued it would save many trips back and forth if they took all three of them together.

"We have their weapons, Johnny. How much trouble are they going to be?"

Sure enough, they had made several, successful individual runs to and from the cage. Until, while collecting the group for showers, Tyson had inadvertently left his stun rifle leaning up against the bars. He had been in the process of unlocking the door when one of the prisoners had grabbed the rifle and had stunned him, just as he keyed in the last of the code.

Unfortunately, for the prisoners, Tyson's paralysed body had slumped forward against the bars, sliding to the floor and blocking the unlocked cage door. Luckily for Tyson, John had been watching the incident unfold on the cargo bay's cameras and was on the scene before the group had been able to shove Tyson's sizeable bulk out of their way.

They had been so focused on moving Tyson that they hadn't heard John enter the room and he had been able to creep stealthily up to the cage, line up one of his targets between the bars, and, with the butt of his rifle, dealt a brutal blow into the back of Captain Craybon's large, bald head without being detected.

Lector's body had dropped like a stone, crashing loudly onto the cage floor, the stun rifle clattering noisily from his limp hand as he did so. The two other prisoners wordlessly turned to face John, wide-eyed in surprise.

"Unlike my sleeping friend there," John had said, pointing his gun directly at the chest of Dauwn Stirling, "My rifle isn't a stunner."

Obediently, the captain had raised her hands above her head. Wane Ash quickly followed suit.

"A wise choice. Now, toss me the stunner through the bars."

With one eye on the barrel of the weapon still pointing unwaveringly at her, Dauwn had inched towards the crumpled unconscious body of Lector and reached down with both hands to pick up the stun rifle.

"You know," John's whisper had been only for her ears, "I would really hate to have to scrub your blood off my favourite cage's floor."

Dauwn had stiffened visibly, then slowly and carefully had picked up the stunner with her elbows and tossed it out of the cage.

After that, the prisoners were escorted one at a time. It had only been a minor incident and John's real concern was with a few nagging questions he had, the likes of which had greatly contributed to his quiet demeanour. Questions that he didn't have the answers to yet.

He wanted those answers badly, but he didn't want to blow the cover of the military special operations operative that was sharing a cell with two other members of the Kings in their cargo hold. There had been a few brief occasions when he had been able to interrogate him, but every time he had started, Tyson had interrupted him, which only fuelled John's frustrations.

"Johnny, it looks like there are four separate settlements on the surface. They're pretty spaced out around the planet, though. I guess it must be to maximise the exploration and mapping process."

"Good job, Ty." John's mood brightened instantly as, at Tyson's words, an idea struck him. "That's brilliant." Now, he wouldn't have to isolate the prisoners on his ship, he could just drop them off at different locations on the planet, and in doing so, could have a long, friendly chat with Wane Ash.

"Finally! I get the recognition I deserve," Tyson said as he made an attempt at bowing while still seated.

John shook his head and let out a long, exaggerated sigh in response. "I'm thinking the best idea would be to break up our little 'party' and drop them off at separate points on the planet."

"Yeah," Tyson agreed. "I don't want to risk moving them all at the same time again."

A wry grin appeared on John's face, but he chose not to comment any further. "Pick out the three most isolated settlements, then plot us a course for the closest one."

It wasn't long before Tyson had locked the co-ordinates into the navigation computer and the blue light was winking at them again. Wordlessly, the captain reached over and depressed the button.

The Broken Eye burst through the heavy cloud cover in a long, smooth, gradual arc, scattering a wide and colourful array of birds as it did so. Relieved to see all the sensors still functioning this time, Tyson scanned the planet's surface.

The thick jungle terrain, stretching as far as the eye could see, was teeming with wildlife and Tyson's screens lit up as the short-range scanners detected life form after life form. Periodically, the dense landscape was parted by wide blue rivers that stood out in stark contrast to the vivid emerald greens of the jungle.

Each of Tyson's chosen settlements were based within a few hundred metres of a rivers and John took great delight in approaching the isolated communities via the waterways, scattering the local animals and sending up spray as he did so.

Even with his showboating, the first two drops went off without a hitch, Tyson staying with the ship as John escorted first Craybon and then Stirling safely into the settlements. Seeing as it wasn't his choice to babysit the ship each time, Tyson was soon complaining he was getting bored while John 'got to have all the fun planeside.' So, somewhat reluctantly, John agreed that they would both transport their last guest together.

They had barely gotten off the ship and secured the cargo door when Tyson spotted a very attractive young woman with long blonde hair who was struggling to carry some large boxes.

"That poor woman!" he exclaimed. "Isn't there any gentlemen around that can help her?" He questioned his two companions and then looked around in a show of concern. Before either John or their "guest" could answer, Tyson continued, "Well, if there are no other gentlemen around, I guess I'm the next best thing." He flashed a grin and was off, walking briskly across the clearing and heading straight towards her.

John laughed at both Tyson and his luck. Now, he had the perfect opportunity to question Wane. He quickly steered him to a small, nearby workshop and paid the surprised workers to take an extended work break in order to give he and Mr. Wane Ash some much needed privacy. As soon as they were alone, John gestured for his guest to take a seat on one of the workbenches that ran along the smooth white wall of the workshop.

Wane sat, waiting quietly.

"I have a few questions for you before we part ways," John began, carefully disguising any note of urgency in his voice.

Wane nodded, "And I have a few of my own."

John smiled, "I think you're forgetting which one of us has the gun."

"Fair enough," Wane shrugged. "Ask your questions first. But be quick about it. I have a mission report to file that's already overdue."

"Let's start with that then. What exactly is your mission?"

Wane hesitated, but only briefly, "My orders," he sighed, "are to infiltrate the *Kings* organisation and to ascertain if there is any connection between them and the crime lord Liebecker."

John paused, "Mikhail Liebecker?"

"Yes, and I can't say I'm surprised that you've heard of him. His power has grown substantially in recent times. He now runs operations in the Alpha, Beta, Delta and Gamma Systems. We need to stop his reach into this system before it's too late."

John swore under his breath, "What have you found out so far?"

"It appears we are already on the back foot. Liebecker has extended an invitation to the *Kings* leader to meet with him at a location of his choosing."

"Can't you and your team just take him out of the picture?"

"The military is a complicated machine," Wane shook his head ruefully, "We allow Liebecker some latitudes in return for certain favours."

John gave a short, ironic chuckle, "Of course you do. That was one of the main reasons I left the core."

Wane shrugged again. "It's not a perfect system. For the most part, it works. I believe it's my turn to ask the questions. Tell me, captain, what code were you?"

John thought about not answering, then, considering all the information he had just been given, replied with a single word, "Frost."

Wane Ash's face went through an impressive display of confusion then, finally, he shook his head in disbelief.

"There has only ever been one designated code 'Frost' and he was the pilot of the …"

"*Blue Shield*," John smiled as he finished for him.

Wane stiffened and his demeanour changed instantly. "Sir," he said in a tone of utmost respect, "I wasn't aware that it was you we were hunting."

"Relax, soldier. There is no way you could have known. And you can drop the 'sir', 'Captain' will do just fine." John brushed the admiration aside with a dismissive wave of his free hand. "Thanks for the information though, surveillance specialist Ash. If you don't mind, leave me out of your report."

"Of course, sir, and if I can ever be of any help, let me know."

"I appreciate the offer, soldier," John looked over at the workers who were returning from their unscheduled break. "For now, you had better go and file your report."

Wane nodded and left quickly, leaving John standing alone, still pondering over the details he had just received.

It took him a little over half an hour to locate Tyson, eventually seeing him come out of a small hut on the outskirts of the clearing.

"Run, Johnny! Run!" Tyson laughed as he sprinted past his startled friend.

He was tucking his shirt into his jeans and looked up to wave at John.

John had just raised his hand to return the greeting when there was a sudden outburst of angry shouting and then a blaster bolt sped over Tyson's head.

John looked toward the small hut, immediately recognizing the blonde woman from earlier. She was half-naked and wrestling for control of the rifle an older man had just fired in their direction. He cursed Tyson briefly and succinctly before, with a grin, he turned on his heel and ran towards their ship.

Not unaccustomed to having to make quick getaways, John had left the ship in standby mode, so, as soon as he and Tyson had fitted their harnesses, they dusted off from the planet.

"Are you going to tell me what happened back there?" he turned to look at his co-pilot once they had safely cleared Mettile's atmosphere.

Tyson glanced down at the zipper on his jeans. It was still open, "I don't know what you're talking about," he smirked, tugging it closed.

"The guy with the gun who was shooting at you, any idea why?" asked John with a smile in his voice.

"Who knows what strange customs these small-town settlers have," Tyson feigned ignorance, studying his screens intently, "No sign of any ships following us. That's good."

"Ty," John pressed. "The woman? What do you know about her?"

"That I can help you with," Tyson sat back in his chair and laced his fingers behind his head. "I think it would be safe to say, I know everything about her."

"Everything? Really?"

"Everything physically at least," Tyson returned with a wink.

"I'm sure you do!" John groaned, double checking no one was following them. "Do you want to tell me why that man was shooting at you?"

Tyson's grin faded. "Now that you mention it, he may have said something about killing the impure vermin that dared defile his daughter."

"Any idea to whom he was referring?"

"Well, he couldn't possibly have meant me!" Tyson objected indignantly. "You know me. I'm much more gentleman than vermin."

John arched a cynical eyebrow. What he did know was that Tyson wasn't about to admit to any wrongdoing anytime soon, so wisely, he changed his approach. "So, what was the girl's name?" he asked.

Tyson contemplated the question and sat, deep in thought for a long minute, before he answered. "I think it was Kiara … or Kirra … Kellon. Ahhh, maybe it was Cliffa. No, no, I'm certain it was Cailah. Or was it…"

John started to laugh, and the more his friend kept trying to remember the young woman's name, the harder he laughed until tears were streaming down his face.

Tyson stopped guessing and started laughing himself.

It was several minutes before either of them managed to gain control of themselves.

"Fine!" John relented, wiping away the last of his tears and gesturing to the screens in front of Tyson. "Have it your way. Can you at least remember how to put a course into the navigation computer?"

Resisting the urge to swear at his friend, Tyson keyed in the course for Caxton. This time, much to his surprise, the computer accepted the co-ordinates.

"Look, Johnny," he said, pointing at the 'destination accepted' banner on his screen. "What do you make of that?"

Before John could comment, however, the navigation button flashed blue. "Finally! Some good luck," he sighed, hitting it without a second's hesitation.

The Broken Eye jumped. Neither of them had time to ponder why Caxton had suddenly become accessible.

Chapter Fourteen

John pulled up well short of the enormous planet and locked *The Broken Eye* into the maximum orbit possible before setting about giving their weapons a final check. Tyson promptly busied himself with running scans, checking the toxin levels of the wide range of gases that made up the swirling atmosphere below them.

"Johnny," he said after a lengthy silence, panic creeping into his voice. "I think you're gonna want to see this."

John finished reassembling the tactical pulse rifle he had been inspecting and walked over to where his co-pilot sat, peering over his shoulder at his screens. "What am I supposed to be looking at?"

"That's just it, there's nothing to look at. Whatever that stuff is down there, our scanners can't analyse it."

"Did you run a diagnostic on the systems? Maybe they got damaged back on Wenwick or something."

Tyson let out a slow, exasperated breath, "Of course, I did. Twice. There's more to it than that, Johnny. Look!" He flicked to another screen.

This one was a topographical map of a section of the planet's surface. Tyson had already zoomed in and enhanced a part of it that clearly showed some sort of artificial structure. "It's a Bio Dome, Johnny," he explained at the captain's confused frown. "One of the largest I've ever seen. And look here and here too," the co-pilot pointed at several different places on the screen. "You can see it has obviously been purpose-built and it is split over several levels."

"It's probably just the old mining camp…"

John had hardly got the words out, however, when Tyson lightly tapped his screen and said softly, "This is a life form scan, Johnny."

Immediately the screen lit up with hundreds of red illuminated markers.

John stared, watching as more and more life forms were detected by the scanners. "What is going on with this planet?" he rasped. "It's supposed to be abandoned and quarantined."

"Quarantined? Maybe," Tyson shrugged. "But abandoned? Definitely not."

John paced the cockpit, then scrubbed at his face with his hands. "Any idea who they might be?"

Tyson studied the map again. After a moment's thought, he pointed to three separate points on the screen. "These must be main airlocks and over here…" He scrolled across to show an open flat area on the map, "… Looks like a good spot to land a ship," John cut in before his friend could finish his sentence.

"Yeah," Tyson nodded. "It should only be a few minutes' walk in a bio suit from there to one of those airlocks."

"Anywhere else we can set down without being noticed?"

Tyson paused before answering ruefully, "Well, I hate to have to say this, but we're going to have to get closer so I can run a more comprehensive scan."

"We have to be careful here, Ty," John warned. "If this is a military base, they will shoot us down the second we break the atmosphere."

"Then I can only suggest we make planetfall way over here," Tyson said as he moved and rotated the map, zooming in on a small flat section farther out from the Bio Dome. "Fly in low and hopefully we'll remain undetected."

John peered at the screen then cocked an eyebrow, looking sideways at his friend, "Is that still within scanning range?"

"Well, no, but we'll know soon enough if we've been discovered."

"Just how far is that second clearing from the Dome?"

"Not far," Tyson shrugged. "Maybe ten, fifteen kilometres away."

John smiled as he did a quick calculation in his head, "Perfect. Great idea."

"Thanks," Tyson replied automatically, then with a confused look, added, "Idea? What idea?"

John said nothing, walking over to his chair and securing his harness with a knowing grin.

Slowly it dawned on Tyson what his friend was planning, "You're not serious?"

John kept silent, kept smiling and simply nodded.

"You want us to hike in closer?" Tyson said incredulously. "You're insane, Johnny. *Hike*? In deadly toxic, life-ending gasses?"

"Hey, don't look at me. It was your idea after all."

Before his co-pilot could object any further, John sent the ship in a spiralling downward plunge, laughing at the stream of swear words that erupted out of his friend's mouth as he did so. Twice, the captain had to alter his trajectory because of the rough conditions, but finally, he eased *The Broken Eye* down safely with only a few minor bumps and scrapes.

He sat back in his chair and looked across at his co-pilot with a grin. "All things considered, not such a bad landing. Wouldn't you say so, Ty?"

Tyson didn't reply: after John was forced to abort the ship's first landing attempt, he had turned grey and closed his eyes, refusing to watch the crazy descent. He had been gripping the arms of his chair so hard that his knuckles shone white. At one point, he even found religion, reciting, *By the light of the seven moons* over and over again. He had reopened his one good eye once, looked out of the cockpit's window, sworn at length, and then screwed his eye shut tight again.

"You're not funny," he finally mumbled.

John unbuckled his harness with a short laugh. "Yeah, I am. And you can open your eye now, we're here."

As the red dust stirred up by their landing slowly settled, John flicked off his harness and brought up all the camera displays on his screens so he could see, from every angle, the exterior of the ship. The clearing was surrounded by a heavily wooded area and there was barely enough room to turn a standard surface vehicle in, let alone land a craft five times that size. The cockpit was mere inches from the nearest tree and the rear cargo door had just enough clearance to open, although maybe not fully. In fact, if it wasn't for

The Broken Eye's ability to take off and touchdown vertically, the landing would not have been possible at all.

Tyson opened his eyes and found himself staring straight at a huge tree that filled almost all of the view out of the cockpit's window. He took a few deep breaths and, with great effort, unclenched his fingers from his chair; leaving behind deep marks dug into the arms.

"You okay there, matey?" asked John, his face flushed from the rush of adrenaline.

Tyson shook his head. "You're insane! I mean, I've always known it that you're not all there up top." He tapped at his own forehead. "But I didn't realize you were totally bat shit crazy."

He unbuckled his harness with trembling hands, then after a few more deep breaths, got to his feet. He stood for several long moments on rubbery legs, steadying himself against his chair. "I think I need to lie down," he finally decided.

"Do you need any help getting to your room?" John enquired, trying to suppress a laugh as he did so.

"Yes," Tyson said, before changing his mind and insisting, "No, no, I'm fine. No thanks to you, you mad bastard." He stalked out of the cockpit noticeably bow-legged and using the wall to steady himself as he went.

John powered *The Broken Eye* down to stealth mode, being careful to leave the ship's shields and weapons still online. He thought it was best not to shut all the systems off, just in case they had been tracked. When he was confident that he hadn't overlooked anything, he stood up, stretched, then resumed his seat; checking the ship's scanners and cameras as he waited and watched for any sign that they had been detected.

After many hours of staring at blank screens and empty scenery, John was finally able to concede they had managed to land undiscovered. Silently, he praised himself for their good luck. It was then he remembered the Ancient's dead body they had wrapped up and placed in the unused crew shower block.

What was he supposed to do with the corpse now? Should he bury it? Burn it and scatter the ashes somewhere?

He considered his options. He looked around the cockpit and spotted the fresh grip marks on Tyson's chair. All his concerns about the Ancient's body fell away and a wide grin spread across his face as he chuckled to himself over his friend's discomfort.

Now that he was no longer worried about unwanted visitors, John was beginning to realize how tired he was. It had been a long couple of days. There was still much to be done, so sleeping was out of the question. In the end, he decided the best option would be to freshen himself up with a shower and into some clean clothes. So, he headed for his quarters, the *Eye's* scanners quietly winking away as he did so.

After his shower, John dried off, wrapped a towel around his waist, picked up his clothes and data pad, then walked down to the ship's laundry, throwing his clothes into the cleaner. He searched the data pad for his music file, selected a song from the list, and pressed play.

Music promptly filled the room. It was one of his favourites. John liked Old Earth classic rock. Very, very old classic rock, mostly from the 20th and 21st century. As far as he was concerned, the best of all music was from original Earth. The song he had chosen, and that was currently blasting through the ship's speaker system, was 'Hound' by the singer E. Presley.

John always argued, much to Tyson's dismay, that his song choices came from an era of music that had never been equalled and would most likely never be seen again. They had a special kind of energy to them and that was why he firmly believed the music of those particular years had been so popular with the masses and had endured for so long. The song finished and went to the next one on the playlist.

The cleaner chimed loudly, signalling the cycle was completed. John put his data pad aside and took his clothes out to redress, savouring the moment. There was nothing much better than pulling on fresh clean clothes, it always made him feel calmer somehow. With a contented sigh, he retrieved his data pad and headed back towards the cockpit.

His music was still playing loudly, filling the entire ship with noise. Once again it was *'Shout'* by *J.O'Keefe,* and it put a noticeable spring in his step as he went.

By the time John reached the cockpit, his friend was sitting in his chair absorbed in his screens. Not that he hadn't been busy with other tasks, John noted, seeing Tyson had set out both of their bio suits ready to go. "Feeling better?" he enquired.

Tyson didn't reply. In fact, he showed no sign of acknowledging John's presence at all. John stepped up and tapped his co-pilot on the shoulder.

Tyson let out a shriek and jumped out of his chair. "Give a man some warning, will you? You nearly frightened me into a coronary!"

The captain didn't hear a word he said. He was far too busy laughing uproariously.

"I'm glad that I amuse you," Tyson said sourly, clearly unimpressed.

John recovered some of his composure and replied, still chuckling, "You squealed like a little girl."

"Well, you shouldn't blast such horrible music all over the ship. Then I wouldn't have to wear these!" Tyson was visibly irritated as he removed a set of noise-cancelling earbuds from his ears and threw them at John, returning to his seat with a contemptuous snort.

For a while, Tyson refused to speak to John, even as he stood in the cargo bay, fully kitted out in his bio-suit, waiting patiently for his friend to fit his. It was, he noted with some surprise, the first time he had ever beaten his friend in putting it on.

John's mood had darkened considerably as he was growing increasingly frustrated with his bio-suit. Every time he went to fit the helmet, it would not lock into place. Annoyingly, each time he tried to secure it, the suit would repeat in its soft mechanical voice, "Please scan new user, to ensure optimal performance." Finally, exploding with a barrage of swearing, John began slapping at the arms and legs of his suit. "I've had this thing for over two years, and now it decides to glitch out on me?"

"You could try running another scan and stop fighting with it," Tyson suggested drily.

John let out a deep sigh and nodded, "Fine."

Tyson, feeling a bit sorry for his friend, reached out with a gloved hand and patted him on the shoulder in a bid to offer some comfort. "If it bothers you that much, we can buy some new suits at the next station."

With a quick shake of his head, John rescanned his DNA profile into the suit. Eventually, much to his relief, the mechanical voice announced, "New user accepted. Please enter a category."

John and Tyson shot each other puzzled looks. "I've never heard it say that before," John said, looking at the choices the suit was offering him. As far as he could see there were only had two options on the menu. "Human" and "Other." With another bemused shrug, he selected "Human" and continued the scan.

After a few moments, the suit's alarm sounded again and the voice declared, "Incorrect selection, please reselect."

A slow smile crept onto Tyson's face. "Finally! Proof that you're not human. I knew it all along. Your taste in clothes, food… not to mention music, all a dead giveaway that you're an *other*."

John sighed, clearly unimpressed. "You're enjoying this, aren't you?"

Tyson smiled but remained silent. He then walked over to his still cursing friend and ordered, "Stay still."

It took him less than a minute to reconfigure the bio suit with new settings.

"Better?"

Not bothering with a reply, John picked up the rifles from the floor and handed the stunner to his friend. He tapped the intercom link on his arm. "You ready?"

"Unlike some people I could mention, I have been ready for the last fifteen minutes."

The captain ignored the remark and opened the cargo bay's doors. John walked down the ramp first and stepped out onto the plush green grass. They were, as their cameras had indicated, completely surrounded by trees, the closest of which was less than a metre away. They were huge, some several metres in diameter, their white barks stretching way up into the sky. Greenish-orange leaves creating a mottled canopy over the two men.

Tyson tapped his left forearm and brought up the map of the area. "The Dome is that way," he gestured in the direction with his rifle. "Johnny? What in the seven moons are you doing?"

The captain was slapping the side of his helmet with the flat of his hand. "The stupid suit has gone haywire! It's saying the atmosphere is breathable and it's trying to disengage the helmet's seal"

"Shit, Johnny! Get back in the ship!"

"Nah, it's okay now," John replied, adjusting the suits' settings and putting it on manual release only. "That'll fix the stupid thing. Come on, let's go."

Numerous small creatures scuttled out of their way as they moved through the densely packed trees; some had grown so close together the men had to backtrack several times in order to find a different path through them. After several long minutes of hard going, the trees began to thin out and became narrower. It wasn't long after that the two found themselves standing in a wide open field of thick, green grass that was littered with small, vibrant yellow flowers.

They consulted the map once again, realizing immediately their course alterations in the trees had brought them a lot closer to the Dome than they had planned.

"Get down!" John yelled over the suit's intercom system as he dove forward into the grass.

Tyson obeyed instantly, following his friend's lead.

Just in time, as large chunks of soil and grass flew past his head, followed by a shock wave of air and sound. Once the sound and wind stopped, Tyson lifted his head. A split-second later John's foot contacted with the side of his helmet and the command, "Stay down until I give the all-clear!" slammed into his ears.

Tyson could only nod mutely, and not because of the kick. What he had glimpsed had taken his breath away.

A ship had landed no more than ten metres away from them! If they hadn't been in their bio suits, they would have been killed; if not by the heat then by the ensuing shockwave.

"We need to low crawl back to the trees," John ordered. "SLOWLY."

Tyson got up on his hands and knees, turned around and started to crawl off.

"Stop! What are you doing?"

"You said crawl," Tyson looked back over his shoulder at his friend who was staring at him curiously. "So, I'm crawling. This is the only way I know how to do it."

John swore, cursing himself more than his friend. He often forgot Tyson was a civilian and hadn't had the training that he had received from the military. "Sorry mate," he apologised. "Okay, here's how you do it. Lie down flat on the ground with your head to one side. That's good. Now bring one leg up near the side of your body and touch your elbow to the knee."

The large man shifted in the grass as he followed the instructions.

"Good job," John continued, trying not to think about the ship's shadow that had fallen over them. "Move your other arm up above your head and bend it to ninety degrees."

"Hey, you're teaching me to commando crawl! That's what it's called, right?"

John resisted the urge to roll his eyes at Tyson's outburst. "Yeah. That's what they call it in the movies. You're doing great. Now place your weight on your bent arm and leg and push your body forward with the bent leg's foot until your leg is straight and your forward arm comes into contact with your body."

Tyson's first few attempts were clumsy and slow, but John noted, he kept low and that was the main objective, so he kept quiet.

The two men had barely reached the tree line before the landing ramp of the ship slapped open. They knelt, taking cover behind the trees, both looking through the sights of their weapons for a better view of the ship.

"Shit, Johnny. Do you see the name on that ship?"

"Yeah, I see it. *The Black Star*. That must be our old friend Captain Rockford."

"Shit, shit, shittery, shit," Tyson promptly unleashed a string of expletives. "Do you see who is with him?"

This time it was John's time to swear. Following Daylen Rockford was Dirkland Wheeler. "What is this? Some sort of asshat convention?"

Tyson chuckled dryly at the joke.

"Well, in any case, we have a package to deliver. Let's hope they ask questions first and shoot second," remarked John.

The two men paused at the foot of the landing ramp before heading off directly towards the Bio Dome. Abruptly, the tallest of the pair, Rockford, stopped and then turned to face the trees where John and Tyson were hiding. He brought up his weapon and peered through the scope.

John tapped his friend on the shoulder and dropped to his stomach. Silently, Tyson did the same.

Abruptly, Rockford lowered his rifle and quickened his pace up to his companion. They both paused as Wheeler looked towards the trees where John and Tyson were hiding. Without appearing to exchange any words, the two men broke into a run, heading directly towards the Bio Dome.

"Do you think they saw us?"

"No idea, but they definitely saw something they didn't like," John said as he rolled over onto his back. That was when he saw, between the distant waving treetops, black clouds moving quickly across the once blue sky. "Looks like rain."

Mere seconds after John had spoken, their world was plunged into darkness.

Great drops of rain fell from the swollen clouds, so large that they broke small branches off the trees on their way down. They pounded the leaves, ripping them off and tossing them in all directions before smashing into the increasingly soggy ground.

John stood up, sliding on the wet grass as he did so.

Tyson also slipped and fell several times before finally he used a tree to haul himself to his feet. "We better get back to the ship before we drown," he said, pressing a button on the base of his helmet.

A crackled response came back from John, "Okay, back to the ship it is."

Two, bright lights fanned out from each side of Tyson's helmet, but they were barely able to pierce the darkness. He pressed the button again, this time holding it on. It was the emergency setting, but even on that, he could barely make out John leaning against a tree less than three metres away from him.

John tried to engage his suit's lights, but they wouldn't respond. He swore and vowed to buy himself a new one as soon as possible. He tried to contact Tyson, but the storm clouds were creating some sort of electrical interference and the intercoms were down. He gestured for Tyson to lead the way and, for once, his friend seemed to understand his hand movements.

The ground was now more mud than dirt. It soon became difficult for them to make headway as the suction pulled at their legs and feet with every step.

Many more branches continued to break off in the downpour and both men had close encounters with a number of them as they fought their way back into the much denser part of the forest. Fortunately, fewer branches seemed to fall here, although the ones that did were much thicker and likely to do greater damage to the men if they were hit.

The thick mud was now at knee height and each time Tyson stumbled, he struggled to regain his balance. John was not faring much better. Their progress was hampered by tree roots and hollows in the ground that had been unearthed by the drenching rains.

There was a sudden wave of movement under John's feet and he slid sideways with the shifting mud. He reached out to try and steady himself but grabbed only air as the ground beneath him dropped abruptly away. As he fell, the light from his friend's suit disappeared from his view, plunging him into inky blackness.

Tyson felt the ground move under his back foot and immediately turned to see what it was. As he turned, he saw the look of total surprise on John's face as he dropped downwards and disappeared. "Johnny!" he shouted, forgetting that his friend couldn't hear him.

He stood, his mind whirling, staring blankly at the spot where John had been. The incessant rain must have caused the ground to fracture and collapse, washing away the grass, the trees, and his friend, all with it. Now only a great, gaping, wound stretched as far as his light could penetrate the blackness. Panic set in and Tyson yelled over and over again into the suit's intercom system. His only reply was the constant crackling of white noise from the storm.

Rain continued to fall heavily on Tyson as he stood, desperately trying to think of what he should do next. His thoughts were finally interrupted by a static-filled, "Ty, get to the ship," over his intercom. Hit by a brief surge of hope, he hollered back until, eventually, he was out of breath and had become aware that his suit's yellow alarm was flashing.

It was his oxygen level. There was no time left for him to waste. As fast as he could, he trudged back through the trees towards the ship.

When Tyson finally reached *The Eye,* he collapsed on the docking ramp, exhausted. His suit had begun alarming red alert in the last ten minutes, and he knew he would only have moments of breathable air left. With his remaining reserves of energy, he crawled up the ramp and slapped his hand on the door's panel. The cargo bay door hissed as it sealed shut. He forced his glazed eyes to focus on the light above the cargo door, watching it turn from red to amber then green. As soon as it lit up green, he unsnapped his helmet and tossed it to one side, gratefully gulping in the ship's clean, filtered air.

***

In his first few seconds of free fall, John had scrambled about with his hands frantically, trying to grab hold of something, anything to stop himself from plummeting further into the blackness. Then, without warning, he slammed into a solid mass, coming to a sickening halt.

For a long, breathless moment, he lay there, a lone rock caught in a raging stream. Water continued to pour over and around him, his only companion the absolute blackness he had been swept into and the hard, unrelentingly surface he was pinned against. The raging waterfall that was pounding on his chest was making it difficult to breathe, even in the bio-suit.

His thoughts drifted to Tyson. He would have put good credits on his friend going comatose after seeing him being swept away. With great effort, he tapped his intercom, "Ty, I don't know if you can hear me, but you need to get to the ship, Ty. Get to the ship."

After repeating the order a few more times, John left his intercom open but heard nothing in response.

He needed some light. He craned his head forward then threw it backward, hoping to hit the button to activate the lights. Nothing happened. So, out of frustration more than anything else, he did it three more times, his swearing getting louder and more eloquent each time he did so.

The final time he cracked his helmet against the wall, John's suit responded, and the emergency lights flickered on, fanning out and illuminating the gloom.

He was in a cavern, caught on a ledge where the pressure from the waterfall was holding him in place in perfect balance. Above him, he could see where smashed and ruined trees had collected, stemming the stream of water. Without them, he would surely have been washed straight off the ledge, continuing to plunge deeper into the hole. However, he also quickly calculated that if the water stopped flowing, he would also drop. How far exactly, he didn't know, but he was almost certain he wouldn't survive the fall.

John tilted his head as far back as he could to try and get a better view of what was behind him. He could just make out a hollow section in the wall. Congratulating himself on his good fortune, he edged himself backward; each movement a battle against the torrent of water.

Eventually, he made his way into the hollow and discovered it was actually more of a tunnel. It was an odd triangular shape and he realised it must have been one of the shafts left over from the planet's mining days. He tried the intercom again; this time he didn't even get static.

It was then his survival training kicked in. *Assess. Adapt. Engage.*

Assess. John checked his suit. He still had healthy air, his levels showing a little over quarter capacity. He had lost his rifle, but he had his sidearm strapped to his thigh and, thanks to Tyson, he also had the position of *The Broken Eye* lit up brightly on his map on his forearm.

Adapt. He knew that by breathing shallowly and restricting his body moments, he could increase the life of his oxygen reserves by at least a third.

Engage. He should follow the tunnel. If his memory was serving him correctly, John was sure all legitimate mining companies were required to dig no further than five hundred metres without an emergency access point.

So, all he had to do now was to go through the tunnel and hope he wasn't at its point of origin. For if he was, there was no way his air was going to last.

John adjusted the settings on his suit, lowering the breathable oxygen percentage by two percent, still well within range but giving him another ten minutes of air. He then stepped, slowly and deliberately, onto the smooth polished surface and started his journey down the long, abandoned tunnel.

***

As soon as Tyson's breathing returned to normal, he snatched up his helmet and ran straight towards the ship's bridge. Red-faced and puffing loudly, he collapsed into his chair, his fingers immediately flying into action. He had fitted both of their bio suits with trackers, taking care and a considerable amount of time to show John precisely how they worked. Praying his friend had been paying attention, he engaged the scan with one hand, simultaneously tuning the ship's intercom system into the frequencies of the bio suits with the other.

The scan revealed nothing at first, then a faint blue dot appeared on the map not far from the ship. Tyson let out a long sigh of relief. John was alive and on the move. But why was his marker blue? Any kind of human life form always showed up as red, except animal ones which were yellow. *But blue?* Tyson pondered it for a moment, then realised why. Of course! He had changed the suit's setting to "Other." As far as the tracker was concerned, John wasn't human.

"Johnny's going to love this when I tell him," he laughed to himself before setting to work about trying to contact his friend.

He sent a message out on every frequency the suit was capable of receiving, being careful to use code just in case the transmission was intercepted. "Copy Cowboy, this is Green Jeans. The homestead isn't far away. Hit me back for directions."

Tyson knew John's love of Old Earth classics extended to Western movies too and was confident he would understand the meaning.

He set the message on a loop and waited.

In reply came nothing but silence.

While he continued to wait for a response, he checked his bio-suit, pleased to see it was functioning well and absorbing oxygen from the ship's air at a good rate; already it was registering half full.

Still waiting silently, but with growing concern, Tyson rotated the map where he was tracking his friend's blue dot. There was something unusual about it. For a while, he tilted it this way and that, confusion clouding his expression until finally, it dawned on him. John was moving all right, but he was moving underground.

***

The first few dozen steps were fine. It wasn't until he stopped and looked back over his shoulder that John's first claustrophobic thoughts set in.

The 'Red Jackal' had sustained critical damage — its shields were down, there were numerous hull breaches and it had lost two of its main thrusters along with half of its port side wing. It wasn't until they re-entered the planet's atmosphere that the assault on their ship finally stopped.

All team members were ordered to use the life pods and abandon ship. He had refused, stating that unless he could stop the ship's rapid descent, the pods wouldn't have enough time to release. Mystic Fox was with him, trying desperately to stop the ship from going into a spin. He was focusing on pulling the vessel out of its dive. Both were fighting together to control the doomed craft.

He eased the remaining thrusters into reverse and hauled back as hard as he could on the controls. Painstakingly slowly the ship responded and began to level out. A brief alarm flashed up in the corner of one of his cracked screens: "lifeboat release successful."

Mystic Fox smiled as he acknowledged the alarm. Then, a blinding flash and the cockpit was torn in half…

John reopened his eyes. His head was pounding as he struggled to focus his vision. His breathing became more and more laboured; prickles of sweat beaded on his forehead and ran down his face, stinging his eyes. His limbs became heavy and stiff. Forcing himself to look forward once more, he closed his eyes and tried to focus. He knew if he didn't control his breathing he would die, right there in that dark, endless abyss.

"Come on, John," he berated himself sternly. He snapped his eyes open and examined the tunnel in front of him, looking for something, anything, to use a fixed point, an anchor to focus on.

As he looked closer at the walls, he realised that there were markings on both sides that formed some sort of a pattern. His mind now occupied, his breathing returned to normal. His limbs felt less tense too. Unfortunately, though, the thought of being buried alive didn't leave him and he was still sweating profusely as he moved forward to follow the cryptic patterns.

So focused was he on controlling his breathing, he lost track of how far he had walked by the time he came to a grinding halt in front of a large stone slab. It was decorated with more carvings. These were much more intricate and complex in their beauty, and tiny, as if they had been etched in by a very small, thin object.

The slab itself was huge —at least twelve feet high and took up the whole width of the tunnel. As far as he could tell, there was no way around it. Scowling, John studied it carefully, looking for any sign of weakness. It certainly looked solid. He pressed his shoulder against it, braced his feet and shoved. It didn't budge.

He tried again, this time pushing with all his might, knowing that if he couldn't get past it he would have to turn back. Stubbornly refusing to accept that as an option, John pushed and pushed until he was red in the face and breathless. Still, the stone did not move.

Feeling hopeless and more than a bit frustrated, he took out his sidearm and shot at it. Much to his amazement, the rock glowed for an instant and two, oversized handprints shone brightly on its surface; one on the top right-hand corner, the other on the bottom left.

John swore. He had never seen a lock of this type before, and although he was by no means a small man, he had no hope of reaching both handprints at the same time. Really annoyed now, he shot at the stone again.

To his surprise, the handprints glowed for an instant then disappeared, reappearing a moment later in different, but still unreachable, positions. Then an idea struck him. If he kept shooting, sooner or later the handprints should appear where he could reach them. Or, at least he hoped that would be the case anyway.

It wasn't until the sixth shot that they appeared close enough that he could reach them both. Quickly, he holstered his weapon and placed a hand in each glowing print. The giant slab groaned and grated noisily, then swung inward, thudding heavily against the wall.

Smiling, at last, John stepped cautiously into the huge, well-lit room that awaited him.

Allowing his eyes time to adjust to the light, he stepped further into the room, stopping in the centre and turning slowly, taking in the sight. He was standing in the middle of a large, hemispherical dome and the sweeping, curved wall had row upon row of recesses set into it.

"Tomb," John whispered into the silence.

He was so lost in amazement at the grandeur of it all that he didn't notice the stone tablet slide silently shut, sealing him in. He wondered where the light could possibly be coming from and then he realised, set within the spaces between the burial places were stones that each glowed faintly, but together shone as if sunlight was emanating from all around the circular room.

More of the elaborate and beautiful carvings adorned the chamber. Wide-eyed, John followed the symbols around the room, tracing them with his fingers as he went. He was certain that they told a story, but whatever language it was, it was beyond his understanding.

It was then he noticed the door had closed, but, for the moment anyway, he was unconcerned and continued to follow the hypnotic scripture. He lost track of time as he traced over all the writings with his fingertips, softly, gently, reminiscent of a lover tracing their mate's body, drinking in every contour. It was peaceful in the chamber and total calmness washed over him. John had never experienced any feeling like it before.

As he reached the final burial place his hand stopped, hovering over a delicate section of the carvings. Before his eyes, the scripture transformed into a single word: *Esheel.*

John's pulse quickened and he began to awake from the trance-like state he had fallen into. The feeling of blissfulness seeped from his body as the name echoed around and around in his brain. He stood, silent and motionless, thinking for a long time, but it wasn't until his bio-suit began sounding a loud alarm that he fully returned to his senses.

John checked his readout. It was a yellow alert warning about his oxygen levels. He turned to face the heavy stone door. It was open.

Not knowing why but not wanting to be trapped inside the room, he stepped closer to the exit. As he did so, Tyson's voice burst over the intercom. It was the same message playing over and over in a loop.

"Copy Cowboy, this is Green Jeans. The homestead isn't far away. Hit me back for directions."

"Ty?" John slapped at his com to interrupt it. "Tyson? Hello? Are you there?"

"Yeah, Johnny, I'm here. Where in the seven moons of Cryos have you been?" Tyson's voice rang back clearly. "You know what? Never mind that now. The storm has passed. That's why we have coms again."

"I fell, Ty," John explained quickly. "I don't have much air left and I don't know where I am. The ground kind of swallowed me whole."

A rising panic clawed its way up Tyson's chest. Never before had he heard John's voice sound so distant and disconnected. "Can you make your way back to where you went down? I'll pull you out."

"I know the way out, but I … I have to come back here."

"Alright Johnny, but let me get you out of there first, okay? I'm on my way."

Tyson rushed to the cargo bay and collected the rescue kit, snapping on his helmet and slapping at the cargo door panel. Minutes later he was running through the thick mud towards the hole where John had disappeared. As he ran, the heavy rain clouds lifted, giving way to the bright sunlight once again.

It wasn't long before he was back at the gap in the tree line and had spotted the hole. It was imposable to miss – a dark, ugly rip in the otherwise pristine landscape.

Tyson hastily secured the rescue rope around the nearest tree, then threw the rest of the connected kit down the hole. He watched as it bounced between the jumble of roots and debris before finally slipping through them, disappearing out of sight.

John reached the entrance of the tunnel just as his suit's red alarm sounded. "Copy, Ty," he called into his intercom. "I don't mean to rush you, but I'm almost out of oxygen down here."

"The kit is on its way down to you now," shot back Tyson. "You should see it any second."

No sooner had he said it that the kit bag landed at John's feet. Without missing a beat, he opened the bag and harnessed himself in. "Good to go down here." John couldn't resist adding, "Just be careful of those trees when you lift me."

"It's all under control, don't worry. Everything's going to be fine," Even Tyson was amazed at how confident he sounded. He could feel himself trembling inside with panic and was trying his best to remain calm as he engaged the lifting device.

It took several tries, but eventually, he found the right angle to lift John safely through the tangle of trees. With shaking hands, Tyson unbuckled the harness, and John fell limply to the ground. That was when he noticed the rip in his friend's suit. Assuming it must have caught on something on his awkward ascent and not bothering to try and explain anything to John, Tyson picked him up, tossed him over his shoulder and ran as fast as he could towards *The Broken Eye*.

***

John awoke to find an oxygen mask strapped to his face. At first, his vision refused to focus, and he had to scrunch his eyes open and shut several times before he realized he was in the medical bay and Tyson had obviously hooked him up to every conceivable machine that he could find.

Unlike his friend, John had never spent much time in his ship's medical facility. He hated hospitals and medical rooms. They all reeked of the same pine disinfectant and the walls were always painted the standard, stark, clinical off-white.

As he lay there, staring at the ceiling, waiting for his vision to return to normal, one of his past hospital visits burst into his mind; a memory he had repressed long ago. It flared in his brain like an angry bruise. Unable to resist its power, he had no choice but to let it run its course.

After finding him hiding amongst the wreckage at the crash site, Altren had wasted no time in taking him to the nearest hospital. Neither of them, however, had expected him to be stuck there for quite the number of weeks that he had.

The medical team had started out by putting him on several courses of medications and steroids to help increase his body mass and strengthen his bones, most of which had become brittle after years of malnutrition and abuse. But only once the senior doctors were satisfied the first round of treatments had been successful, they really get down to work.

Firstly, they had to reset his nine broken ribs. After that, painfully realign all the bones in his legs and arms that had never been given the opportunity to heal properly in the past …

One of the machines John was hooked up to, gave a long beep and the memory faded. He sat up and began pulling off some of the probes that his friend had stuck all over his forehead and face.

It was then he noticed he was only wearing his compression shorts and he swore, tugged off the mask that covered the lower part of his face, and was just pushing himself up off the pristine, white cubicle mattress when Tyson entered the room.

"How long have I been out?" he asked before Tyson could even open his mouth.

"Um … five days, give or take a few hours," the co-pilot replied, still looking a little shaken. "By the seven moons, Johnny, you scared the shit out of me!"

"Five days?" John repeated, apparently unconcerned by the news he had alarmed his friend. "And no one had discovered us?"

"Nope. No one has had had a chance to. There have been continuous storms since we landed. I managed to secure a few scanners to some of the trees around us and outside the dome. No one else has landed or exited the Bio Dome since we arrived." Try as he might, Tyson was, as always, unable to stop the involuntary wince he made whenever he saw John's uncovered skin. His body was littered with scars.

Once, after they had spent a long night emptying a wide variety of potent and powerful bottles of alcohol, as was their custom following a particularly lucrative cargo haul, Tyson had asked him how he had gotten them. He would never forget the answer John had given him.

He had paused, frozen in thought for a long time. Eventually, he had locked his friend's eyes with a hard stare and said, "Evil exists in the universe and if you're lucky, very lucky, you will never have to see it up close as I did."

Then, as if he never had spoken, he burst into song. One of his favourites about a hundred green bottles of beer standing on a wall.

Not knowing how to respond, Tyson had joined in singing along with his friend.

Neither man had spoken of it again since.

"Do you remember what happened?" Tyson asked, focusing on their current situation instead.

"I know I caught the sleeve of my suit on the trees and I remember my oxygen alarm was going off," John shrugged. "The next thing, I woke up here."

"What? You mean to tell me you don't remember me carrying you heroically through a torrential storm, wading through thick knee-high mud, fighting for my very own life to save you?" Tyson exclaimed in an exaggerated display as he described his bravery.

"Gee thanks, Ty," the sarcasm was evident in John's reply. "Did I ever tell you that you're my hero?"

"You can make all the jokes you want. I know deep down that you mean it and you're welcome," he finished with a stiff bow.

The captain nodded and smiled at his friend as he stood up. With a barely perceptible wince, he collected his clothes that Tyson had put on the chair next to his bed and dressed.

Chapter Fifteen

John was still smiling to himself as he inspected his bio-suit a short while later. The rip in one arm was large and jagged, and he knew he was lucky to be alive. If it hadn't been for Tyson's quick actions, he was certain he would have suffocated.

A screeching siren erupted throughout the ship, wiping the grin from his face and spurring him into action.

"Ty, what's going on?" John called, slapping the com on the wall.

"Oh, it's nothing," Tyson replied after a brief pause. "It's been going off the last few days or so."

"Can you shut it off now?" John had to raise his voice to a yell as the alarm blared louder and louder with each cycle.

This time Tyson took even longer to reply, "I'm overriding the system now."

Abruptly the siren stopped mid-cycle.

"Ty, exactly how long has it been doing that for?" John sighed, relieved to be rid of the noise.

"Ever since I brought you back to the ship."

"And you're only mentioning it to me now?" John asked, clearly frustrated.

"Well in my defence, you were unconscious and near death when it started."

John let out a long, deep breath and somehow managed to calm himself down before asking slowly, "What is the alarm for?"

"That's the thing, Johnny, this time it said critical alert."

Beginning to grind his teeth in his growing frustration, John finally asked, "TY, what area of the ship is it originating from?"

"The filtration bay. In the oxygen scrubbers."

John swore as he released the com button. Without the scrubbers working properly, the poisonous gases from outside would be allowed to enter the ship's air. It wouldn't be a slow death, but it would be a very unpleasant one. "Stay in the cockpit," he ordered. "I'm on my way to take a look now."

He got as far as the corridor of the main crew shower room when he came to an abrupt stop. The sight that greeted him there caused his throat to constrict, his mouth to dry out, and sent a cold shiver down his spine.

A purplish red webbing covered the walls, ceiling, and floor, stretching as far as he could see down the corridor. Small, bright yellow and black-winged spiders jumped and glided through the tangled glistening mass, adding more and more to the web right before his very eyes.

John stepped closer to examine the web in greater detail. A single, thick cord ran out from under the shower room door. "Esheel," he muttered as he remembered where they had placed the alien's body for safekeeping.

At the sound of his voice, the activity from the cluster of spiders stopped. They grouped together and turned to face John, appearing as one large, menacing, and very focused animal.

Thousands of tiny eyes followed him as he walked up to the shower block door. Then, as if acting on command, the spiders separated. Advancing upon him. Hundreds of legs running towards him, over and through the webbing, all of them coming to an abrupt halt, some only inches from his face.

John stood as still as he could, trying to show no fear. He had never been afraid of any animal, but these were different from anything he had ever seen before. Up close, he could see their black unblinking eyes, but more unnerving were their double sets of fangs. They were huge in comparison to the rest of the creature. So much so, that John noticed that they were forced to walk on their hind legs to keep their balance.

For a long moment, the spiders and John examined each other, until a single spider slowly lowered itself down from the ceiling, stopping just above his hand. With a controlled and gradual movement, John turned his hand over, facing his palm up. The lone spider dropped lightly onto his hand, bobbing up and down on its legs several times before running up his arm then stopping on his neck, searching.

John resisted the urge to slap it away, mindful he was under the watchful eyes of its many brothers and sisters.

Without warning, the little spider sunk its fangs into the scar on John's neck and delivered a full dose of its venom into him. John couldn't see the small trickle of reddish-blue blood that escaped from the four puncture holes it left in his neck, but he did watch in surprise as the small spider immediately shrivelled up and fell to his feet...dead.

Quickly John covered his neck. Strangely he felt no pain from the spider's venomous bite. The only sensation he had experienced was from the initial puncturing of the fangs through his skin.

Instantly, the hundreds of spiders began backing away from John, as far as the walls of the corridor would allow them. Sensing it was some kind of test, he relaxed, then carefully took his hand away from his neck.

It was no longer bleeding. In fact, he could feel no wound on his neck at all. No bite marks. Nothing. The only thing that convinced him that he hadn't imagined it all was the small, wet tell-tale stain on his shirt.

Tyson's voice broke the silence. "Johnny, you okay down there? Everything okay?"

John tapped the intercom on the wall. "Yeah, everything is fine." He struggled to keep his voice from betraying him. "Nearly done down here. How are you? You okay?"

"Uh-huh, all good. We do have another alarm though Johnny. Unless you fix the filtration problem soon, we only have another twenty-six hours of air left."

"Okay. Thanks for the update. I'm on it," he replied mechanically, part of his brain still trying to determine what it was that had just happened.

He had no time to dwell on it now. He had a ship to fix.

John approached the shower room door with caution. He had no idea if there would be more unwanted guests behind it. Flattening himself against the wall alongside the door, he turned the handle slowly, then nudged the door wide open with his foot. He waited a few seconds before peering around the corner into the room. John quickly realised it was the Ancient's body the spiders were after. It had been wrapped in layer upon layer of black and purple webbing and was in the process of being hoisted up towards a large hole in the ceiling, leading towards the filtration room.

On instinct, John reached up and smeared the remainder of his blue blood from his hand onto the strong corded silk that held the alien's wrapped body.

He watched, fascinated, as the thick cords wilted and turned black, weakening, and then, one after another, rapidly breaking away.

John pulled at the last few remaining strands, catching the still tightly wrapped body as it fell, and gently placed it on the ground. "Esheel," he apologized to the man hidden inside. "I have not forgotten my promise to you."

As he turned to leave the room, John did not see the faint glow that pulsed from inside the cocoon in response to his words. He had to tear his way through the thick webs as he made his way to the filtration bay, where finally he keyed in the passkey and the door slid open. The room was infested with more of the black, winged spiders; these were much larger than the others.

John stopped just inside the door. As far as he could tell, there were a couple of things that could have triggered the alarm. Firstly, most of the hydrogen baths were completely covered with purple webbing and, secondly, there was another large hole in the ceiling, through which a large percentage of the spiders were now hurriedly retreating.

He started ripping at the silk that covered the tanks in an effort to free up the filtration units. He had torn away most of the webs when a splashing sound came from behind him, making him turn sharply to look back towards the centre of the room where the last and biggest of the tanks sat. A chill ran down his spine. He watched as, gradually emerging from the water, was the queen. Her bright blue abdomen shone in the muted, flickering light of the filtration bay and black water dripped lazily from her protruding four-inch fangs.

John watched in a mix of fear and awe as they twitched and sliced at the air. Every single one of the eight eyes in her unmoving, flame red head targeted directly on him.

Slowly, she climbed down from the tank, each movement precise and deliberate. Her eyes still locked onto John, she then lifted each of her blue hairy legs, one at a time, and shook off the oily black water.

John's right hand instinctively flew down to his hip, finding nothing but an empty space where he wore his gun and holster. Swearing, he scanned the room for anything that could be used as a weapon against the huge spider in front of him. Before he could assess the room properly, however, the queen, tilted her head slightly to one side as if examining him, then burst forwards in an incredible display of speed. In that instant, John moved into a defensive stance. The muscles in his arms and back flexed as the muscles in his calves and thighs contracted like coiled springs ready to react at a moment's notice.

She stopped. Inches separated them. His heart pounding heavily in his chest, John stood his ground, waiting for the creature to strike. Several long minutes passed as the two of them continued to face each other. The spider stood motionless.

John could feel his body pulsing with adrenaline, the urge to strike the creature first increasing with every breath he took. Years of extensive training was the only thing keeping his emotions in check. Finally, the spider moved, so slowly it was barely perceivable at first. Her forward front leg moved gently up from the floor directly in line with John's chest. Lightly she tapped the tip of it on the thick blue liquid that stained the front of his shirt. Without warning, the queen suddenly darted sideways and ran off, stopping just outside the door and turning back briefly to face John.

He watched as she tapped her front feet expectantly and then whirled back around facing the corridor. As the last of her hair-covered legs disappeared from his view, John let out a long, controlled breath, allowing all the muscles in his body to relax before continuing to clear the remaining webbing away from the tanks.

He had just set them all on a cleaning cycle when, to his surprise, the queen spider ran back into the room. She danced about excitedly on the spot for a moment, almost as if she was trying to get his attention. Then, again, she turned and ran back out the doorway. This time, John followed her out of the filtration bay, closing the door carefully behind him as he went.

As she scuttled along through the corridors, the huge arachnid turned her head back from time to time, seeming to want to check that John was still behind her. Occasionally, John would shoot her a reassuring grin, and by the time they reached the crew's shower room, he was beginning to feel an odd fondness towards her. Here she turned abruptly again and went inside.

Without the slightest hesitation, John followed. His defences shot up again as he watched her rush over to the cocoon he had placed there so carefully earlier. But he soon relaxed as he realized the care the queen was taking to peel away the layers of silk that covered Esheel.

Her razor-sharp fangs sliced effortlessly through the strong corded fibres until all that was left covering the Ancient alien's body was the same blue blood that stained John's shirt. When she had finished her work, the queen skittered away from the body on the floor and moved off into the corner of the room.

John was still unsure of the spider's motives, although he had no doubt she was intelligent, and she had clearly taken great care not to harm the Ancient alien's body while cutting away the webbing.

Originally he had thought the spiders he had encountered were planning to use Esheel for food, but now he wasn't sure that was the case at all. A look of confusion crossed John's face. If the spider queen had meant him harm, she would have attacked him already.

"Okay," he asked eventually, looking in the spider's direction. "What are you trying to tell me?"

The large spider slowly manoeuvred herself between John and the alien's body then rested one of her front legs on Esheel's blue blood-soaked body. With equal deliberation, she extended her alternate front leg and tapped John lightly on his matching blue-stained shirt.

"Are you trying to say we are the same?"

She lowered both of her legs and replied with an excited, erratic dance.

John nodded, "Okay, I understand. I'm trying to take him home, but I need to do something first."

The spider pressed her abdomen flat to the floor and started violently vibrating all the hairs on her body. Instantly, thousands upon thousands of black, winged spiders flooded out of the hole in the roof above them, swarming over every inch of the room.

John now had no way out of the room. The only exit was completely blocked by a wall of spiders.

The queen reared up on her hind legs, displaying her savage fangs in all their hideous and terrifying glory.

His entire body beginning to prickle with sweat, John cleared his throat. "*Or* I can take our mutual friend's body back first."

Seeming to be satisfied with the new arrangement, the queen lowered herself back down and strummed her eight legs against the hard flooring. In an instant, all the smaller spiders filtered out of the room back up into the broken ceiling.

John knelt down and with great care picked up Esheel's body; the spider queen following him closely as he led the way to the cargo bay.

He was just opening the access doors when Tyson's voice crackled over the ship's intercom, "Johnny? Are you okay?"

"I'm fine. Although I seem to have made a new eight-legged friend," John replied, looking up to see the camera in the cargo bay zooming in on him.

"I can see that. You sure you're okay?" Tyson's voice trembled as he spoke.

"Yes," John assured him. "Everything is fine. My new friend here would just like me to take Esheel to his final resting place."

"*What?* Are you serious?"

"Yes, she was very insistent." As he spoke, thousands of small, winged black spiders poured in through the open cargo bay doors behind John.

"What in the seven moons?" Tyson exclaimed. "How many more new friends do you intend to make?"

John looked around at the large population of spiders now crawling around his cargo bay. "I think they are eager to go home. Although, I don't know how they got on board in the first place."

"I think I know how they did it," Tyson said, sounding sheepish. "It might have been when I was getting you to the medical bay."

"You left the doors open again, didn't you?"

"I may have. But it was only for a few minutes, while I was heroically rescuing you."

John laughed, "Fine, okay then. Hey, do we still have a spare bio-suit down here in the locker?"

While John and Tyson talked, the spider queen reached up and tapped the panel on the doors, sealing John and all the spiders inside the cargo bay. Tyson realised what was happening a moment too late and the rest of the spiders swarmed the panel on the other side of the room, activating the opening sequence on the landing bay doors before he could do anything to stop them.

John dropped Esheel's body and ran towards the storage lockers. The spider queen, however, moved faster and immediately blocked his path, again performing an agitated dance in front of him.

John took a deep breath and spoke in a firm, measured voice, "I need to get to that suit. I cannot help your friend if I am dead."

Tyson's voice yelled over the intercom, "Johnny! Hurry! I can't override the sequence."

As the last airlock seal was broken, the planet's deadly atmosphere flooded into the room. Tyson could only watch helplessly as his friend coughed and heaved against the poisoned air. Struggling to breathe, John stumbled for a few steps and then pitched forwards unmoving.

Tyson exploded from his cockpit chair and rushed towards the cargo bay. He paused only briefly to snatch up his bio-suit, wrestling it on as he continued down the corridor. It was not an easy task to do on the run, but by the time he reached the outer bay's doors, he was snapping his last glove into place to successfully complete the suit's seal.

Inside the bay, the queen strummed her legs against the floor and the mass of black spiders scuttled towards the two, lifeless bodies, spinning their webs around them in a masterful display of synchronised efficiency.

Tyson wrenched off the panel next to the locked doors and threw it aside, getting to work on the manual override system. He could see the spiders through the monitor that was set into the door and he looked on in horror as both John and Esheel were rapidly encased in thick, purple cocoons. The panel in front of him lit green and he heaved on the manual lever, the door creeping open agonizingly slowly.

As soon as their task was complete, the swarm of spiders crawled underneath the two wrapped bodies and lifted them. Realizing he was too late, Tyson screamed into his helmet. As he struggled to force the door open further, the spider queen turned its large red head towards him, fixing him with a brief stare before straightening up and marching off down the ramp into the forest. Carrying aloft their securely wrapped cargo, her thousands of little children followed her.

Refusing to give up in his fight with the door's override lever, Tyson eventually burst through the narrow opening and stumbled into the empty cargo bay. Swearing to himself, he keyed in the door's code, sealing it shut tightly behind him. He knew there was only a little over a day of breathable air left on the ship and, if he had any hope of getting off the planet, he couldn't risk any more of it becoming contaminated.

He stood there for several minutes just staring out into the forest, trying to formulate a plan. Then John's words came back to him, "My new friend here would like me to take Esheel to his final resting place" and Tyson knew at once where the spiders were headed. They had to be taking them back down into the ragged hole in the ground that he had pulled John out of.

Not wanting to waste another vital second, Tyson grabbed the rescue kit and spare bio-suit out of the locker, stuffing them into the first pack he found in the lower drawers. Spying the spare blaster and holster John had stashed there, he decided to take that too and fastened it around his waist. After a final, quick suit check, he slung the bag over his shoulder and headed out down the ramp and into the forest to find his friend.

***

The rain had stopped but the sky was still covered in heavy, dark grey clouds.

Tyson was making good progress and it wasn't long until he found the place he was looking for. There was no sign of the spiders, however, the jumble of branches that had previously blocked the hole had now been securely bound together with more of their purple webbing. The result was astonishing in the grey, muted sunlight. The whole structure gleamed deep purple and maroon as it stretched across the large open hole.

Examining the curious bridge in more detail, Tyson noticed two, thick sinewy cords of webbing threaded down from the bound trees deep into the darkness below.

Cautiously, he stepped onto the structure and jumped up and down on the spot. Once he was satisfied it would hold his weight, he lowered himself to his hands and knees and crawled over to the thick dark ropes that hung below him. He activated his suit's lights, then grabbed one of the dangling, thick silk cords in both hands and lowered himself into the unknown depths.

It felt like he was descending into the cavern for ages and Tyson was glad to feel solid ground under his feet again once he reached the bottom of the ropes. Looking around from where he stood, he discovered he was standing at the entrance of an unusually shaped tunnel.

Tyson could not ever recall hearing of triangular tunnels, but it certainly looked solid enough. As he walked through it, he spotted the occasional small, black-winged spider scurrying along the walls out in front of him. It was unnerving but did at least confirm he was heading in the right direction.

After a while, the sight of the spiders no longer bothered him, and he noticed instead that there were markings on both walls of the tunnel. He was familiar with many different languages but not one of the intricate carvings had any similarity to anything he had seen before.

It wasn't long before he found himself standing in front of a large, half-opened rock door that was sluggishly closing. He slipped through with barely more than an inch to spare.

Congratulating himself on his excellent timing, Tyson stepped quickly away from the door as it slammed shut behind him. Immediately, he let out a yelp of pain as a blinding, bright light caused his cybernetic eye to briefly flare and shut off. Squinting with his one good eye, it took a moment for Tyson's cybernetic eye to be able to see again. Gradually though, he became accustomed to the intense light that he could soon see was being given off by glimmering stones.

Cautiously, he began examining the room, looking for an exit or any sign of his friend. His cybernetic eye was the first to detect inconsistencies in the light, but as Tyson walked closer to the wall of burial cavities, he could soon clearly see that two of the stones were shining in a different colour to the others. He approached the closest one. It was a very bright blue and the cocoon inside the recess was slowly dissolving.

He watched, mesmerised, as the purple webbing fell away to gradually reveal the form of Esheel, resting peacefully inside the recess. Only once the cocoon had fully disappeared, the blue glow stone then blinked out, turning the same dazzling white as the rest.

Tyson moved to the second. The coloured light was now alternating between bright blue and vivid red. As he got closer, he could see that this cocoon was still intact.

He reached out with his hand. As soon as his fingers made contact with the cocoon, the webbing reacted, dissolving much faster than the other one had. Fumes from the rapidly disintegrating layers rose and fogged Tyson's helmet visor. By the time it had cleared, he could see John's body, pale, and motionless. A loud screech rang out from behind him and the room was plunged into darkness.

Tyson swore as he turned around, activating his lights and fishing in his bag for the gun as he scanned the room. Hundreds of black, winged spiders of all sizes began to drop gracefully from the ceiling in front of him, effectively blocking his escape. He looked up, his heart skipping a beat as the huge, hairy, blue bodied spider gradually descended from a thick cord of webbing that trailed out of her spinnerets. The eyes in her big red head focused directly on him.

With a gulp, Tyson took several involuntary steps backward and promptly bumped into the chamber's wall, where a strong hand reached out and gripped his arm.

Tyson screamed in terror as he turned to face his would-be attacker. There was a peaceful but amused look on the Ancient alien's face.

Tyson opened his mouth to berate him for scaring him but, before he could speak, Esheel released his grip on his arm and stepped towards the large, hairy spider that was doing an excited danced on the spot.

In what, to Tyson, looked like an affectionate gesture, the alien patted the big red head of the spider as he passed it on his way to the door. He then touched the door's surface in several places, and it slid noisily open. All of the smaller black spiders immediately ran, jumped or flew through the open door.

The large, blue spider ran towards the door too, but stopped short and turned back to face the Ancient alien.

Briefly, Esheel spoke to the spider in a language Tyson didn't recognise, then abruptly she ran off into the tunnel after the smaller ones.

Esheel walked back past Tyson, stopping in front of where John's body lay. He knelt and placed one hand to one side of John's neck, the other over his heart. After several long moments had passed, he finally stood and turned to face Tyson, "Your friend is quite resilient."

"Then, why isn't he moving?"

Esheel's amused smile did not waver for an instant. "It will take time for him to recover fully. Your ship, I believe, will provide more favourable conditions for such a return to health."

"Hang on." Irritation was creeping into Tyson's voice as he demanded, "What did your spiders do to him? And why does he look all pale? Are you sure he's okay?"

Esheel stepped up to Tyson to halt the flow of questions. "Forgive me. I have not made myself clear. I know you mean well, but time is of the essence. We can no longer discuss this."

The alien's hands moved with such speed that Tyson didn't see them as they flew up to strike either side of his helmet simultaneously. He didn't hear them or feel them make contact either. In fact, Tyson felt nothing at all as he crumpled silently, and surprisingly gracefully, into a heap at Esheel's feet.

Chapter Sixteen

Tyson woke up on one of the medical bay's beds to find someone had removed his bio suit's helmet. He sat up and looked around the room. Esheel was sitting quietly on a chair in one of the corners and opposite him, on an identical bed, lay John.

John's monitoring equipment was displaying all his vital signs and Tyson could see, although they were weak, his friend was still alive.

"I see you have returned to us. I must apologize but your friend urgently needed a more compatible environment to recover in."

Tyson sat, still dazed, the memory of past events slowly returning to him. "You hit me," he said at last, with only a small amount of accusation in his voice. "Why?"

"Your questions were wasting valuable time."

"So, you decided knocking me out was the answer? *That* was your best solution?" Agitation quickly replaced anything else in Tyson's tone.

"It was more expedient for me to carry you both back to your ship," Esheel replied calmly. "You humans walk very slowly in the suits that you're wearing."

"You could have warned me!" yelled Tyson.

"As I said, time was of the essence and after you lost consciousness, it became very quiet and peaceful."

Tyson shook his head in disbelief. "By the seven moons, you and Johnny are one and the same."

Looking even more alien-like than usual, Esheel moved his head around in several, short sharp movements before straightening back up and saying, "It is true, he carries the same biomaterial as I do, however, by no means does that make us 'one and the same'. Please clarify your comment."

Tyson scrubbed at his face in frustration and muttered, "Never mind. I retract my statement."

Esheel stretched as he stood, remaining silent for a long moment before replying, "As you wish."

Tyson climbed off his bed and walked over to stand beside John.

"I must be leaving now. Your friend will recover; however, it may take some time. Let him know I am grateful to him." Tyson nodded.

"My thanks are to you also. John is fortunate to have such a faithful companion. I believe my gift will benefit you both greatly in your trials forward."

"Wait." Tyson looked up sharply. "What gift? And what do you mean by *trials*?"

Esheel gave a small tight smile in response and inclined his head. Then, he turned on his heel and promptly strode out of the room.

A few minutes later, Tyson heard the unmistakable beeping of one of the secondary airlock hatches opening. He tilted his head to one side, waiting to make sure he heard it hiss close too, his shoulders slumping in relief at the sound and what it meant.

Esheel had left the ship.

For the first two days, Tyson checked John's bed's readout every two hours. After that, he decided to reposition the medical bays cameras so that one was pointing directly at John, while the other could be zoomed in or out to read his medical bed's vitals screen. Satisfied he could adequately monitor the situation from his screens up on the bridge, Tyson soon had his visits to the medical bay down to only a few times a day.

As the days stretched on, the gaps between his trips to John's bedside got longer and longer. Some days he didn't go in at all.

Following Esheel's departure, Tyson kept the ship locked and secure. The foul weather had passed, and most days were clear-skied, so much so that he wished the planet had a more favourable atmosphere so he could go outside without his bio-suit and feel the pleasure of the sun's warm rays on his skin.

A week crept by, and then ten days. Tyson filled the passing hours with cracking and modifying the code of the White Lace security program. After that he performed several small modifications to the ship, he then set about repairing John's bio-suit. Finding himself with still more time to kill, he tinkered with its settings, beginning to wonder how long it was going to take for John to regain consciousness.

As the days passed Tyson noticed the activity around the Bio Dome was increasing. When they had first arrived, there had been only a half dozen ships in the vicinity, now there were more than twenty. Finally, however, exhaustion got the better of him, and he put the ship into silent mode to run it on minimal systems and to avoid detection from scans. Once he was satisfied they were safe, Tyson went to his quarters and slept.

Loud blaring alarms startled him awake so abruptly that he actually fell right out of his bed. As he scrambled to his feet, he could see his whole room was lit up bright red from the monitors on the walls.

The alarm was coming from the medical bay. John was awake.

By the time Tyson arrived in the medical bay, John was sitting up rubbing his face vigorously. He stopped as soon as he realised his friend was in the room. "Hey Ty," he offered in an affable, sleepy voice. "I feel like I've slept for a week. What's been happening?"

"Shit, Johnny, you scared the crap out of me. I thought you were going to die," Tyson replied as he felt all the tensions of the previous days leaving his body.

"You can't get rid of me that easily," grinned John. "Where are my clothes?"

Tyson pointed to the locker in the corner of the room. "I put them in there for if ...*when* you woke up."

John padded his way across the room and began dressing. As he was putting his blaster in his leg holster, he looked up, his grin stretching wider. "I feel fantastic. I might have even lost weight. See? I am a notch tighter in my waist belt. Although, my neck is still as itchy as a bastard." As he spoke, he scratched at the wound on his neck, neither he nor Tyson noticing when something shifted under his skin, away from his fingers.

"Can we now, please, just deliver the package and get out of here?" asked Tyson.

"Oh right, the package. I'd forgotten all about that. Yes, I've had enough of this planet to last me a lifetime. If we never come back here, it'll still be too soon."

"Agreed," said Tyson with a nod.

The two men stood in the cargo bay partly dressed in their bio suits. Once he was sure Tyson wasn't paying him any attention, John plucked the top off the small bronze box that he had received from the Oberon Rodney's courier and sniffed at the contents. It had no obvious smell. He carefully swirled the black liquid contents around in its container. It moved rapidly, much faster than anything he had seen before, and a small amount of it spilled out onto his fingers. Remembering what happened last time, John vigorously rubbed his hand onto his shirt sleeve. To his relief, this time it didn't burn. With a sideways glance at Tyson and a guilty look on his face, he quickly replaced the top back onto the box and popped it into his suit's pocket along with the small DNA scanner.

The substance was very sticky and being that it didn't burn him like the other one, John concluded that it was harmless. So, as a result, he could only think of one way to remove it before Tyson had realised what he had done and got all judgemental on him about it. Quickly, and discretely as he could he wiped the black fluid on his trouser leg.

Tyson turned around just as John had finished removing the last traces from his hand. "What are you doing?"

"Me? Nothing," John smiled back at his friend.

"You're looking very guilty."

John's mind raced to come up with a clever answer. For once, it failed, so all he could was say the first thing that came to him. "Well, I was just thinking, have you ever noticed the way hands move? The fingers, in particular, are fascinating."

John waved at his friend very slowly staring at it as he did so.

Tyson shook his head very slowly, "You are a strange man, Johnny, a very strange man."

John shrugged and went back to tugging his bio-suit on.

The two men each had a blaster holstered to a thigh and, on Tyson's insistence, a backpack, complete with their data pads, suit repair kits, and medical packs. John thought it was all a bit extreme, but seeing as so far nothing they had done had gone to plan, he chose not to share this opinion with his now paranoid friend.

They only just made it off the landing ramp before a volley of black-tipped, surface to surface missiles slammed into the hull of *The Broken Eye*: John recognising them a split second before the impact.

The Merloc missiles detonated, causing a blast so enormous it sent both men hurtling into the surrounding trees. John recovered from the disorientation first, and without a moment's hesitation, he grabbed at his friend's suit, hauled him up over his shoulder and ran as fast as he could further into the dense trees.

Seconds later a secondary, even larger, explosion incinerated what remained of their ship, taking with it a large part of the forest.

John had barely made it out of the blast zone before the shock wave had them both airborne once again.

They crashed to the ground with a heavy thud. Tyson began getting to his feet, but John pulled him back down to the ground roughly, raising a single finger to his helmet in the universal signal for silence. Tyson nodded and lay flat and still.

A squad of six burst out of the surrounding trees, scanning for movement, their black bio suits standing out in stark contrast to the white-barked trees and yellow green hues of the leaves that now littered the ground.

John and Tyson hunkered down, motionless and barely breathing, beneath a large, severed branch of one of the bigger trees. As the black-clad team searched the area, they came within inches of where they lay, but they were not detected. Finally, apparently satisfied the area was clear, the team moved closer to the impact site where there was now nothing more than a wide, smouldering crater. *The Broken Eye* was completely destroyed.

John began moving slowly away, heading towards the Bio Dome and signalling for Tyson to follow him. The two men crawled for several kilometres before John stopped. Tyson, red-faced and sweating beneath his helmet, was glad for the rest.

John rose to his feet and looked back at where their ship had been. The expression on his face behind his helmet's visor was unreadable.

Without a word, Tyson followed his movements. Someone had obviously detected their ship and decided to remove any and all potential threats.

There was a part of John that appreciated how effective the Merloc missiles were, as there was nothing more than a large hole of scorched earth where the Broken Eye had been. Not a single scrap of debris remained. Hit with a fresh concern, John searched his pockets and retrieved a vial from each breast pocket along with the scanner. He sighed in relief as he saw they all remained intact, carefully placing them securely back into his pockets.

***

Tyson stood, still mute, as he surveyed the area that once held their ship. *His* ship. It had been totally annihilated, reduced to a charred hole in the ground. Not even a single metallic slag remained of the destroyed vessel.

John tapped the com on his suit. "Ty, we'd better get moving."

"Uh, yeah sure, Johnny," Tyson shook himself out of his reverie. "But where do we go now?"

"Well, we still have the vials to deliver and with any luck, there's a ship out there just sitting, *asking* to be borrowed by a couple of careful guys like us."

"And what do you propose we do? Walk up to the main door and knock?"

"I was thinking along the lines of a more discreet entrance."

Tyson's shoulders slumped as he replied, "Sure why not? It's not as if we have much more to lose."

"That's the spirit!" came back John's cheerful retort as he turned and strode off towards the Bio Dome.

Chapter Seventeen

It took them several hours, but the two men eventually successfully slipped unnoticed into the Bio Dome via a poorly patrolled service entrance. Avoiding the elevators, they took the stairs down to the first sub-level, where John quickly located the service centre showers and locker room. Here, they stashed their backpacks and bio suits, putting them on auto-refill, before changing into some overalls.

On their way out, Tyson slipped his data pad into one of his pockets, zipping it closed as John helped himself to a clipboard and riffled through its contents.

"Finally, some good luck!" he smiled as he showed his friend what he had found.

"A map. Yippee for us," Tyson drawled and picked up a pair of safety glasses. He tapped them on the side and darkened them to an almost solid, yellowed mirror-like surface to hide his cybernetic eye. He slipped them on with a grin. "What do you think?"

"Very nice. And not just a map," John indicated for his co-pilot to look closer at the clipboard. "Look! A fully operational ship service bay. Right on this level!"

"John, I hate to break it to you, but my ship is way beyond needing a few spares," Tyson replied sarcastically.

"Oh, I don't know," John shrugged. "With a quick re-shape and a fresh coat of paint or two …"

"You're really not funny, you do know that, right?" chuckled Tyson.

"Sure I am. But what I really meant is, that there will be ships there being repaired and or serviced."

"Ahhh," nodded Tyson with a wink. "And we could steal one."

"Steal?" echoed John, clearly insulted by the proposition. "I don't steal. I simply acquire items no longer wanted or needed by their previous owners."

"Is that right?" enquired Tyson, more than a little amused by his friend's feigned disgust. "Sounds a bit like stealing to me."

"The fact that they don't know they no longer want them is hardly my concern," grinned John.

The two men headed off towards the service area. John kept the clipboard tucked close to his side as he walked.

"Hey," Tyson asked after a brief silence. "How come your uniform has white sleeves and mine has black?"

"This is hardly the time to discuss fashion, Ty."

Tyson would have pressed the issue further but the pair both immediately lapsed into silence as they saw a buggy rapidly heading towards them, its intent obvious. The four men in the approaching vehicle were clearly on a mission to intercept them.

"Shit, they're heading right at us. Should we run?" Tyson quickly surveyed the area and, to his rising dismay, not finding a single escape route.

"Try and relax there, Cyclops," John hissed. "It's a big place and I doubt anybody knows everyone here. Just follow my lead."

"Relax, he says. Yeah, sure. No problem. It's not as if we are creeping around a super-secret criminal organisation's base in maintenance overalls as a disguise. Yeah. Sure, John, no worries. I'll relax my ass off," Tyson's voice was strained by panic as he spoke.

The buggy slowed and came to a stop right in front of them. The driver was the first to exit, followed promptly by the three others that occupied the passenger seats.

The short, black-haired, neatly presented driver took a step towards John and gave a sharp nod.

John noted that they were all wearing similar overalls to his and Tyson's. The three men at the back had grey sleeves. The leader, the man who had stepped forward, had yellow. John quickly assessed this as a type of rank as he returned the nod and waited.

The dark-haired man spoke quickly, "Sorry sir. We hoped to have the vehicle back before the end of our shift."

Tyson shifted uncomfortably as the three other men hung their heads and stared at the floor.

John continued to stare at the man in front of him and simply said, "Go on," as he scanned each man's security tag that was displayed on his right chest pocket.

The man spoke even more rapidly, "Sir, It's my fault, sir. These men were just following my orders. We just received a batch of new ships for retagging and refitting, I was trying to get a head start. That's why I took it, sir."

John frowned. "This is not standard operating procedure and you men did take my assigned vehicle without proper authorization."

The four men now all stood in silence at his harsh tone as he continued, "Is this the example you wish to set for new recruits?" John motioned to Tyson, who stood stiffly clearly looking terrified of John.

The tallest of the men spoke, "Sir, no sir. Will you be formally reporting us? What I mean to say is, will this be on our permanent record?" His voice quivered as he spoke.

John looked all four men in the eyes, one at a time, "If you men have learnt from your mistake, I believe we can leave it as a note in my private files." All of the men visibly relaxed. "However, I do require a driver as this fresh recruit has not been issued a STC."

"STC? Sir?"

"Security Tag, son, STC."

"Sir," stammered the taller of the man once again. "It's Security Clearance Tag, not Security Tag Clearance."

John who now looked very irritated replied, "Perhaps you would all like to go on report after all?"

The two men who stood either side of the taller man both delivered a savage elbow into the man's ribs. Before he had a chance to crumble under the attack, however, they caught him, propping him back up to a standing position.

The movement had happened so quickly Tyson wasn't sure that it had happened at all, it was only the red face and tears that were running down the man's face that gave it away.

The short man who was obviously the leader spoke again, "Sir, no sir."

John frowned heavily as a deadly edge crept into his voice, "I need a volunteer to drive this vehicle. Both the recruit and I are new to this facility."

The short man took a step forward. "It would be my honour to drive you, sir."

The frown on John's face lightened a little. "Excellent, you other men report to the mess hall for two hours of volunteer clean up duties. That will be all. Dismissed."

The three remaining men glanced at each other in a collective understanding that things could have gone much, much worse. Then they quickly headed off together towards the mess hall area.

"Where to first, sir?" said the crewman.

"I think a brief tour will do. It will give this boot here a good overview of what is expected from him."

"Sir, yes sir. This way." The crewman led the way to the buggy and opened the front passenger door for John. He waited until he was seated, then walked around the front and climbed into the driver seat. Tyson entered the rear seat and, after fumbling with the seatbelt for a long moment, he finally snapped it closed.

The crewman's quick tour took a little over an hour. John and Tyson were dropped off by the main service hangar before John dismissed the young driver.

When the vehicle was at a safe distance away, Tyson asked, "Why did you want to be dropped off here? Aren't these ships all broken in one way or another?"

John started walking into the hanger as he answered. "Two reasons. The first is that I want to see what modifications they are doing with these ships, and the second is, they will hardly expect someone to take one from out of here."

"Okay, so you're saying that only a mad bastard like you would think of trying to steal one of these hunks of junk?"

"True, some of these should have been stripped down for parts and scrapped years ago, but occasionally you can find a ship worth restoring."

Tyson stopped dead in his tracks "Oh shit, Johnny, look," he said as he pointed to the far edge of the hangar bay.

John fought the urge to run, as he walked as quickly as he could without drawing and unwanted attention from any of the maintenance teams that were working in the hanger. Tyson followed closely behind.

The shell of *The Vulture* sat in the middle of what was obviously the scrap pile. Its wings had been severed and the main cockpit was lying several feet away, upside down and stripped of all its components.

"My ship," John whispered hoarsely as a tear slipped down his face.

Tyson stood next to his friend and said, "By the seven moons, Johnny. I'm so sorry."

A voice spoke from behind them, "Sir, we could use your help over here."

The two men turned around. In front of them was a huge specimen of a man, at least six foot eight, and all of it was bulging muscles. He was also saluting.

John returned the salute. "How can I help you?" He paused as he looked at the man's uniform. It was unlike all the others he had seen so far. A black, fitted grey top that threatened to split under the pressure his salute was putting on it. His black pants had silver piping along the legs and cuffs.

"SP Griffon, sir!" he said as he finished his salute. "I was unaware of your arrival until I heard of some core men talking of your arrival in the mess hall."

Tyson leant a little closer to John and whispered, "SP?"

John nodded, "Myself and this new recruit were offered the opportunity to visit. How may I help you, Special Projects Griffon?"

Tyson stood to attention and executed the best salute he could muster as John replied.

Griffon's eyes flicked to Tyson as he acknowledged the hurried and sloppy salute. "At ease recruit. To be honest sir, we are having some problems with some recent modifying the commander has requested on personal ship. As you can imagine, he is a man best not displeased."

"I would be happy to help," responded John with a smile.

"Fantastic. Follow me please," Griffon led the way to his awaiting transport vehicle.

The instant John and Tyson were buckled in, it burst into action, complete with a flashing amber light and siren. After a frantic dash through the hangar the little buggy stopped abruptly.

"Here we are," offered the specialist as he pressed his palm into a nearly invisible wall panel.

A door appeared instantly and opened. Tyson looked inquisitively at it.

"It's one of my ideas…" began the Specialist.

Before he could finish, Tyson interrupted, "You fused camouflage tech into the ship?"

"Exactly."

"How did you achieve it? I mean any fluctuation in the power supply would render it unstable, not to mention the cooling supply need for sustained use."

For the first time, the Specialist looked at Tyson. "I now understand why you were invited." He smiled warmly, "And here I thought you were just an A.P.E."

Tyson smiled back as he searched his memory. He remembered John saying that he had been employed as an Armed Personal Escort for extra credits on his downtime between missions.

The three men walked into a separate well-equipped hangar where nine highly modified ships were parked spaciously apart. One had a team of at least a dozen men working on it. Some were holding data pads, others were arguing about power flows and output consumption, and another group was standing in front of a schematic holographic display looking completely baffled on how to proceed.

As the three men approached, John said, "My cadet has a good understanding of components and programming. He is at your disposal."

"Thank you, senior chief. This is our Commander's favourite ship, *The Dragon's Dawn*. It's a two-man fighter class. However, all the modifications we have been asked to make will either ignite the fuel cell, lower shield capacity or compromise life support. None of which will be acceptable to the Commander."

John studied the hologram screen for a few minutes in silence as he flipped through all the ship's settings and systems. "Looks like your work crew could do with a break. Perhaps they take one now, while the cadet and I take a look with some fresh eyes?" he offered.

Without another word, the specialist let out an ear-splitting whistle. All the workgroups stopped what they were doing and lined up in front of Griffon, each of them snapping a perfect salute.

"Men, you are dismissed. Return here in two hours. That is all."

The workgroup disbanded rapidly and left the area.

The Specialist's wrist intercom chimed. "By the moons, I'm due to give my weekly report."

"Go do your report. We will assess the ship and inform you of our findings on your return."

"Thank you, senior chief. I'm in your debt," Griffon performed a quick sharp salute and headed off.

"Well," said John. "We may as well take a look now that we're here."

Tyson gave a sly grin, surveying the ships one at a time as he replied, "Yeah, you never know, we may even find ourselves a new home."

"My thoughts exactly," replied John.

Two hours later, to the very second, Specialist Griffon returned with his team.

John and Tyson had not been wasting their time. They had completely removed, rewired and fully customised the ship's cooling system into a smaller, far more powerful version and were currently in the process of refitting the craft's fuel cells into the newly created space.

John ignored the approaching maintenance team and continued his work.

The group, including Specialist Griffon, waited and watched in silence. Tyson was holding a fuel cell in his hands, wearing thick padded gloves as a precaution against the highly corrosive contents of the cell. Five of the cells had already been installed and Specialist Griffon was amazed that the two men had accomplished so much in so little time.

John was lying prone on the top of the craft, propped up by his elbows as he called down for another cell. Tyson stepped closer and handed up the fuel cell. Without looking, John reached down and gripped it with a gloved hand. Then, with practiced precision, he reached inside the ship and slowly guided the cell into place until he heard a faint click.

Wordlessly John stood up, crossed the ship to the stair platform, and climbed down.

"Sir," saluted Specialist Griffon along with his team.

John, as a sign of respect, saluted the team back in a flawless salute of his own. He then led the specialist and his group over to where Tyson was standing. "This updated schematic we have created," he said before anyone else could speak, "Includes all the new modifications we have made." He paused as Tyson brought up the information on the hologram display, and still no one spoke. "In red, you will see the alterations we have made. Be sure to note the new power and cooling output levels," John waited until he was sure that the team had seen the improvements before continuing, "The yellow indicates the newly created areas you will need for the rest of the requested modifications you have been asked to perform."

"Sir?" A voice from the back of the group piped up cautiously.

"Yes?" John enquired mildly.

The voice from the back continued, "What about the vessel's programming? Surely with all the changes you have made, a new system will have to be created?"

Tyson stepped forward to answer the question and John smiled warmly as he stepped off to the side to allow his friend full use of the hologram screen.

After a solid hour of explanations and answering questions, finally, the group ran out of questions, largely regarding how they had managed to not only increase the unused capacity space of the craft but also reduced power consumption and thermal output from the fuel cells.

After a long minute of thoughtful silence, Specialist Griffon ordered his team to continue with the rest of the Commander's modification requests, all of which were now possible thanks to the senior chief and his recruit.

They had barely set to work when a shrieking siren pieced through the hangar.

Griffon and his crew instantly downed tools and everyone inside the bay turned to watch as the far wall split open, the enormous panels sliding back to reveal the workings of a hydraulic landing platform that was slowly lowering.

Tyson edged closer to John and whispered, "I was wondering how they got the ships in here."

It had been on John's mind too, although his focus had been on how to get the ships back *out*. He nodded and gestured for Tyson to remain silent.

The platform came to rest and then rotated, with surprisingly little noise, to allow the new ship to be moved into the hangar.

It was *The Scarlet Blade*.

"How in the seven moons did she find us here?" Tyson just barely managed to muffle the shocked gulp that escaped him at the sight.

John shook his head, answering in a tense, hushed tone, "It doesn't matter now. We just need to deliver the vials and get out as quickly as we can." He gave the hangar another quick sweep, assessing the other craft. "We got lucky this time, Ty. All the ships here are flight ready."

"Lucky? How are we lucky?" questioned Tyson. "If the *Scarlet Blade* is here, so is Breanna Gomez. This is bad, Johnny, real bad."

Again, John motioned for silence. Keeping his expression as neutral as possible, he turned to Griffon and enquired, "Another of your Commander's ships to be refitted?"

"No sir. This one belongs to one of our Commander's guests. She was very unhappy about our quarantine protocols and insisted that if she and her crew had to sit in the medical bay for three days, then the least we could do would be to service and refuel her ship."

Tyson brightened up a little on hearing this. "The Senior Chief also suffered delays by going through your process, but rules are rules," he finished with a grin.

"They have been our guests for two days," Griffon confessed with a wry look. "And they are getting more disorderly by the hour."

"Can you not place them on disciplinary action? Or throw them in the brig for a day or two?" asked John, hoping that they could be delayed further.

"Unfortunately, no." Griffon looked almost as disappointed by his reply as Tyson did. "You see," the Specialist explained. "They are paid contract retrievers from the Beta system."

"Beta system?" echoed John. "They're a long way from home then."

"All I know is, it must be serious business. The Commander hates bounty hunters, and for him to extend courtesies like offering the use of his personal hangar, well, something extremely important must be going on."

John nodded his understanding, while discretely indicating to Tyson he should move away.

"Specialist Griffon," Tyson immediately took the hint and nodded towards the other craft in the hangar. "May I have your permission to walk around and take a closer look at these ships? Some of the improvements your team has achieved are very impressive."

Griffon's smile widened, "I see no harm in that. All I ask is that you return upon the hour. The Commander has already requested to meet the two men responsible for making the modifications he desired to his favourite vessel possible."

"Thank you." Tyson gave the two men one of his very best salutes and walked off.

"If you don't mind me saying so, senior chief, your recruit has one of the poorest salutes I have ever encountered."

John didn't bother to hide his smile at the remark, "That's the trouble we find with mature intake cadets, lack of discipline. Although, that being said, there are a great many benefits in other areas."

"Yes," the Specialist agreed, watching Tyson disappear from view between two of the ships. "His knowledge of programming and systems is most impressive."

Tyson waited until he was sure he was well out of sight before he retrieved his personal data pad from his pocket. Within minutes, he had tapped into the complex's system. Taking care to remain hidden as he walked, he began searching for the Commander's private hangar's inventory.

It wasn't long before he had all the listed specifications, along with all of the modifications that had been done to each of the nine of the ships currently inside the bay. The ship's classes meant little to him, so Tyson decided he should walk among them and look them up by their names.

The biggest ship Tyson dismissed as a potential new home for he and John almost immediately. It was a large freighter named *Midnight Titan,* and with its sleek design and widest array of offensive weapons he had ever seen on such a ship, it was a tempting choice. But it, like the medium freighter next to it, *The Red Hornet*, was in too awkward a position. Tyson quickly determined that neither could easily be manoeuvred out onto the hydraulic landing platform. The next two freighters were very different from each other in design and construction, but somehow the pair were listed as the same 'medium class.'

Tyson could clearly see that both ships were missile capable and both, like the freighters, had top-end forward and aft guns. As he walked between them, he thought about how much John would love to have a ship that could fire missiles.

Still, even with that in mind, and though he liked both their names *–The Crimson Tiger* and *The Black Flacon* – the latter painted a light blue that reminded Tyson of a summer's day back on Earth 2, he had to dismiss them too. They were still too far from the landing platform.

The last four ships were all in a much better position to be moved into the elevator platform with minimal effort. Three of them, however, were single occupant fighter class, all streamlined, and, if the data pad was to be believed, all were incredibly fast. All three had different modifications.

The White Cobra, its name displayed in a pearl white paint, had superior shields beneath its nondescript grey hull. The second, *Silver Phoenix*, had an impressive increase in second stage acceleration speed. The last, covered in camouflage green with its name in a cool yellow, *Grey Mongoose*, was equipped with what Tyson thought was really an excessive number of weapons, both forward and aft. But, anyway, all were far too small to be of any real use to him and John.

He moved on again. Thinking hard.

The last ship, and the one that was in the best position for a quick take off, was painted in a deep purple with golden, shimmering lettering on its hull: *Blue Warlock*.

Tyson studied his data pad with growing interest. It was a hybrid and had the cargo space of a small freighter coupled with the speed and firepower of a fighter class. According to its listed specifications, it also had excellent shields – something that Tyson always held in the highest regard.

Yes, he nodded firmly to himself, scanning the rest of the notes displayed on his data pad. It would suit them perfectly. As he probed deeper into the intricate, inner workings of the base's computer systems, a familiar name soon popped up – *White Lace*.

Tyson's favourite, most recently hacked and reverse-engineered security system. He smiled and with a few, deft strokes of his fingers had soon overridden all the security protocols in the private hangar. He then wasted no time installing his 'improved' version on every ship there, knowing that, in the next update cycle when they interfaced with the whole building, it would spread through the entire complex.

With a satisfied grin, Tyson locked his data pad and tucked it safely back into his pocket. He then threaded his way back through the ships, this time making sure he was seen by other workers in the area and returned to where John and Specialist Griffon were still deep in conversation.

"Welcome back recruit." John looked up to greet him as he approached them. "Did you find your walk helpful?"

"Yes sir," Tyson replied with a curt nod. "The Commander certainly has a fine and very well-maintained collection."

The Specialist's wrist intercom chimed. As Griffon took a step away to look at it, Tyson gave John a quick thumbs up and a smirk, his movements so quick and smooth, no one else would've had time to register the gesture.

"Sir," Griffon addressed John as he moved back towards them. "If you and the recruit could follow me, your presence has been requested by the Commander."

John smiled, "Lead the way," as they both fell in step behind the Specialist.

It was the break he had been waiting for. The Commander had to be Hector Gibbs. His whole plan hinged around that assumption. Although John's smile wavered briefly, it was only now he realised he never did get the Commander's actual name.

"Specialist Griffon," he quickened his pace until he was level with him. "I am curious to know your Commander's full name. I am wondering if we haven't perhaps crossed paths throughout our respective careers."

"He is known only by his rank," Griffon replied.

"He must have a name though. Surely, everyone does," Tyson said but then fell back slightly, realizing how disrespectful he sounded.

There was a long pause and John sighed, "I must apologize for the recruit. He does tend to forget his place from time to time."

Griffon nodded but it wasn't until they had walked back out of the hangar and reached the waiting Jeep before he finally replied, "The Commander's name is Stapleton. Mitchell Stapleton."

It felt exactly as if a bomb had exploded inside John's head and he climbed back into the Jeep and sat, staring straight ahead, the name reverberating through his skull.

Mitchell Stapleton. He would never forget that name as long as he lived. Or rather, *The Black Nova Butcher*, as he and his old team from his core service days knew him. John wracked his brain, his heart hammering painfully in his chest. Had they ever met face to face? Yes, he concluded after a frenzied moment, they had.

Shit, John swore to himself internally. *No, wait…*

His brain whirled faster. He had been dressed in full combat kit at the time, including a blast face shield. He remembered it clearly now.

The last time he had seen Stapleton was when John and his crew had been escorting him onto a maximum-security prison ship. They had turned him over to the guards on the ship and, shortly thereafter, had left. They had heard he had gone on to detonate one of the guard's weapon packs with the presumed intent of causing a distraction. The explosion he had created had ripped through the convict ship and he had escaped.

John hadn't cared. He had fulfilled his part of the mission. Besides, everyone had assumed Stapleton had died out on that barren planet. That had been over eight years ago.

John allowed himself to relax slightly, knowing there was no way he could be identified by the man. Still, it didn't solve the problem he was now confronted by – where, in the seven moons, was Hector Gibbs?

John was lost in thought for most of the journey, the sound of Specialist Griffon unbuckling his seatbelt and announcing, "Here we are gentlemen. Please follow me," finally jolting him out of his reverie.

Tyson had never heard of Mitchell Stapleton or the *Black Nova Butch*er for that matter, so he stepped out of the jeep and followed Griffon towards a large, guarded doorway, still smiling and with no idea as to whom, or what possibly lay behind it.

Griffon presented his arm to one of the two, burly men at the entrance. "These two are with me," he nodded as the guard waved a small scanner over his exposed wrist. The device chimed loudly then flashed green.

"You are clear to enter," the guard nodded, and Griffon led the way through the door.

They entered what looked, to John anyway, to be the operations control room for the base. Tyson smiled at the handful of workers who glanced up to see who they were. Most, however, like the Specialist and John, either continued with their tasks or stared straight past them, uninterested.

The trio approached another doorway. This one was unguarded, and it slid quietly open to reveal a small, thickset man with intelligent blue eyes waiting there to greet them. He stepped out into the control room with three, very alert and intense looking bodyguards at his heels.

Tyson took a barely perceptible step closer towards John.

"Ahh Specialist Griffon!" the man called out jovially. "Are these the two men who achieved the modifications to my ship that your team said were impossible?"

Griffon stood bolt upright, saluting sharply as he replied, "Commander! Yes, sir Commander."

"Very good. You are dismissed, Specialist Griffon. I'm sure we can all get along just fine without you."

"Yes sir, Commander," he repeated as he spun on his heel, saluted John and left without another word.

Tyson continued to eye the bodyguards warily as the Commander continued in the same, affable tone, "Why don't we take this to my private stateroom."

Chapter Eighteen

It was sparsely decorated. Aside from the two cherry red armchairs John and Tyson were directed into, the only really large pieces of furniture in the stateroom was a huge antique desk and matching chair, which the Commander strode over to, making himself comfortable while gesturing to two of the guards to take up position on either side of the closed door, the third remaining menacingly by his left shoulder.

Ignoring the obvious attempt at intimidation, John began admiring the desk. "That looks like some sort of Old Earth Prime forest timber," he noted.

"It is," nodded the Commander, "One of a kind, I believe."

"I remember seeing something similar in the Alpha System, many years ago," John went on thoughtfully. He stopped short of saying it had been in the Secretary of Defence's office following the well-documented Battle of Orion, but the Commander didn't appear to care anyway.

The Commander smiled at John's declaration and spoke calmly and fluidly to the pair. "Gentlemen, my name is Mitchell Stapleton. As you are aware, I am the Commander of this facility. There are two things I would like to discuss with you both. Firstly, I must thank you for your efforts on my ship. I believe in rewarding all under my command generously for an outstanding effort. However…" he paused to let the statement hang in the air between them.

Tyson swallowed hard and a sick feeling began to bubble up in his stomach. *Had they been discovered?*

John, obligingly, filled in the pause, "However, we are not under your command."

"Exactly." Stapleton tapped the edge of his desk and instantly both John's and Tyson's pictures appeared, shimmering and floating above the desktop, with bold lettering underneath detailing bounty rewards and crimes committed.

"And that," the Commander continued, "Brings me to the second item I wish to discuss. It seems you owe a powerful man a lot of credits. A man with whom I am closely associated."

Tyson turned white as he thought about all they had been through. Surely they could not be caught now. Not like this.

"I ask myself," Stapleton's chair creaked noisily as he leant forward. "Why two, heavily sought-after men such as yourselves would take the time to repair someone else's ship instead of simply stealing one to make their escape?"

John hesitated.

"I assume that the pile of slag just outside the perimeter of my Bio Dome was once your ship?"

"Yes," John nodded. "The ship was ours. We were lucky to escape before your men destroyed it."

Stapleton shrugged his broad shoulders. "The Bounty Hunter Breanna Gomez requested the destruction of the craft known as *The Broken Eye*. It was a request I could not deny. After all, this base is supposed to be a well-kept secret."

John replied casually, "And, as for your ship, it was too fine a craft to be left without making the modifications you ordered. Besides, the time spent working on it gave us a good chance to blend in and help us to plan our next move."

Before Stapleton could enquire as to what that move might be, Tyson asked, "Are you going to kill us? Or hand us over to Breanna and let someone else do it?"

"Killing can be so messy. I believe we can come to another, more agreeable, arrangement."

"May I ask a favour of you first?" John enquired.

"You may ask, of course. That doesn't necessarily mean it will be granted."

"I understand," John nodded, pausing purposefully before continuing. "Do you know of a Hector Gibbs? I have a message for him."

Sure enough, a spark of recognition flashed in Stapleton's eyes. "Yes. He is the director of environmental research here." He tapped lightly against a different section of his desk and spoke loudly to someone in another room, "Director, if you could come directly to my stateroom, please."

Neither John nor Tyson heard a reply but there must have been one as the Commander then said, firmer this time, "No! Now, Director. Thank you."

The Commander looked up from his desk and gestured to two of his bodyguards, "Find the director and escort him here immediately."

The guards left the room in such haste, Tyson actually found himself sympathizing with Hector Gibbs. Whoever this Director of Environmental Research was, he was glad he wasn't him right at that moment.

"So, about this *other arrangement?*" Tyson enquired as they waited for the Director to arrive.

"Yes," Stapleton nodded amiably. "I believe I can help you out with your, shall we call it, *misadventure,* with regards to the cargo that you owe Liebecker. I'm afraid you would still have to pay out the bounty hunter yourselves. She has, of course, wasted a great deal of time chasing you across the systems."

John nodded, "That is very generous of you. What would we be expected to do in return?"

"All that I ask is that you both stay as my guests for two years and to lend your expertise in overseeing all of my personal ship's modifications."

Before John could answer, Tyson quickly replied, "Let's negotiate. Two years is quite a long time. How does six months sound?"

The Commander let out a low cackle. "Mr. Blake, I do enjoy your humour. My counter-offer is one year, and I allow you to live."

There was an unmistakable edge to his voice and the smile vanished from Tyson's face. He glanced across at John, who was shaking his head slowly.

"A generous offer, Commander," John said softly, knowing a refusal would only result in both their deaths. "We will, of course, accept your terms."

"Excellent!" the change in Stapleton's demeanour was immediate. "Then it is settled. I look forward to our continued acquaintance."

Neither John nor Tyson shared his enthusiasm at the new arrangement. They were not given time to dwell on the unfortunate situation, however, as the two bodyguards soon returned, a disgruntled looking Director sandwiched between them.

"So good of you to join us," the Commander's smile stretched. "One of my guests here has a question for you, Director Gibbs."

Hector Gibbs was a tall, sinewy man. He wore a long, white lab coat over a sharp, grey suit. Both of which appeared to have been tailored expertly for him. His face was lined from lack of sleep and his intelligent red-rimmed dark brown eyes darted around the room in anticipation before finally coming to rest on John.

John stood, the guards eying him closely as he rose slowly from his chair and stepped towards the Director. He unzipped the pocket of his overalls and both guards instinctively reached for their weapons. "I am unarmed," he assured them as he withdrew the two small vials and presented them to Gibbs.

Hector hesitated at first then reached out and wordlessly took the vials from him. John reached back into his pocket, again indicating to the guards there was no danger, this time removing the small DNA scanner. "Director," he said with more politeness than Tyson had heard in a long while. "Would you kindly place your hand on here? If you please"

Gibbs did as he was requested, and the unit flashed a multitude of colours before finally beeping softly three times and lighting up green.

"Thank you," nodded John, returning the scanner to his pocket, indicating to everyone in the room that the transaction was now complete.

As John walked back to his seat, Tyson noticed the Director had turned very pale. "Is something wrong?" he asked. "Is that not what you wanted?"

Hector Gibbs had turned very pale as he stammered, "You have been carrying them unsecured this the whole time? How ... How long have you been carrying them around like this?" Gibbs was looking from the vials to John and back again.

"They both had separate cases at one stage, but circumstances changed, and I had to minimise what I was able to carry," explained John.

It was then John noticed that it was quite obvious the vials were only half-full. He didn't think he'd spilt that much of either. But then, he couldn't be sure how full they had been to begin with.

No one else commented on the amount in the vials. If Tyson had noticed any irregularities, for once he was keeping his mouth shut about it.

The Director held each of the vials up to his right eye, and John realised that he too had been fitted with a cybernetic eye.

"How are the samples, Doctor?" asked the Commander.

Doctor? Tyson's ears pricked up and he silently wondered what kind of doctor the director might have been.

"The composition is exactly what was promised, and the sample quantity is even more than what I had hoped for."

John allowed himself to relax a little.

"I'm glad everyone is happy," Tyson slapped his hands against his armrests to announce loudly. "I, for one, haven't a clue what that stuff is, and I don't care either. The guy who originally hired us to deliver it threw himself out of an airlock into open space. So really, when you think about it, the less I know the better."

"Commander, it has been a long day, could we be shown to our new quarters?" John enquired.

"Sir, there is one small favour I'd like to ask," Tyson grinned as Stapleton gestured to the guards to take them out of the room.

"And, that would be?" asked Stapleton with curiosity in his voice.

"Could John and I be there when you tell Breanna that our debt has been paid and the bounty lifted?"

The commander chuckled, the first time in many years. "Yes, I'm sure that can be arranged."

The guards all looked so surprised by the sound of his laugh that, Stapleton had to remind them sharply to, "Escort the guests to their living quarters!" They all jumped instantly to attention as they ushered John and Tyson from the room. The Director left the room with them, mumbling something about "further analysing the contents of the vials." They walked in silence through the long corridor.

Tyson attempted to make conversation with the bodyguards, but after a while their simple "yes," "no," "that's classified information" answers caused him to give up.

John abruptly stiffened and fell backward to the ground. There was a loud crack as his head contacted sharply with the highly polished floor. Ignoring the guard's shouts, Tyson instantly dropped to his knees to help his friend, but at that same moment, John's whole body began shaking in a wild and uncontrollable seizure.

Unable to do anything to stop the violent spasms, Tyson knelt by his friend's shoulder, peeling off his shirt and rolling it up to put behind John's wildly jerking head. As he leaned over, for a second, he thought he saw something moving beneath the skin on John's neck. He blinked, looked back, and it was gone.

The guards swiftly alerted the medical team and by the time they finally arrived, the spasms had stopped, and John was beginning to regain consciousness.

"Name and rank?" one of the medics bent down to ask, shining a light into John's eyes.

"Captain John Alexander," mumbled John, and even Tyson looked surprised, eventually complying with the guard's repeated order for him to move away with a puzzled expression on his face.

The guards, arguing briefly over whether or not to pull Tyson away, swiftly alerted the medical team and by the time they finally arrived, the spasms had stopped and John was beginning to regain consciousness.

"I think we better take him down to the medical bay," one of the other medics nodded, searching through the pack by his feet and withdrawing an instrument he took care to conceal from Tyson, "As a precaution."

"I'm sure he'll be fine," Tyson insisted and then let out a small, "Hey!" and rubbed at the side of his neck. "What was that for?" he turned around to ask the first medic, standing behind him with an empty syringe in her hand.

"Just a precaution," she shrugged. "You and your friend here will need to be quarantined for further testing."

"Is that ... really ... necessary?" mumbled Tyson before sinking into a deep and surprisingly pleasant sleep.

John awoke to the sound of soft music. He tried to sit up, but it hurt his head too much, so instead he stayed reclining comfortably on what appeared to be a very expensive medical bed.

He quickly discovered that twisting his head from side to side only caused him a small amount of discomfort, and as his eyes grew accustomed to the bright lights, he soon was able to determine he was in a padded room.

After a few more minutes of careful head turning, the pain gradually lessened.. John found out he had been dressed in a light grey jumpsuit that had "Medical bay only" stamped on it.

The credit chip on his left hand had been removed and the cut on his neck where Esheel had cut him had been reopened and stitched closed professionally. A voice interrupted the music: John recognised it as Hector Gibbs. "Good afternoon John, how are you feeling today?"

John was in no mood for small talk. His head still ached, and it felt like the padded walls were beginning to close in on him. "What's going on? Why am I in here?" he snapped.

"You have been placed into solitary for your own protection and also for the safety of others." There was a note of condescension in the Director's voice as he continued, "I see you have been in contact with the serum in the vials, John. You must understand both of the vials were developed separately and were to be kept apart for a very good reason."

"I don't know what you're talking about," John laid his head back on the pillow and closed his eyes.

"You can feign ignorance as much as you like, *Captain*. My team and I have run many scans and tests and I know that you are lying. You have been exposed to *both* serums."

John shrugged, refusing to open his eyes.

"Perhaps you are not as intelligent or as dangerous as our Commander would have me believe."

"Dangerous?" John echoed, lifting one eyelid to squint at the ceiling. "Me? Okay."

"I have a theory …"

John was sure he could detect a note of irritation creeping into the Director's voice, but his bored expression did not alter for a second.

"I believe that you *accidentally* came into contact with the serums. I also believe you have no clue as to what you have been exposed too. However, what no one here can understand is how you survived without professional care. Or why your blood shows traces of an unknown DNA structure."

John's drawled, "Maybe I'm just special that way," which only served to annoy Gibbs further.

"Special indeed!" he growled over the intercom. "And we require more of the DNA structure to stabilise the serum in the activation vial!"

Growing tired of the conversation, John finally hauled himself upright to declare, "I don't care about your serums. The transaction was completed. You have no right to keep me here. And where is Tyson?"

"Don't worry. Your friend is safe and unharmed, for the moment anyway. Unlike yourself, he seems, annoyingly, completely human. My team has tried several interrogation techniques on him." There was a loud sigh, "However, he just keeps passing out before we can get anywhere."

John smiled. They weren't much of a medical team if they had failed to detect the chip behind Tyson's cybernetic eye that allowed him to drop off to sleep whenever he wanted. It had been John's idea. Although the fitting of Tyson's cybernetic eye had been successful, he had unfortunately immediately begun to suffer badly from headaches and insomnia in the months following the surgery, and no amount of medical intervention had been able to help him. John had seen chip technology in a variety of applications and had suggested Tyson give one a try. After an initial reaction of, "You have got to be kidding me? *More technology*? That's your answer?" he had agreed to undergo the procedure. After the first two days of solid sleep, the headaches vanished, and his sleep patterns returned to normal.

"You know what?" John held up his hands in mock surrender. "If you want more of this unknown DNA, just take it out of me now and let us both go about our business."

"What do I have to say to make you understand?" The Director's voice had taken on its condescending tone. "Let me try and simplify things for you. We need a complete DNA sample. The one inside you is fractured. Think of it like slicing an up apple into twelve pieces, then removing five of those pieces and trying to make the apple whole again. It just doesn't work. Every other person we have tested the serums on has died a most gruesome death. That DNA holds the key to our success, and I think you might just know where I can find more of it."

"I can't help you."

"Then I'm sorry to have to say this, but you leave me no choice. Perhaps injecting your friend will help jog your memory. You will have six hours between injections in which to change your mind. And I will remind you, everyone we have tested this on has died in a great deal of pain and I assure you, quite horrifically."

"Wait," John stood up and looked around frantically, trying to see where the Director's voice was coming from. "Ty has nothing to do with this!"

"Six hours, John. The clock starts as soon as the first injection is complete."

"You son of bitch!" John yelled at the walls. "We brought you the vials! We did what we were asked!"

"And now I'm asking for just a little bit more," the Director's voice glided around the room. "See, I told you your friend was unharmed."

One of the padded walls lit up with a display of Tyson strapped to a medical bed. John looked on in rising panic as the Director dripped three, sluggish drops of grey liquid into a micro-syringe and injected it directly into Tyson's prone arm. Remembering his own, painful reaction to the first serum, John cringed as his friend immediately began writhing around, the bed's thick straps straining against his bulging muscles.

"Your friend has now been injected with the primer agent," Gibbs turned to face the camera, lowering his medical mask and giving John full view of his smiling face. "This will target weakened DNA strands and strip them of their protective sheaths, leaving them vulnerable for re sequencing." He stepped back so John could better see Tyson, screaming now as he fought against his restraints. "I'm led to believe this is a very painful process. However, I can assure you it is not normally fatal."

Gibbs' face moved back into view, his lips contorting into a cruel smile, "Unfortunately, the same cannot be said about the second vial."

"Stop it!" yelled John. "Stop it now!"

"Only you can stop your friend's suffering," the Director looked back at Tyson and gave his head a sad shake. "Tell me where to find the DNA structures and all this will end."

John's shoulders slumped in defeat. "Fine," he mumbled.

"I'm sorry, I didn't quite catch that." Gibb's mocking face took up almost the entire screen. "You'll have to speak up. Your friend here is terribly noisy, I'm afraid."

"Let him go!" John shouted. "Give him a ship and let him go." He sighed and continued in his normal tone, "Then I will tell you how to get what you want."

"No, John, you will take me to the source," demanded the Doctor.

"Agreed," growled John between gritted teeth "I will take you there!"

There was a brief laugh and then the screen shut off, each of the padded walls in John's room looking the same once again.

A long silence followed, and John began to think the mad doctor had either killed Tyson or was changing the deal. A solid hour had passed before he concluded that Hector Gibbs was not firing on all thrusters, and both he and Tyson would be lucky if they didn't live out the rest of their lives as his unfortunate lab rats.

"Captain Alexander!"

John startled as a loud voice hailed him over the intercom.

"This is the Commander. We accept your terms. Mr. Blake has been gifted a ship that is being prepared for launch as we speak."

"Show me proof," John demanded. "I want to see him alive and leaving this place before I do anything for you."

In under a minute the screen reappeared and this time the image was of Tyson strapped securely into the pilot's seat. "Ty!" he cried out in relief. "TY? You okay?"

"Yeah, Johnny," Tyson sounded a bit groggy, but he looked otherwise okay. "They shot me up with some weird stuff that burned like the fires of Orion, but I'm all right now. I don't like this though, Johnny. I don't like it at all."

"It's going to be okay, Ty," John reassured him firmly. "You just get out of here and don't look back."

"Johnny," Tyson's tone turned almost apologetic. "They've locked it on autopilot to the nearest starbase. I can't reach it."

"That's okay. Didn't you once tell me this planet would end up being my tomb?"

"I'm sorry I can't help you, Blue," Tyson abruptly began speaking in a much more jovial voice. "Hey! Remember that time we met our tall friend and his war pet? Those sure were fun times. I'll lock it in and remember them always."

"Enough of this!" interrupted the Commander. "Launch him now!"

***

Given the quality of the ships in the hangar, Tyson was surprised at just how bad the craft he had been bundled aboard was. It looked very old. Some of its techs were so outdated he was sure he'd seen similar parts on display in at least one museum on Earth Two when he was attending boarding school, and it had the outward appearance of a ship that had been around all of the seven systems at least once, perhaps even twice.

As the Commander issued the order to launch, he considered crossing his fingers, convinced the hull would never withstand the pressure of open space. One of the screens in front of him lit up and Tyson was surprised to see an image of John, strapped to a medical bed in a padded cell. It was, like everything else on the ship, a poor quality, but it was definitely John.

Ignoring the other screen that was flashing warning messages about stress levels throughout the ship, Tyson watched as John as he lifted his head and looked as if he was sniffing the air. The image crackled and reset, clearer this time so that Tyson could see some sort of gas was pouring into John's room through the ventilation system.

"No!" Tyson yelled, even though he doubted anyone was listening to him. "JOHNNY!"

He watched helplessly as John's head sagged onto his chest and he suddenly felt a fit of rage building within him. He burst ferociously into a round of swearing, accessing anything and everything on board the ship that he could.

It was futile and Tyson knew it, and eventually all he succeeded in doing was cutting off the feed from the base, causing the lifeless image of John to disappear.

***

John watched the launch from inside his room, marvelling at the way the aged rust bucket held together through the planet's atmosphere. He was roused out of his thoughts when he heard his cell being pumped full of gas and took a tentative sniff. Instinctively, he took a breath, holding it for as long as he could. Whatever it was they wanted to do to him, he wasn't about to make it easy for them.

John could feel his lungs starting to burn but still, he fought the urge to take another breath. Just once, he thought to himself as he eventually lost consciousness and collapsed to the floor, just once it would have been nice to have someone pleased to meet him!

***

John awoke to find himself sitting between two bodyguards, opposite a smiling Dr. Gibbs, in the back of one of the Bio Dome's fleets of jeeps. All of them were wearing bio suits but John's hands and feet were securely bound.

"It's good to see you awake, John," Hector continued to smile pleasantly at him. "Our scans tell us that sometime, while you were on this planet, you were exposed to unknown DNA. I believe you know where that was and that you will direct our driver there. Now."

John nodded. "Take me to where my ship was. You know, the one your team blew up?"

"Not *my* team," Gibbs retorted lightly as he leaned over to speak quietly to the driver and the jeep roared to life, heading out of the dome towards the surrounding tree line.

It didn't take long for them to reach the site. John was helped out of the jeep by the guards and they stood back, letting him shuffle among what little was left. He kicked about the crater for a few minutes then reached down and picked up a small, black ball with many coloured wires inside.

"What have you found there?" enquired Gibbs.

"Just a gift from Ty," John replied with a shrug. "He kept on insisting it was a piece of 'lucky' Alien Tech. All it seems to have done is be indestructible."

"Does it have a use?"

"Not that I found. I did use it once to keep the cargo doors open, though, when they kept auto-closing." It was a lie, but even though he wasn't sure it would ever work again, John still did not want Doctor Gibbs getting his hands on it.

One of the guards went to take it off John, but when he offered no resistance, Gibbs waved his man away.

"Thank you," said John as he put it in one of his suit's pockets.

After a few more minutes of foraging, John finally looked up and pointed into the trees. "Your jeep won't fit through here. We have to go the rest of the way on foot."

Neither the guards nor Gibbs appeared happy at the news, but with a few muttered words to each other, they agreed and followed John into the wooded area.

After what felt like days but was only a few hours, Gibbs called, "Time for a break." All three men were perspiring heavily inside their suits as, even though the mud had dried, there were a great many fallen branches and exposed roots to negotiate. The Director and his guards sank gratefully onto a fallen log, Gibbs checking the time and wondering if the captain wasn't just leading them on a fool's errand.

Having been quite enjoying his ramble, John stood on one side of the log and watched the group, their shoulders heaving as they tried to catch their breath. He had just broken a sweat and was wondering why the others were having so much trouble keeping up.

While they were sitting down, the men all checked their oxygen tanks. Both the bodyguards had used a little over a quarter of their supply while the Director was closer to using up a third of his. John's tank display, however, had hardly moved at all.

The guard that had been given the task of checking John's tank tapped the display with a padded finger. Nothing changed.

The guard shrugged and muttered, "The thing's probably faulty. No matter. You only need to make it there. It doesn't matter if you don't make it back."

"Thanks," John smiled as the guard went back to his seat on the log.

Soon though, they were moving once again through the thick undergrowth. This time, however, whenever John stopped or took too long navigating the terrain, one of the guards would shove him in the back with the butt of his rifle and bark at him to , "Keep moving!"

Finally, John reached the hole he had fallen into. It was covered with downed trees and branches and, as he peered over the edge between the tangled messes of leaves, it seemed a lifetime ago he had been there.

One of the bodyguards sat opposite John, his rifle pointed at his chest, while Gibbs and the second guard set about tying and securing ropes to the surrounding trees for them to abseil down.

The others were so focused on their task that only John spotted the slight movement in trees behind them. He couldn't quite make out what it was, but he didn't want to draw any attention to it either. He leapt to his feet and began hopping about, shouting, "Cramp. Cramp. Leg cramp!"

The guard across from him immediately got up too, watching him for a few seconds before grunting, "Sit your ass down," and clubbing him with the butt of his rifle.

As John fell to the ground, he rolled onto his side and so was able to see the black swarm as it emerged from the surrounding jungle and attacked the guards and the Director.

It took mere minutes for the thousands of black, winged spiders to do their work. The suits of the bodyguards lay in shreds. One of them was still heaving and lurching as he tried breathing in the planet's fatal air. The other had already died from suffocation as the spiders had ripped open his suit and rushed into his open mouth, ears, and nose. He had convulsed in a desperate attempt to expel them, his own hands clawing at his exposed flesh as he fought to rid himself of his body's invaders. To no avail. Following his death, the spiders slowly exited the man's now lifeless body the same way they had entered.

Gibbs had tried to run from the chaos, but, unfortunately for him, he had come face to face with the spider queen. He had frozen in fear at the sight of her. She was craned back on her hind legs, displaying her long, terrible fangs in all their hideous glory.

John stood up slowly and shuffled over to where one of the guard's bodies lay. He eventually located the key to the restraints and freed himself. Still taking his time, he gathered up the guard's rifles and approached the now shaking Director.

The queen lowered herself to the ground and waited. John stretched out his hand with his palm facing up and the huge spider tottered over to rub the side of her massive head against it. He smiled, flipped his hand over and gently stroked the creature's thick, red hairs. The queen shook her head in obvious pleasure and then backed away into the forest, all of the smaller spiders following her. Gibbs stood still and in shock.

John shoved him into a sitting position as he said, "I have some questions for you, doctor."

The Doctor was very compliant in his answers. Now, John knew everything. From the creation of the Penchell serum, manufactured as two parts of a whole. The first vial was created to remove weakened or damaged DNA strands by removing the protective sheaths, leaving them open to be repaired or replaced with healthy ones. This, Gibbs went on, meant that the medical applications were incalculable. Potentially it alone could save billions of lives.

Unfortunately, Stapleton had other ideas for its application. He had decided to fund a brilliant group of geneticists with questionable morals to formulate a second serum. This one would alter the DNA strand structure to create a Customised Programmable Enhanced Human.

They had achieved this seemingly impossible task on paper and had handed on their findings to a third party at the Harmon space station. After being generously compensated, the geneticists were located, one by one, and eliminated.

Soon after the arrival of the research results at Harmon, Stapleton arranged for the creation of the second serum in one of his laboratories on the starport. Arrangements were then made for the first serum, in the Alpha system, to be stolen. Once the thief had secured a reliable courier, the thief was located and then poisoned with a slow acting but powerful hallucinogen.

"Unfortunately for us," Gibbs finished with a wry look. "Somehow he remembered my name and not our planned designated courier to bring it to us here."

"So, this was all for your Commander to create some sort of elite army?" asked John in amazement.

"Not only Stapleton. Liebecker was also in on the deal. They were going to finalise the partnership when Liebecker arrives but," sighed Gibbs. "Without the full DNA structure, the plan will be a failure."

"Where did you send Tyson?" John demanded. "And what is the name of that rust bucket you put him on?"

"Your friend has been sent to Harmon Station and that 'rust bucket' is *The Bronze Hook*,'" Gibbs replied, sounding offended.

"Why that ship? And why send him back to Harmon?" John prompted Hector with the muzzle of the gun.

"*The Bronze Hook* is well travelled but unfortunately also very overdue for its much-needed repairs and maintenance. If the ship makes it to the space station, Breanna Gomez will be waiting there so she can collect his half of the bounty. We covered your side, as we told her you were dead."

"Okay. One last question before I let you go."

Gibbs looked nothing short of amazed. "You're letting me go?"

"Sure," shrugged John. "Why not? You have no weapons and not much air left. If you do happen to make it back to the Bio Dome, it will be nothing short of miraculous."

The Director brightened at the news. He knew all he needed to do was transfer the remaining oxygen from the two guard's tanks into his own and he would have air to spare by the time he made it back to the base. "What was your last question?" he asked, careful not to sound too cocky.

"You said the serum worked on me; I want to know what it did."

Gibbs paused, appearing to consider John's query. "Well," he finally said. "From what we can tell the first vial behaved as it is meant to do and identified and stripped the weakest DNA strands, readying them for the second dose. You then received this dose, which should have killed you, and it must have tried to replace the removed strands with a vastly enhanced and strengthened DNA Sequence."

"And what did that do to me?"

Gibbs looked embarrassed as he replied, "From what we can tell, absolutely nothing. Yet. I could see from your scans where the pieces were replaced, but so far there is no evidence of a positive result." He cleared his throat awkwardly.

"So, you're saying this whole experiment of yours was a failure?" taunted John.

"It wasn't the success we hoped for, but in time and with more research, I am confident we will secure a favourable outcome."

"You're not giving up on it then?"

"The Commander is not one to abandon a projects," Gibbs said firmly, unfazed by John's show of surprise. "He just finds better people to assist him in achieving his goals."

"You are continuing your research then!" John said as he shook his head in disbelief.

He hadn't worded it as a question, but Gibbs answered John anyway. "I most defiantly am. Without me, his whole plan would be set back years in research alone." He stood up as he spoke, pride ringing in his voice. "And now I will assume I am permitted to leave. I have answered all your questions, after all."

"Yes, you have," John replied, walking off towards the fallen bodyguards.

Gibbs looked on in horror as, without a single word. John kicked both bodies over so that they were lying face down before calmly putting a round from his rifle through each of the oxygen tanks. "No!" he cried out. "You said you would let me live, and yet you have just ensured my death!"

"My good doctor," John clarified with a tight smile. "I said I would let you go, as in setting you free. I have done so, however, I don't believe I said anything about allowing you the air to make it back alive."

"You broke your word to me! You lied!"

"As I said, I have kept my word. Unlike you," John pointed out smoothly, "Who said the bounty on Tyson and I had been paid. Consider us even." He turned and left, leaving Gibbs behind him in a crumpled, sobbing mess.

John found his way back to the crater that was *The Broken Eye*, the jeep had been flipped over onto its side and the driver's suit was ripped and torn in multiple places. *No doubt the work of his spider friends,* he thought to himself as he continued towards the Dome.

Slowly and silently crawling on his stomach, John entered through a different service entrance that he and Tyson used before. Once he located the same locker room, he swapped out his bio-suit for one of the pilot's black bio-suit that he found in the changing rooms.

He checked where he and Tyson had stashed their backpacks; luck was with him. They were still there, but he could only carry one without drawing suspicion. He searched both packs. Both had the same contents minus Tyson's data pad. John took two medical packs out of his backpack - Tyson had packed three in each as a precaution - and jammed in his thigh holster and blaster, along with the heart of the relocator. Barely managing to force the clips, it shut. John quickly scanned the room. He then hid himself among the rear lockers as he accessed his data pad.

Tyson had sent him all the files of his most recent activity. It was an activation code for a ship in Stapleton's personal hangar, but there was no, name only a docking number. Even if John got the craft out of the hangar, and onto the surfaces launch pad, there were still over a dozen ships docked outside. He needed to know the ship's name. It was too risky for John to enter the base any further, in case security had been tightened. He scanned the pad for a further hint, a list of names popped up, John realised they were the names of the commander's personal ships: *Dragon's Dawn*, *Midnight Titan*, *Red Hornet*, *Crimson Tiger*, and *Black Falcon*. John's frustration grew with every name, nothing was familiar. Still, he kept scrolling. *White Cobra*, *Silver Phoenix*, *Grey Mongoose* and the *Blue Warlock*.

Still nothing, however, if the stats he was reading were correct, the ships had undergone extensive modifications; all were impressive.

John wracked his brain when something clicked. What did Tyson say to him before he left? Something about a war pet and locking it in? John concentrated harder on what Tyson had said. He called him Blue... that was it! *The Blue Warlock* was the ship.

After slipping the data pad back into its slot in the backpack, John shouldered it on and crawled out silently the same way he had come in. He reached the landing platform that was directly above the Commander's hangar and hid amongst the landing gear of a heavy freighter that had just arrived, knowing it would be at least an hour before maintenance did an inspection. He retrieved his data pad and keyed in Tyson's override code, selecting *The Blue Warlock*, and waited. After a long five minutes, the entire complex was plunged into darkness, and soon after, the emergency light activated as the Dome's exterior door closed.

"Nice work, Ty," John muttered to himself with a grin, "I think sometimes I don't give you enough credit."

All the ships which were out on the landing platform with him suddenly started to move, rolling slowly in every direction. He had to quickly jump up onto the landing gear of the one he was nearest to avoid being crushed beneath its oversized wheels. After five minutes of complete chaos, and a lot more swearing, all the ships eventually ground to a halt.

As he climbed back down from his hiding place in the freighter, John realised the hydraulic platform that led into the hangar below had now been cleared. He watched as it began to disappear from view. Their distribution appeared completely random, some had even been moved out as far as the surrounding tree line.

John hoped that the platform was heading down to collect *The Blue Warlock* for him, but before he could check on his data pad, the doors to the Bio Dome abruptly reopened and dozens of people dressed in bio suits surged out, rushing towards all of the moved ships. Just as the fastest of the pilots reached the landing area, the perimeter lights flared to life and a siren blasted. The ground parted once again and a ship, being lifted by the hydraulic platform, came into view, stopping level with the ground. Spurred on by the sight, the black-suited pilots ran for their ships, frantically trying to gain access to them. There seemed to be some sort of mass malfunction, however, as not one of the craft would open for any of them.

Hiding his smile, John began walking briskly towards *The Blue Warlock*, which was looking even more impressive as it sat proudly on the landing platform amidst the chaos. He tapped his data pad against its hull and instantly the cargo bay doors opened. Unfortunately, the sudden movement trapped most of the unsuspecting pilots. With a large smile now displayed across his face, John boarded his new ship and made his way up to the bridge. The pilot's seat was, not surprisingly, extremely plush and comfortable. John quickly made himself at home, adjusting screens and pulling up all the information he needed for take-off. In one screen he could see several crews had managed to finally gain access to their craft and had begun to perform their pre-flight checks; he decided he may as well do so too. After a few minutes, he was satisfied that the craft was safe and in good working order, so he closed and locked the cargo bay doors. He glanced across at the empty chair and wondered if Tyson was okay.

As he warmed up the engines he saw the Commander, flanked by several burly bodyguards, heading towards him. Without further thought, he pushed the thrusters to half, taking off so rapidly that the guards didn't even have the time to aim their weapons at him.

The Blue Warlock broke through the planet's atmosphere within seconds.

A message appeared simultaneously on the main view screen. It was from the Commander. Keeping an eye on his other screens for any alerts about approaching vessels, John scanned it for viruses and lockout codes. It was a program that Tyson always insisted he kept on the data pad as another of his 'safety precautions'. John was happy to let it run and give him the all-clear before he opened the message.

It read simply:

Captain Alexander,
Well played, sir. Well played.
Mitchell Stapleton.
P.S. You owe me a ship.

John smiled. The Commander might have been a monster, but he certainly had style. He closed the file and checked his screens again. No one was following him.

He searched the star maps and located Harmon Station, plotting the fasted course there he engaged the autopilot. A moment later all of the engines were brought online, and the *Blue Warlock* performed a wide, sweeping arc over the planet and powered off towards the distant station.

Chapter Nineteen

John enjoyed his time getting to know his new ship. He managed to get the scanners to identify his bio signature and secured all the systems so that only he could access them. He spent some time in the engine room and made a few small adjustments as he familiarised himself. He was very pleased to see the crew areas were fully stocked and were all perfectly functional. There was even the room to carry modest cargo if required.

In the last hour, he had showered, shaved, and cleaned his suit, knowing the station must be close. While redressing, he had chanced upon three credit sticks, hidden away behind a hidden panel in the captain's quarters. Each of them held 10,000 credits. He took one out and put in his pocket, leaving the other two securely hidden away as he returned to the pilot's seat.

A pleasant tone sounded as the ship reduced its speed, remaining in autopilot. John smiled and magnified the screen. There it was. Harmon Station.

While *The Blue Warlock* went through the auto docking sequence, John went down to the medical bay. Something Dr. Gibbs had said was still bothering him. Stripping down to his underwear, he stood on one of the scanner platforms and initiated a scan. Coloured lights pulsed around him in every direction as the platform gradually turned three hundred and sixty degrees. The process took a little over eight minutes and it wasn't until the end that John realized he'd been holding his breath the entire time.

He shrugged on his bio-suit and went back up to the cockpit to wait for the results. As he sat down in his pilot's chair, a prompt appeared on his screens:

To initiate docking registration, please enter through landing bay door number twenty-two for the final stage of authorization scanning. Thank you for your compliance.

A thought hit John. If the ship wasn't registered in his name, or a company he was working for, the ship would be impounded. He would then be arrested, and the rightful owner notified.

Swearing softly, John reached out to tap the 'abort landing' tab on his screen, but as he did so the results from his scan appeared. In that moment of distraction, the ship's autopilot selected 'resume docking' before he could hit abort. Cursing himself now for not putting it into manual override the moment he had sat down, John hoped he could talk his way out of the predicament once he had docked.

Seeing as there was little he could do about it now, John brought up his old DNA scan which he always carried on his data pad, and put it alongside the one had just done, selecting 'compare scans' from the menu.

Instantly the computer displayed the report on his screens. John could only recognise some of what it said, as it was all in medical terms and, unfortunately, that was something he was not fluent in. He highlighted what was familiar.

Subject has undergone significant gene manipulation. Bio scaffolding has occurred with unknown Deoxyribonucleic acid *agent. Core physiology and metabolism Deoxyribonucleic acids have been irreparably recoded.*

John knew that Deoxyribonucleic acid meant DNA, but that was all he was certain of. He saved his new profile to his data pad, renaming his old Scan as J.A.1 and his new scan as J.A. NEW. He then uploaded it into the ship's computer and deleted the old one. Now all officially recorded files would be updated with his new scan file and, unless people had a reason to compare them with his old ones, which he highly doubted, no one would ever know the difference.

The docking sequence finished, and a pleasant female voice said, "Welcome to Harmon Station, Captain John Alexander. All permits and registrations have been registered and confirmed. Enjoy your stay."

John smiled. He should have known Tyson would have previously hacked in and altered the ship's registration and ownership certificates. He reached down and retrieved his thigh holster and blaster from his backpack. Standing up, he unzipped his pocket, taking out the heart of the relocator and placing it down on the chair next to his. He then fastened the holster around his leg, checking the hand blaster had a full charge and was in good working condition before sliding it snugly into place.

John made his way through the station until he found the same clothing shop he had visited before.

This time as he walked in he was greeted by a tall, dark-skinned woman with bright red hair that was shaved close to her skull on one side but grown very long on the other. John's immediate opinion was that it made her even more attractive, although the smile she offered him was a little half-hearted, "Hello. Welcome to Van Hallens Boutique."

John's eyes scanned her black, tight-fitting top and located her name badge. "Hello, Skylar. I'm John, and I'm hoping you can offer me some assistance today."

She took a half-step backward and gave him a long look, before tucking the data pad she was holding into her suit's inner pocket. "Hello John," her smile broadened as she lingered on his name a little longer than was necessary. "What sort of assistance do you need?"

"As you can see, I require some more appropriate clothing. I am to meet my friend Oberon at the Nobles Bar in a few hours." John let the statement hang in the air and waited.

"You're friends with Mr. Rodney?" she inquired incredulously.

"Yes. I'm his private courier and we meet quite often in his private booth. You know the one, at the back of the Nobles Bar?" John ventured. "He drinks whiskey with his most valued staff members there every quarter. Or so I'm told." He made a show of looking purposely around the store. "Or maybe I have the wrong establishment."

The young woman gathered her composure and tried to hide the surprise that was evident on her face as she smiled a much bigger and much more welcoming smile. "Not at all John, you have the correct place. So, you say you're in need of some fresh clothes?"

"Thank you, Skylar," John nodded and gestured down at his pilot suit. "And yes, I am in need of something a little more befitting for drinks with my friend."

"If you'd like to follow me, I'm sure I can help you with that."

Skylar walked with uncommon grace and John quickly found he enjoyed following her, watching the way she moved towards the back of the store. She stopped abruptly and turned to face him, catching him out while he was looking at her buttocks.

John knew he was caught so he just grinned and said, "I was just admiring how closely your skirt fits you."

She gave him such a practiced smile in return, John was sure he hadn't been the first one she had caught looking at her rear end. "Here are our finest quality suits, John." Again, she paused on his name. "Do you have a preferred colour or style?"

John looked up and down the rack, choosing a jet-black suit with a long, blood red-trimmed coat to start with. He then selected a tight-fitting, black, button-up shirt, before pulling out a purple and black striped waistcoat to complete the look.

Clearly pleased with his choices, Skylar glanced down at his feet and then queried in her politest tone, "And will you be requiring any footwear?"

John smiled broadly, "Yes, in fact, I do."

Skylar gathered up his clothing selection and scanned each item into her data pad, efficiently replacing them on the suit stand, "If you would please like to follow me again."

"Indeed, I would," chuckled John softly as they headed off to another section of the store.

He was positive she was walking much slower this time, and the effect was utterly mesmerising.

"And here we are," she said as she stopped and spun around, brushing John's arm with her breast as she turned. "Oh, I am sorry," she apologised.

She didn't sound particularly sorry and John looked deep into her soft, liquid brown eyes and replied, "Don't be. I'm not." Her eyes flared for a moment as she returned his smile. He reached over and pointed at a pair of blood red shoes with a fine silver trim, "I think I can see what I like right in front of me."

"A fine choice, sir," she blushed slightly, added the shoes to her data pad and nodded. "Of course, they come with complimentary foot coverings."

"Excellent. I think, black for those."

Putting the last of his order in, Skylar sounded almost disappointed as she asked, "Will that be all for today, John?" He nodded and then she added, with a renewed twinkle in her eye, "Would you perhaps like to change now into your new selection now?"

John smiled and produced the credit stick from his pocket, handing it to her as he replied, "Yes, thank you. I would like that."

She waved the credit stick over her data pad. It chimed softly and flashed green. Skylar smiled and handed it back, now much lighter in credits. "Your garments have been selected and sized to you from your previous visit with us." Again, she looked John over from top to toe, tapping on her data pad one last time before returning it to her suit pocket. "Sorry," she said, this time sounding like she meant it. "But unfortunately, I am very late for a meeting. I must leave you now. You can claim your items by the front entrance. I have included my business card among your new clothes, should you wish to contact me for any reason ... day *or night*."

John raised a curious eyebrow as she winked seductively at him, patted his forearm lightly then walked off to the rear of the store. "You don't want to see the finished look?" he called after her.

She stopped and turned back, but only repeated the words, "Remember, day *or* night," before whirling around again and striding away.

John located the fitting rooms and, as promised, there were his new clothes. He changed quickly, then removed his holster from his bio-suit and modified it with swift, practiced precision. In moments, his new, cross draw holster was all but invisible under his new long coat. He threaded the holster's strap through the belt loops on his trousers, fastened the clasps, and slipped the blaster inside. After a few minor adjustments, it was securely resting against his left hip.

John admired his new choice of attire in the four, full-length mirrors that the room had. Inside his long coat's left inside breast pocket was Skylar's business card complete with her after hour's number printed on the back, with those words again: *anytime day or night.*

After he left the store, it didn't take long for him to locate a service courier. He paid the going rate and gave instructions for them to take his bag to his ship's docking pad and leave it in the storage area next to it. Now, free from the burden of his old clothes, he headed for the Nobles Bar in the hope of finding Oberon.

It took John even less time to find the bar and, as luck would have it, there were still a few tables free. He sat at the one that offered him the best view of all the entrances, including the private booths, and waited.

Within minutes of him sitting down, a waiter appeared and asked him if he was available to join Mr Rodney and his guests in his booth. Smiling, John stood up and followed the waiter through the rapidly filling bar into the private area beyond.

The waiter stopped in front of double doors and pressed his hand flat against one of the panels. A pale green glow appeared around the man's hand and the doors slid open silently. He stepped to one side and looked at John. "Would you like a drink brought to you, sir?" he asked. "Your usual perhaps?"

"My usual?" John enquired with a faintly amused smile.

"Yes, sir," replied the waiter. "Daylarian scotch with dry ginger, unless my records are incorrect."

"Your records are correct. Yes, my usual then. Thank you," John nodded as he entered the room alone.

The room was mostly as John remembered from his previous visit. This time, however, Breanna Gomez and another, heavily built man with black cropped hair and intelligent blue eyes were already seated at the only table. He hadn't expected to see them there and they both looked back at him in surprise as he approached them. As he drew closer, he noticed that their weapon holsters were empty, and their feet had been tightly bound to the legs of their chairs.

The table had four other empty seats and in front of each one was a name plate. John pulled out the chair by his name, reading each of the others as he sat down:

Breanna Gomez - *Owner of Crimson Blade / Retrieval expert.*

Quaid Ashford - *Security officer Crimson Blade / Retrieval specialist.*

Carson Pine - *Chief council of legal affairs Harmon Station.*

John Alexander - *Owner of Blue Warlock / Exotic goods courier (Dec)*

Tyson Blake - *Computer systems expert / Exotic goods courier*

Oberon Rodney - *Chief executive of Harman Station.*

John smiled at Brianna and Quaid, just as the waiter appeared carrying a tray with three full glasses on it. He placed one in front of each of them. "Sir," the waiter addressed John. "Could I trouble you for your weapon?"

He hesitated for a split second.

"I would prefer to not have to use force and restrain you as I have done to our other guests."

John removed his blaster slowly and smoothly from its holster, wondering how the waiter had managed to remove both Breanna and Quaid's weapons, let alone confine them to their chairs. He placed it carefully onto the waiter's empty drinks tray and smiled, "That won't be necessary. It's no trouble at all."

They were sitting quietly, sipping their drinks and avoiding conversation when a tall, dark-skinned, finely dressed, bald man with small, round glasses entered the room. He crossed to the table and sat down in front of his name plaque Carson Pine. Shortly after his arrival, the waiter appeared again, placing a drink in front of Pine and informing them all, "Mr. Rodney and his last guest will be arriving shortly."

Carson Pine thanked the waiter quietly and produced a data pad from his jacket pocket, placing it carefully on the table in front of him.

The waiter then smiled around at them all, wished them a pleasant evening and returned to his position behind the bar.

Everyone remained silent at the table as the minutes passed by. Occasionally, one of them would gesture to the waiter for another drink and he always responded with a warm smile, promptly delivering the new beverage. John was halfway through his fourth drink when Oberon and Tyson arrived together. Tyson was wearing a yellow jumpsuit with *Harman Station* stamped across the chest in bright red letters. He had been fitted with ankle and arm restraints, along with a suppression gag over his mouth.

At the sight of him, Breanna yelled, "You had no right to take him off MY ship! He is MY cargo!"

Carson spoke softly, "Miss Gomez, please control yourself. You will find we have every right. It is stated in the landing agreement - that *you* signed - at the end of the document, paragraph three, section A." He spun his data pad around, so that both Breanna and Quaid could see it, and highlighted the corresponding section of their landing agreement.

"You're wrong!" spat Quaid. "It says here that no one under contract to Harmon Station may be detained unless authorised to do so by the chief executive!"

Both Oberon and Tyson were seated now, and Oberon was enjoying the first taste of his favourite whiskey. Apparently unconcerned by Quaid's accusations, he placed his tumbler on the table and said, "Mr .Alexander and I had a contract and I offered no such authorisation to detain anyone."

"What does that have to do with you boarding my ship and removing my cargo illegally?" Breanna asked with fire in her voice.

Carson turned slightly to address Breanna directly. "Do you currently have any outstanding bounties on Mr. Alexander?"

"No, the bounty was paid by a third party. I was also informed, by the same third party, that he was deceased. All other outstanding bounties have also been cancelled, upon notification of his death."

"Correct and agreed," Carson nodded. "We have the same information. I will add that the last time Mr. Alexander visited our station, he had a legal will and testament drawn up, which in the event of his death, clearly states all business holdings, contracts and debts shall be transferred to Mr. Tyson Blake."

Although Tyson couldn't speak through the suppression gag, his eyes widened in surprise.

Seeing as he had only been on the station for a few hours, John smiled slowly as he enquired, "When did the finalization of the transfer take place?"

"Oh, I believe it was only a short time ago," offered Oberon as he cocked an eyebrow in John's direction.

"We still have an outstanding bounty on motor mouth there," Quaid said, pointing at Tyson.

"I believe there are sometimes, shall we call them, early release options on bounties?" Oberon enquired pointedly.

"The amount owing on Mr. Blake is thirty thousand credits. Twenty thousand more for the early release and cancellation of the bounty," stated Breanna flatly.

Carson looked across at his boss. Oberon lifted his glass, taking a slow, measured drink before placing it back on the table. Only then did he nod his approval.

Carson picked up his data pad and tapped it several times before he spoke, "Fifty thousand credits have been transferred to your account."

He passed the pad over to Breanna. She read the screen, a smile forming on her lips. She too nodded and pressed her palm against the pad's surface. It beeped its acknowledgment of the transaction.

Carson tapped the pad once more and returned it to his suit pocket.

Oberon gestured to the waiter and he returned with a fresh round of drinks for everyone. Once he had placed all the glasses on the table, the waiter tapped the surface of his empty serving tray. There were a series of faint clicks from beneath Breanna and Quaid's seats as their feet restraints slotted back into the legs of their chairs.

With a smile befitting someone who had just earned themselves a tidy pile of extra credits, Breanna pushed up the sleeve of her red jacket and keyed a code into a small screen she had strapped to her arm. Instantly Tyson's restraints fell away, including the mouth gag. Quaid carefully gathered them up, folding them neatly and stashing them away in his suit's pockets.

Tyson coughed and spluttered for a few seconds before regaining his composure.

"Now," Oberon enquired mildly. "If all parties are satisfied, perhaps we can share a drink like civilised adults?"

They raised their glasses to toast the conclusion of their 'business transaction' and then lapsed into silence. Carson finishing his drink first and stood up, thanking everyone politely before leaving the room. Breanna and Quaid were the next to get to their feet.

"You understand it was nothing personal, right?" She sneered at John. "You and your friend were worth a lot of credits to me, that's all."

"Yeah, right," retorted Tyson. "Nothing personal? You've been chasing us for months."

"And if I'd known how much trouble you guys were going to be, or how much time you were going to cost me, I swear I never would have bought the damn contract!" Breanna replied angrily.

"I'm sorry our freedom was such an inconvenience to you," Tyson drawled sarcastically.

Breanna took a long, slow breath. "This was my last job as a contracted retrieval agent," she informed them, a note of pride creeping into her voice. "With this deal, I'm free and clear. Now, I can go freelance and pick my own jobs."

Far from being impressed, Tyson drained what was left of his drink and said, "We were your last contracted assignment? Gee, lucky us."

"Freelance?" Oberon interjected with a surprising warmth in his tone. "That is quite an achievement for one so young. May I be the first to offer you my congratulations."

Breanna smiled.

Quaid, however, sounded almost petulant as he asked, "Are we free to go now?"

"Of course, you are," nodded Oberon, still smiling pleasantly.

"Do we get our weapons back?"

It was the waiter who replied, having returned to the table to collect the empty glasses. "Mr. Ashford and Miss

Gomez, you'll find your weapons have been sent to your storage locker by your ship."

Breanna nodded her acknowledgement to the waiter and thanked Mr Rodney for his time, leaving the room with Quaid following closely behind.

Tyson turned to John. "Johnny," he said, deeply apologetic. "I'm so sorry. I didn't want to leave you there. I tried to turn the ship around, but I couldn't do it. The ship wouldn't respond to anything I did."

"It's okay, Ty."

"But, Johnny, you looked real bad."

"I'm okay, really."

Tyson shook his head. "No," he insisted. "You don't understand. You must have been lying there for over three hours. I watched you. There was no movement. Nothing. You..." his voice wavered, "I thought you were dead."

"Ty," John said patiently. "We spoke. Remember? When you were on the Bronze Hook? We talked. You told me about *The Blue Warlock*."

"After that John, they gassed you. They left the live feed on to my ship. I saw it all."

"Ty, it was probably a trick to stop you coming back for me. Ty, look at me, I'm alive, the gas wasn't fatal. It just knocked me out for a while."

Oberon regarded the two men for a long moment, then he said, "Gentlemen, this is a time for celebration, is it not?"

John smiled, "Of course, you're right, my friend. And I suspect I owe you quite a debt."

"Yes, you do," Oberon agreed with just the hint of a smirk. "However, I shall consent to subtracting it from the balance of the credits I owe *you* for the completion of your delivery job.”

John nodded, “Of course. So, what will the final balance be?”

“If I am correct, and I usually am, you will be left in debt to me for thirty-five thousand credits.”

John let out a low whistle. “That's quite a sum.”

Tyson shoved his chair back roughly and got to his feet. “You still have a lot of explaining to do Johnny. You know that right?”

“Okay Ty,” John held out a hand to try and placate him. “Can we talk about this later?”

Tyson reluctantly nodded his agreement. “Fine, but first, may I speak with you for a moment Oberon?”

“That is Mr. Rodney to you, Mr. Blake,” Oberon said smoothly. “As I don’t feel we are acquainted enough to be using first names. Yet.”

Tyson stiffened slightly at being rebuked but quickly re-composed himself. “Mr. Rodney,” he began again, “I have about thirty thousand credits that I can give you right now so that we can pay off most of the debt that we owe you.”

Oberon reached inside his thick, deep green jacket and produced a data pad. “Yes. That would be acceptable, thank you, Mr. Blake,” he said warmly.

Tyson ran the back of his hand across the data pad. It chimed and verified that the amount of thirty-one thousand had been successfully transferred.

“Thank you, Mr. Blake. It seems the outstanding balance is only four thousand now.”

Tyson nodded but John was looking on with confusion. “They didn't take your chip out?” he asked. “They took mine.”

"Like I have been trying to tell you, Johnny," Tyson sighed impatiently. "All sorts of weird shit happened."

Oberon cleared his throat loudly as he stood up. "Gentlemen, I will leave you to talk. It seems you have a great deal to talk about. John," he inclined his head in John's direction. "If you would be so kind, could you contact me when you are free. I have a business opportunity I would like to discuss with you, at your leisure of course." He reached out to pat John kindly on the shoulder. "And I am so very pleased everything worked out." He offered them both another of his warm smiles and left the booth.

Slumping back down into his chair, Tyson waved the waiter over and ordered a large, blended Lishten iced coffee. John looked at him inquisitively, but Tyson said nothing. The waiter delivered the drink and left promptly. Tyson snatched up the glass, slammed it down, and waved for another.

"Ty," John finally asked cautiously. "What's going on?"

"Johnny, I thought you died in that room," he replied bleakly. "And there's more I haven't told you about."

"Okay," said John calmly. "Then tell me."

Tyson let out a long breath. "When I got the feed reestablished, I saw your body thrashing about on the floor and that bluish-red shit you call blood, it was everywhere."

"I'm fine, Ty. Like I said, it was probably just a show they put on to scare you into not coming back."

"Fine, okay. Well, you tell me how they knew about your blood then?" challenged Tyson. "And how did they know about your credit chip? When they didn't know about mine?"

"They did thorough tests and scans, Ty. They knew."

"Tests and scans for DNA sequences," Tyson conceded. "But not for implants. They are totally different and, given what we paid for them, they should be totally undetectable."

"Well okay fine. If you say I died, I must have. But answer me this, how do you explain me in front of you now?" stated John in frustration.

Tyson's drink arrived and he downed a large portion of it in one gulp. "There's still more."

"There is?"

"Yeah. It was your own body that pushed out the implant... and then the wound on your neck opened up, and then..."

"Then what, Ty?" John pressed after a short pause.

"I couldn't see much after that, but that's weird right?" Tyson finished on a long, shuddering breath.

"Okay," John said thoughtfully. "Anything else?"

Tyson sighed again, finishing his drink. "To be honest, I don't know. All I know is people rushed into the room and started trying to revive you. The images weren't great, but it kept streaming for three hours. Three hours, Johnny. Even I could tell that they thought you were dead the whole time."

"Like I keep telling you, it was all a sham." John picked up his own glass and took a drink. "No one comes back after being dead for that long."

"Yet here you are!" stated Tyson.

"Yes. Here I am."

The two men sat for a long time in silence, thinking.

It was Tyson who spoke first. "So, what now? I assume you got away in *The Blue Warlock*?"

"Yes, it's a fine ship. Nice work on that."

Tyson gave a sudden grin. "Hey! I guess it's my ship now, what with you being declared dead and all."

John laughed. "We might have to rectify this me being dead. It could cause a whole lot of trouble."

"Trouble? Like what?"

"There are some people I know might be upset about it. They deserve to know I am actually okay. And then," he paused, "There's my military record."

Tyson raised a curious eyebrow.

"Well," John explained. "Certain parts of my record could be released, as a sign of respect to my years of service."

"How would that cause trouble?"

"Old wounds run deep, my friend. Some people could seek retribution on my family and friends."

"Aah," Tyson nodded on the 'friend's part of John's statement. "Shit. Well, in that case, let's go and resurrect you from the dead."

"You read my mind."

"So, Johnny, just how broke are we?" Tyson eyed his empty glass, wondering if Oberon was picking up the tab.

"I may have found a credit stick or two hidden on the Warlock. Why do you ask?"

"It's this jumpsuit," Tyson confessed with a grin. "It itches, you know…? Down there," as he looked down at his crotch. "And I'm hungry."

John laughed. "Why am I not surprised to hear that? Fair enough. Let's get back to the ship and get you sorted out."

"I can't tell you how relieved I am to hear you say that."

The two men stood. John finished his drink and banged the glass on the table. "Thank you!" he called to the waiter as together he and Tyson headed out of the deserted bar towards their new ship.

Chapter Twenty

For the following several months, John and Tyson decided to call Harmon Station home. John wanted to make sure that, firstly, any outstanding debts were well and truly settled and secondly, that all the paperwork pertaining to his unfortunate, premature death was filed correctly. He had explained, as well as he could, his altered DNA to Tyson and had insisted his friend pull all the drives from *The Blue Warlock* and replace them with fresh ones.

Tyson had obliged, splicing and updating John's personnel file with the new data. He had taken it further, without John's knowledge, and sent a copy of the two sequences, via a secure and encrypted courier, to his mother in the Delta system. He had added a note. Careful not to reveal too much information, he had simply asked her if she knew anything about how the alterations to the serum in the vials had been achieved and what the possible consequences were.

He did consider telling John what he had done, but decided against it, figuring there was no real harm in asking. Besides, it was his mother, and if anyone knew how to keep secrets, it was her.

While he waited on her reply, Tyson set about attempting to prove John was still very much alive. He was surprised by how difficult the task turned out to be with the many, many forms and the exorbitant expense.

Fortunately, somehow Oberon had heard about them 'helping' to modify one of Mitchell Stapleton's ships, a seemingly impossible task by all accounts. He was so impressed by their skills he offered them work on his three private vessels. The work was challenging, but it paid too well for them to turn it down.

John poured almost his entire earnings into fixing up *The Bronze Hook*. Initially, he was amazed that it had managed to get Tyson all the way to Harmon Station without breaking apart. But he soon saw the potential in the aging vessel and set about injecting life back into the old derelict ship.

Once a week, John met with Oberon for drinks, even after all the modifications on his ships were completed. To Oberon's surprise, he found John's company refreshing after his day to day dealings with the station's issues. The man certainly had an edge to him. Oberon put it down to his years of military service and he almost always found a way of making light of any situation.

Tyson spent most of his evenings frequenting the station's many restaurants and various bars. After being accompanied home on more than one occasion by several attractive young ladies, Tyson soon made quite a name for himself throughout the station. It wasn't long before he was known as, and at times loathed for being, a playboy with deep pockets.

After the repairs to *The Bronze Hook* were completed, John began heavily modifying the craft. As long as the credits came in, the work continued, and after several months it boasted a Novak 2 engine and an impressive pair of forward-facing, A Class pulse lasers, accompanied by two rear-mounted B Class beam lasers. He had even found time to install the heart of the relocator. This time not only did he put a new red button on the main cockpit's console, but he also installed a new warning light below it.

John had even managed to install a small gym into a re-purposed recreational room. Satisfied he had done all he could, John had the whole ship repainted and renamed: *The Silver Falcon*.

Tyson kept insisting that he had missed the meeting where the name change was discussed. Until that is, John produced a video of him snoring through it. John went on to explain that there had been the agreed forty-eight hours cooling-off period for any new names to be submitted and it wasn't his fault Tyson didn't check his video mail often enough. Tyson went quiet for a while. It stayed The *Silver Falcon*.

"You know, I've thought about it, and you're not funny," Tyson complained, as he fired up the navigation computer, marvelling at what a fantastic job he had done.

"Sure I am," John activated both of the newly installed modified seat harnesses on the cockpit's main chairs and grinned as Tyson let out a yelp of surprise when his automatically adjusted at the same time, "I'm hilarious."

It was on the men's last test flight around the station that Tyson finally succeeded in getting the video mail accounts working properly. The program had conflicted with his newly modified and improved White Lace security system and it had taken several weeks of coding and rewriting to rectify the problem. As soon as John logged onto his video mail, one from Lyle Gregson came up highlighted on his screen.

The message was text-only and was brief:

John,

The investigation into the incident concerning Sergeant Wheeler has been reviewed and all charges against you have been dismissed.

Take care

Lyle.

John read the Email out to his friend, who was in the middle of scrolling through his own mail.

"See, Johnny. I knew it would all work out," grinned Tyson. Suddenly, a video mail appeared from his mother marked "urgent." Not wanting John to hear what she had to say just yet, Tyson connected his earbuds to his screen and opened it.

His mother's face filled his screen. She had dark circles beneath her deep brown eyes and her usually immaculate, blonde streaked hair was pulled back in a rushed bun perched on top of her head. She spoke quickly and without pleasantries.

"Tyson, I need your help. Have you heard from your father? He has disappeared from his business trip to the Gamma system. No one can locate him, and I fear something terrible may have happened to him."

Tyson had never had a good relationship with his father, and his mother was well aware of it. He knew she had to be getting extremely worried if she was asking him for help. On the screen, she reached out toward him to end the call, but hesitated a moment before continuing, "Those samples you sent me, where did you get them from? They are very intriguing. Is the test subject still alive? I am sorry it has taken so long to reply. Just after I received your video mail our research station was quarantined for the third time this month and again, we were all held for the duration of the suspected outbreak." Tyson sat, glued to the screen as his mother continued, "It is believed that during our research of molecular cloning several plasmids mutated and became corrupt, thus creating a new strain of microbial bacteria. It is nothing to be concerned about as there is no evidence that it survived the lab's decontamination. My staff and I all tested negative and have gone back to our research. I only mention this because the sample data you sent me may hold the genetic scaffolding agent we are trying to create, and I would love a tissue sample if possible. Please respond as soon as you can." *End of message.*

Tyson sat in shock after hearing the video mail. After several minutes, he still wasn't sure who to be more concerned for his missing father or his mother.

John could see a deep furrow in his friend's forehead and tapped him on the shoulder. "You okay?"

"Ahh, yeah. It's my parents," Tyson admitted, finally pulling out his earbuds. "One is missing and the other …"

"Go on," John prompted after a long silence.

Tyson sighed and finally came clean about sending the data to his mother for her professional opinion as a genetic erosion specialist. "Don't worry," he assured him. "I didn't mention where I got the sample from. Unfortunately, now she sounds very interested in obtaining a tissue sample and, on top of that, my father seems to have gone missing somewhere in the Epsilon system."

John inhaled deeply as he took all the information in. He wasn't angry that Tyson had sent the data off to his mother. In fact, if anyone would know what he had been exposed to and how it might affect him, it was her.

"Okay," he said after another few minutes of silence. "So where to first? The Epsilon system? Or to visit your mother in the Delta?"

While John waited for Tyson's response, he retrieved his data pad from his chair's storage pocket and connected it to the *Warlock's* control systems. It wasn't long before he had plotted in a course as close to Caxton as he could and set the autopilot for remote take-off via his pad. He then accessed the ship's main view screen and wrote:

To whoever finds this ship,
This is the property of Commander Mitchell Stapleton.
Here is the ship I borrowed. I believe this will find us even.
Regards.
Captain John Alexander.

Smiling to himself, John engaged The Blue Warlock's auto-pilot from his data pad and watched patiently as it slowly decoupled from the station and headed off on its journey towards Caxton.

THE END

Acknowledgements

My parents and siblings, who encouraged me to indulge in my science fiction ramblings.

The Inklings Writing Group and for their feedback and enthusiastic support.

To my friend, Dean, who enjoys my eclectic ways and provided great feedback and suggestions.

To my wife Christy who always enthusiastically supports all of my new projects and my boys Alec and Blake.

About the Author

B.J Valli has worked many years in the mining industry as a process operator. The long hours and shift work are the reason this novel has taken many years to complete. Then again this also has allowed him to brainstorm ideas well into the early hours of the morning of which, not all would make the final draft.

He joined a local writers group and with their help and guidance he has now completed Warning! Malfunctions May Occur, his first novel. He lives in the South West of Western Australia with his wife and two sons.

www.ingramcontent.com/pod-product-compliance
Lightning Source LLC
Chambersburg PA
CBHW050144120726
47903CB00002B/485